CASTLE IN THE CLOUDS

BRIAN CROSS

Griffin Publishing

Castle In The Clouds

Copyright © 2010   Brian Cross
ISBN 978-0-9558559-3-1
Griffin Publishing, Peterborough, UK

This book is a work of fiction. Names, characters and incidents therein are entirely the product of the author's imagination and any resemblance to actual persons, living or dead, is entirely coincidental.

No part of this book may be reproduced, stored in a retrieval system, or transmitted in any form, or by any means, electronic, mechanical, photocopying, recording or otherwise, without prior permission of the author.

Early Twentieth Century
An Island near The Northumberland Coast
Chapter One

To Thomas Llewellyn's unaccustomed ears the sudden noise sounded like a firework cracking the May air, disturbing the peace of an island and the small sixteenth century castle he'd just bought. It seemed idyllic; he hadn't counted on unruly elements shattering the rustic charm.

But then striding along the castle's upper gallery and glancing through a window, Llewellyn saw the reason for the disturbance, as an orange flare from a sea-going vessel ripped through the grey sky.

He trod a flight of stairs, opening an oak door leading onto a former gun battery which now provided a roof garden with a spectacular panorama.

But it was the sight of the sinking ship which caught his eye.

Viewed from a distance it seemed small, its stern largely submerged in the high seas while the bow appeared marooned above them; and then as a klaxon sounded repeatedly he watched the island's lifeboat crew assemble before setting out to sea.

Llewellyn felt a hand on his shoulder and smelled his sister's cologne blasting across his nose.

'Is this what possessed you to buy the place Thomas? So that you could watch real life dramas unfold? No theatre can adequately portray the real thing, isn't that a fact? Prey – let us take a seat and watch.'

'Shame on me should I ever consider such a thing; shame on you that you actually propose it.' Llewellyn removed his sister's heavily jewelled wrist. 'Come Dorothea, if there is nothing we can do to assist, there is little point in witnessing some wretched soul's demise – we shall go inside.'

'Do so if you wish Thomas, but you are not my keeper; nor am I one of your City pawns.'

Dorothea gave Llewellyn a defiant dark-eyed stare. 'I intend to watch the show unfold.'

Llewellyn met that stare momentarily; dressed in her black cape, its hood veiling her dark curly hair, her prominent nose the only distinctive feature, Dorothea seemed every inch the sorceress. There were times when her support was invaluable, but there were occasions when her behaviour was insufferable. Such a time was now.

Llewellyn closed the door on her, took the gallery steps and made his way down to the lounge where he stood by a Gothic window and stared out across the island, surveying the scenery, wild now in the developing storm. He reflected on his decision to purchase the castle as a second home, and how it would fare under the auspices of his sister, to whom he'd entrusted the day to day supervision.

The plan was for Dorothea to manage his staff of three which consisted of David Hambleton, the butler, who had made the move from London to undertake the task; Mrs. Simms, who had been recruited from amongst the Northumberland island's residents as cook, along with John Gibbings, the young gardener cum handyman, who he'd been assured was both a gifted gardener and industrious worker.

The acquisition had been at considerable expense, but as a prominent banker it provided him with a prestigious residence to dine, accommodate and impress his influential clients. They could not fail to be so.

With the wind buffeting its stout walls Llewellyn commenced a routine evening inspection of a castle that had been expertly redesigned by a leading architect to resemble a fortified house. Its many rooms were mainly small in nature and encouraged intimacy, but the castle also contained areas where entertainment could be provided for important guests.

Llewellyn was examining the wide entrance hall, with its exposed pillars and red herring-bone stone floor, when he heard Dorothea's hurried footsteps behind him –

'Thomas – our drama appears to have been played out with success – come, witness a happy ending.'

Llewellyn shook his head, but nonetheless allowed Dorothea to snatch his hand and lead him back to the roof garden – 'Behold, a fair maiden is rescued…'

He followed his sister to the parapet; below on the shores, visible in the fading evening light the lifeboat had come ashore. And embarking from it, shawl wrapped around her shoulders and supported by four boatmen was a tall, slim woman. As Llewellyn watched, for a second the setting sun slipped behind racing clouds and reflected her long red hair.

The wind whipped that hair around her face and as she swept it back he saw her profile. Her face was full and healthy looking, and the straight nose gave her a refined look; he could see at once her elegance and class.

Dorothea watched his chest swell. 'Fair takes your breath away, does she brother? Can she be that pretty?'

'It was the wind, nothing more,' Llewellyn said, aware that his reply had been curt. 'I was merely curious.'

Dorothea said nothing further as Llewellyn returned inside, but her eyes followed the party all the way to the village.

Chapter Two

Llewellyn slipped on his black tuxedo, examining himself in the mirror before heading down the castle's steep cobbled slope and making for the garden where he'd spotted John Gibbings tending the flowerbeds.

Hands on hips, Llewellyn took a quick look around the spring bedding. 'Good morning Gibbings, fine job you're doing with the grounds.'

'Thank you sir.' The dark haired young gardener looked up, squinting in the sunlight.

'Bad do last night, by all accounts,' Llewellyn continued, 'though I gather you chaps rescued at least one poor soul.'

'Aye,' Gibbings straightened, mopping his brow, 'though the crew perished with the ship, I'm afraid.' He hung his head before glancing up with renewed zest. 'Have you not heard sir?'

'Heard? Heard what?'

'About the young lady we rescued.'

Llewellyn fingered his moustache, interest heightened. 'I've heard nothing Gibbings – only what my sister has told me – please be kind enough to elaborate.'

'The whole village is talking sir; it seems the young lady's famous.'

Llewellyn stiffened, was this man deliberately testing his patience? 'Gibbings, just who *is* this young lady?'

The gardener scratched his head. 'Verona something, Day I think.'

'Veronica Day you mean? The violinist?' Llewellyn was astounded.

'Aye – some kind of musician they say.'

Some kind of musician, Llewellyn bit his lip – how ignorant these chaps were. 'Well thank you Gibbings, keep up the good work.' Questions finally answered, Llewellyn left him to the gardening. Walking back up the castle slope, Llewellyn was acutely aware of what a precarious task it could be. The cobbles, still slippery from the overnight rain, glistened in the sunlight but one faulty step could send a person slithering down, or worse still off the rock face to serious injury or perhaps death.

What if a fate of this magnitude were to befall his guests? The consequences would be unthinkable. There was no doubt some kind of rail needed constructing.

Llewellyn paused at the top and turned his attention to the sea, the mountainous waves of the night before had subsided; it was difficult to believe that such a drama had been played out little more than twelve hours previously, not far out to sea. A drama that, distastefully, his sister had followed to its conclusion.

He thought again of the attractive young violinist who had so captivated him as she'd disembarked from the lifeboat. Veronica Day was a household name in the world of classical music, was it chance or fate that had caused her to end up here? He wondered whether she was fully recovered from her ordeal and for how long she'd be in their midst.

Llewellyn joined Dorothea in the dining room where Mrs. Simms was in the process of serving morning coffee from a tray.

'Mrs. Simms has just presented me with some interesting news,' Dorothea said, accepting a cup and placing her cigarette holder in a tray, 'though I don't doubt you've elicited the information from your little chat with Gibbings…'

Llewellyn sighed, taking a seat at the table opposite her; sometimes his sister's tone could be so tiresome. 'If you're talking about our famed violinist, Gibbings has indeed enlightened me.'

Dorothea gave a coy smile, mainly for Mrs. Simms' benefit. 'And I thought my brother had suddenly developed a healthy interest in gardening.'

Llewellyn brushed himself down. 'Really, do try to curb your sarcastic wit Dorothea.' He acknowledged as Mrs. Simms handed his coffee. 'Upon reflection, I'll take this up to my study; I've some important papers to peruse pending my return to London.'

'Oh, *do* excuse me, a trifle touchy this morning, aren't we dear?' Dorothea smiled at his irritation.

Llewellyn watched smoke mushroom from her cigarette, he was on the point of retribution but such recourse would be unbecoming in Mrs. Simms' presence.

To reach his study Llewellyn would need to pass through a central feature of the castle, The Long Gallery, with its stone pillars, its string of fine paintings along one wall, while the other afforded fine views over the North Sea. It was in The Long Gallery and out on the roof garden that Llewellyn planned to entertain his affluent guests.

The study consisted of a long rectangular bedroom he'd adapted for his personal use; its window gave a sweeping view across the island shore, and enabled him to see across to the village.

It was to this window that Llewellyn went now, cup and saucer in hand, and as he stood there sipping his coffee he saw the figure of a tall woman taking the coastal path towards the castle – warmth spread through his veins that wasn't supplied by the liquid.

It was caused by the sight of the woman – that woman was the violinist, Veronica Day.

Llewellyn placed his cup on his desk and put his hands on the window ledge, urging her to come closer, so close he could establish contact. But she wasn't hurrying; her demeanour was perfect, refined and elegant; her long legs raking over the rough track that served as a road.

He followed her progress along the shore, watching the wind whip through her red hair, the shawl of the evening before had disappeared and in the warm spring sunshine she wore a long green dress, wide in the arms so the wind rippled her sleeves.

She was closer now, so close – midway between village and castle – that there was excitement building within – he could not forego this opportunity to meet with her.

He checked in the mirror, fingered his finely trimmed black moustache, combed his short dark hair and then adjusted his tuxedo. That a woman should have this affect on him was unnatural but he couldn't forget that moment when she'd come ashore, the mere sight of her had been enchanting.

Llewellyn couldn't get her out of his head.

Down the castle slope he went at some pace, but upon reaching the curve which would bring him into her sight he slowed, if only to encourage her forward – he didn't want her progress disturbed –

And there she was, barely thirty yards from him, and he could witness first hand her exquisite beauty.

She stopped on his approach, made to turn away as he hurried after her. 'No please,' he called, trying not to alarm her, 'continue with your walk, do not turn back on my account.'

She looked at him hesitantly, sideways on – in the morning sunlight he thought she looked magnificent. 'I thought I might be trespassing when I saw you coming towards me.'

'Not at all, the coastal path carries on by.' He offered his hand. 'I'm Thomas Llewellyn, owner of the castle, and you are?'

'Veronica Day.' She placed her hand in his and he shook it gently.

Llewellyn cupped his chin. 'The name sounds familiar.' He thought he saw embarrassment in her smile. 'I play the violin.'

'*The* Veronica Day – of course, how ignorant of me; what brings you to our small island?'

'A great tragedy, Mr. Llewellyn – a shipwreck…' she shuddered, looked out to sea. 'I'm not sure I want to talk about it,' then shrugging apologetically, 'it's difficult to believe when you look at the sea now.'

'Exactly what I was thinking just a few minutes ago…'

'I beg your pardon?'

'Oh I'm sorry Miss Day,' Llewellyn stammered, caught out. 'Well, I've been fed the barest bones of the incident – you understand on an island like this news travels fast. Might I offer you the comfort of my castle for a while?'

'No, thanks all the same; I found myself in need of some fresh air, getting out here just calms my nerves. You know I thought I was going to die, until I saw the lifeboat – one brave man plucked me out of the sea…'

'Don't distress yourself any further.' Seeing the anguish on her face Llewellyn gently guided Veronica away from the sea; his arm around her back he turned her towards the castle. 'What will you do now – how long will you stay?'

'No longer than it takes to recover from my ordeal, and to await the arrival of my brother in a few days time. From here we travel to Edinburgh, I have an engagement there you see.'

Llewellyn looked into her solemn green eyes, immediately aware of their clarity. 'Was that where you were bound?'

She nodded. 'Unfortunately I lost most of my belongings – even my violin.'

'A shame – a great shame,' Llewellyn muttered, then with great conviction, 'but you have survived my dear, others did not – that is the thing.'

'I feel sorry for those who drowned, but yes – you are right – ah, it is such a fine day after such an awful night – how strangely disturbed our weather has become.'

'Yes indeed.'

Veronica took a step away. 'I will not detain you any longer Mr. Llewellyn, I feel refreshed now – the villagers have been kind enough to provide me with lodgings. I shall return there and rest awhile. It has been a pleasure talking to you.'

'Likewise.' Llewellyn took her hand and kissed it. 'I hope we will meet again.'

'Perhaps, Mr. Llewellyn, we will.' A smile spread quickly across her face, her eyes shone and Llewellyn felt the warmth in them.

Chapter Three

Llewellyn returned to the castle entrance to find Dorothea emerging from its shadows. 'Well brother, that was a chance encounter, was it not?'

'Will you keep as keen an eye on the household as you do my activities, Dorothea?' Llewellyn pushed past her, embarrassed and annoyed by her snooping – he felt her eyes burning the back of his head as he descended the stairs to the lounge.

'Of course I shall, as you well know.' Her voice sounded hollow, resounding from the stone walls of the narrow stairway. 'But one cannot fail to notice your interest in the young Miss Day.'

Llewellyn loosened his tie; Dorothea's words were as sharp as her voice. 'Miss Day has experienced a troublesome ordeal; she felt the need for a peaceful walk. I merely consoled her and introduced myself.'

Dorothea followed him to the lounge window, where he stood, hands thrust into the pockets of his breeches. She stood alongside, drew on her cigarette, gazed across the gardens and fields beyond. 'A peaceful walk perhaps, but I sense there to be another reason for the path she took…'

'Which is?' Llewellyn turned, inhaling her acrid breath. She gave what he termed her "cocky" smile, dark eyes alive with mischief. 'Do not concern yourself brother, time will tell.'

Unprepared to indulge himself in his sister's ambiguities, Llewellyn returned to his study. He longed to re-establish contact with the lovely Miss Day before she left the island, and in so doing, perhaps he could recompense what he deemed her biggest loss.

He tugged the gold-threaded cord at the side of his desk and soon acknowledged the presence of his silver haired butler –

'Ah, Hambleton, I wish to avail myself of your infinite London knowledge…'

'Sir?'

'Please close the door Hambleton, I wish our conversation to be private.

'Good, now – whereabouts in London am I to acquire a classical violin fit for the use of a renowned performer?'

'Sir – I do not…'

No Hambleton.' Llewellyn directed a forefinger at his butler. 'Please do not advise me that you are unaware of the tragic events of last night…'

'No sir, indeed I am not.' Hambleton drew a finger across his lip. 'I was merely going to suggest that you look in the opposite direction for your musical equipment.'

Llewellyn shook his head – everything of quality derived from the Capital, it was a known fact.

'Sir, if you please – might I suggest Edinburgh as an alternative. Transportation of suitable merchandise from the City might prove a lengthy business. By selecting Edinburgh you would not be forfeiting quality and I can arrange delivery of a fine instrument within two days, I have no doubt of that. But I do doubt that Miss Day will be long on this island – if you wish to impress her then I suggest Edinburgh sir, a mere seventy miles away – London is many times that.'

'I seek not to impress her,' Llewellyn said loudly, then adjusting both his tone and tuxedo, 'you understand I seek to address a great misfortune; spare no expense on my account and do all you can to ensure delivery within two days. Edinburgh it will be.'

'I shall attend to it sir.'

Llewellyn nodded as Hambleton departed, and satisfied with the wisdom of his butler's suggestion, strode to his dark oak cabinet, whereupon he poured his finest scotch and gazed out to sea.

***

Two days later, Dorothea sat in the dining room, eyeing her brother from under her heavy lashes. 'Should you not be making preparation for returning to London, Thomas? Your train is but one hour away.'

Llewellyn was stirred from his thoughts, eager anticipation of the arrival shortly, of a violin from Edinburgh. 'My profound apologies for not informing you, dear sister – I shall be staying a while longer.' Llewellyn derived satisfaction from a brief flicker of his sister's eyelids and a sudden tic in her cheek, which often exhibited itself when she was irked.

'What might I ask induced this change in your normally meticulous planning, a certain washed-up violinist?'

'Spare me your humourless taunts, Dorothea, and improve upon your nature. We are to receive a guest at dinner this evening.' Llewellyn watched Dorothea's lips tighten and twist. 'Yes, Veronica Day, and we are to be treated to a private recital in the gallery.'

'Without an instrument, Thomas? From what I understand she lost about everything but the clothes she wore.'

'It is being arranged.' Llewellyn smiled at Dorothea's discomfort, 'and before you exercise your razor sharp tongue, I seek to improve Miss Day's fortunes, nothing more.'

Dorothea placed her cup down and tilted her head back, fixing him with a long, unblinking stare. 'And has Miss Day any knowledge of this?'

'Do not concern yourself on that account.' Llewellyn took in the tautness of his sister's facial muscles with pleasure. 'It is as good as done.'

Satisfied with having gained the upper hand over Dorothea, Llewellyn left her to simmer, and his spirits were further raised when the Stradivarius violin arrived at lunchtime, Hambleton being as good as his word. Hambleton had established contact with a specialist supplier who had knowledge of Veronica Day's career and had provided the ideal instrument.

With the violin in his possession Llewellyn immediately set out for the village in his trap, drawing the pony to a halt in the main street outside the address Mrs. Simms had provided for him.

He knocked and heard the sound of footsteps within, and was shortly greeted by the violinist, wearing a long floral dress, her hair tied back so that her refined features were fully displayed.

'Why, Mr. Llewellyn…'

'Miss Day, please excuse my unannounced arrival, but I felt I had to compensate for the tragic consequences of your demise.'

'I'm not sure I understand you.'

'Please bear with me for an instant.' Llewellyn went to the back of the trap, lifting out the cased violin. 'Please accept this as a gift from me, a token of my deep sorrow at your losses and…'

'Oh but I cannot; really I cannot…' Llewellyn saw her glance down, saw recognition of the manufacturer's label. 'It is too much, I cannot justify receiving it from you.'

'Oh but you can,' Llewellyn focused on her green eyes, jewels in her face. 'For I ask something in return.' Before she could respond he held his free hand aloft. 'I only ask that you perform at the castle, a private recital. It would be a privilege and an honour to receive you and to hear you play.'

Veronica was silent, Llewellyn thought she might not accept, but in a singular graceful movement she stretched her limbs, relieved him of the instrument and nodded. 'Then I do accept, if only to express my gratitude. When would you desire my presence, Mr. Llewellyn?'

Llewellyn fingered his moustache, looking directly into her fine features, her soft, flawless skin, feeling a tremble from head to foot. 'If it pleases you, this evening; following which we will enjoy dinner.'

She raised her brows, looked uncertain. 'Why, such short notice; I need to familiarise with my new instrument…'

'And I need to return to London at similarly short notice; the opportunity might not arise again.'

'Then I will begin rehearsal immediately, and will attend the castle at?'

'Six o'clock would be excellent.'

Llewellyn bade Veronica Day farewell, for six short hours at least.

But farewell, with regard to her, was not a word which figured prominently in his thoughts.

Chapter Four

Veronica Day sat in the small drawing room caressing the strings of her new violin before running her fingers over its russet surface. How kind it had been of Mr. Llewellyn to go to the trouble and expense of purchasing a replacement violin for her – and to be able to acquire one so similar to her own treasured instrument – surely he must have some form of expert knowledge on the subject; she thought to question him later.

She turned her attention to the four walls, each of them mounted with three rectangular paintings, all of sea-going vessels, with several depicting lifeboats in action at the scene of a troubled ship. One such painting, of a stormy evening in failing light, with the wind seeming to hurl huge buckets of swirling foam over the bows of a distressed craft, brought re-charged memories that smashed their way into a mind unwilling to receive them. She'd need to come to terms with the tragedy, with the loss of life that had ensued thus leaving her the only survivor, but not yet. Too soon; far too soon.

But as she struggled in the sea, sucking in air, spitting out water, she'd seen the lifeboat bearing down on her, its bow plunging through the heavy tide.

She had no trouble recalling that instant, or the sight of a young man perched ready to jump, which a second later he had – in one expert movement diving alongside and then drawing her towards the boat where they'd both been pulled to safety.

Truly, that was one moment she would never forget. From enquiries in the village she'd learned the man's name was John Gibbings, that he could be found most days tending the castle grounds where he worked as a gardener.

She'd been on her way there, to thank him personally for his bravery when she'd encountered Mr. Llewellyn – an imposing and distinguished looking man upon first reflection, descending the castle slope. She'd thought at first she'd been trespassing and had been about to turn heel, but he'd bade her continue and then, reluctant to reveal the true intent of her visit she'd declined. During their brief encounter however, she'd sensed that Mr. Llewellyn had taken an instant liking to her, and in truth, was looking forward to her evening at his castle, notwithstanding her usual apprehension in unfamiliar company.

***

'Do not worry dear brother; your appearance is as usual impeccable. Our distinguished guest cannot fail to be impressed.'

Llewellyn gave a start; Dorothea had been standing at his half-open door as he examined himself in the mirror. 'Dorothea,' he snapped, turning on her, 'please find a more deserving outlet for your tasteless sarcasm; we are most fortunate to be receiving a personal recital from a renowned musician, please remember that.'

Dorothea raised her heavy brows, lifted her face and with a smirk, said, 'Using an instrument you went to untold length and cost to acquire for her.'

Before Llewellyn could deliver an appropriate retort Dorothea had swept away along the gallery and down the castle stairs, leaving him irritated beyond measure.

Nevertheless, despite his sister's humourless broadsides, Llewellyn was determined to look his best to receive their visitor, thus he departed the castle in pony and trap wearing a dark blazer, white shirt and bright flannel trousers; out of keeping with the costume of the island but entirely in keeping with his own standard of dress.

He drove along the coast road before entering the village and, pulling up at her lodgings, jumped down from the trap to be received by the tall woman with flaming red hair who'd so captivated him. Attired in a white satin shawl and full length lilac dress she presented a picture of immeasurable beauty.

Llewellyn caught his breath at the sight of her but she seemed not to notice, as he took her violin case in one hand, and with the other gently guided her up into the trap.

'I trust you will enjoy your evening at the castle,' he said, letting go of her hand reluctantly and taking up the reins. 'It is quite a special place you know.'

'I'm quite sure it is,' she said, adjusting her dress around her long legs, 'and that I shall enjoy it; likewise I trust you will enjoy my recital.'

'Of course, I shall.' Llewellyn gave a broad smile, tweaked his moustache, then forced his attention to the road; out of the corner of his eye he saw Veronica in her seat, her back held straight against the padded bench; she had perfect poise as well as natural beauty.

To the east, the sky was blue, and along the open approach to the castle the sea seemed filled with green jewels. And he, Thomas

Llewellyn had invited the finest jewel of them all to his castle, for an evening never to be forgotten.

Chapter Five

Waves rippled gently below, reflecting on the gallery's lime coloured walls as Veronica Day played, the setting sun inflaming her red hair and shimmering on the bow she stroked so finely.

Sitting on a long oak bench with Dorothea at his side Llewellyn watched, enthralled, as Veronica recited Vivaldi, Beethoven and Tchaikovsky in what she explained was a romantic interpretation of violin solos. Llewellyn wasn't an expert in the world of music but he loved the fluency that caused her bow to glide over the strings and the resonance she created in the gallery's high interior was electrifying.

With Veronica playing to his right, and directly opposite through the windows, the sun a large mellow pumpkin sinking into the horizon, the castle he'd so recently purchased took on an atmosphere altogether different from anything he'd experienced. It was as if the castle and Veronica had combined to create a special magic.

'Absolutely beautiful,' Llewellyn exclaimed when she'd finished; this was followed by a noticeably reserved 'most impressive' from his sister. But Llewellyn hadn't been aware of any comment from Dorothea; in fact, only the arrival of Hambleton announcing dinner forced his eyes from the radiant Veronica.

'I must say Miss Day, your playing both astounded and moved me,' Llewellyn enthused over a salad dinner prepared by Mrs. Simms.

'Why thank you Mr. Llewellyn.' Veronica placed her fork down and took a sip of wine. 'You know your choice of violin was perfect, how on earth did you know which to get?'

Llewellyn lowered his knife and fork, ran a napkin over his lips. 'A man in my position has many useful contacts Miss Day, need I say more?'

'No indeed, it is enough for me to know you bought it, and once again I thank you.'

'Indeed you should Miss Day.' The heavily-jewelled Dorothea held a wine glass to her lips, downed the contents in one gulp. 'My brother is not always so charitable.'

Llewellyn coughed and glanced out at the garden, smarting, but unwilling to rise to her bait. 'Come, come, Dorothea, none of your mischief – ah,' he said, looking down at the gardens for a change of subject. 'Nine o'clock and our gardener is still working. Good chap that.'

'Pardon?' Veronica followed Llewellyn's eye, coming to rest on a slim, dark curly-haired figure busily watering the flower beds. She rose to her feet, the speed of her movement surprising Llewellyn. 'I do hope you'll excuse me but that young man down there is the one who pulled me from the sea. I really must go and thank him; I may not get another chance to do so.'

Llewellyn flapped a hand across his face. 'No, no, don't trouble yourself to do that, I'll have the butler fetch him up.'

Veronica smiled but shook her head. 'I think that would be inappropriate. His bravery demands that I should attend him. I cannot do him justice by having him come to me.'

Dorothea raised her eyebrows, glanced at Llewellyn who sighed. 'If you feel you ought to do so then please allow me to accompany you down the slope, it is rather hazardous. I need to erect some kind of stair-rail forthwith.'

But Veronica waved away his offer. 'No please, do not trouble yourself. I assure you I am quite agile for a woman; it will present no problems.'

Llewellyn nodded reluctantly. 'Then hurry back, your company is much appreciated here.'

His heart-rate increased as she left the room and he knew it wasn't caused by the digestion of food. He'd seen by the ease that she'd coped with the ascent that Veronica Day's abilities weren't restricted to the violin, but he hadn't wanted her out of his sight any longer than necessary.

'The lovely Miss Day has a very peculiar attitude Thomas.' Dorothea's acidic voice cut into his thoughts like a freshly sharpened blade. 'Gibbings is, after all, a *servant*, servants come to us.'

'To us, Dorothea perhaps,' Llewellyn looked into his sister's unblinking eyes, 'but it seems that the young lady does not conform to your philosophy. She has courage, I give her that.'

Dorothea shook her head, a mass of dark curls mushrooming about her face. 'Do not set your stall at her door, Thomas...'

'Dorothea,' Llewellyn said through clenched teeth, 'please do not talk in riddles. I have suffered enough of your antics these past few days to last a whole year.'

'Then perhaps you have deserved it,' Dorothea hissed, her face close, taunting him. 'You're besotted with that woman; I saw it from the first time you watched her come ashore. You think it purely by chance, a blissful accident that you encountered her outside the castle? That she was merely out for a stroll when fate took a hand and led her straight to you?'

'Dorothea!' Llewellyn slapped his hand on the table and felt pain shoot through his fingers. 'She was taking a walk following the effects of a trauma.'

'Poppycock, think again Thomas,' Dorothea shouted over him. She swung to the window, pointing to where Veronica approached an unsuspecting gardener. 'She was looking for Gibbings.'

***

Veronica reached the gate of the walled garden, lifted the catch and slipped through. John |Gibbings had his back to her, watering plants with a large spouted can.

She shut the gate and saw him jump in alarm, clasping her hands to her cheeks. 'Oh my, I'm so sorry – I thought lifeboat people were supposed to have nerves of steel.'

'Oh Madam,' he straightened, 'you surprised me, I was just tending to Mr. Llewellyn's plants.'

'I can see that, and don't call me Madam, I'm Veronica.' She dropped her head and then gazed directly into his eyes. 'The woman you saved from the sea?'

'Aye,' he put down the can and shuffled uneasily. 'You feeling better?'

'Feeling better?' she shrugged. 'A little. But I came to say thanks. If it hadn't been for you I wouldn't be standing here right now.'

She felt his brown eyes study her. 'Any of the others could have done what I did.'

'That's not the point, thank you John Gibbings.' She held out her hand. 'Well, go on, take it.'

'My hands Ma – Veronica.' He looked tentative. 'They're dirty like...'

'Well of course they're dirty, you've been working in the garden – I'm not afraid of a little dirt.'

'Strikes me you're not afraid of anything Madam – I mean Veronica – you were the coolest casualty I've ever seen and I been doing this for some years.' He finally took her hand loosely, 'Now you'll have to wash it – the Llewellyns' are…'

'It's okay John, I'm sure there is a washroom...' she looked around the garden, 'this place is a credit to you, such an array of flowers and blooms, and all so tidy.'

Veronica breathed in the freshness of the evening, the scent of the flowers, saw the tumble of waves beyond as they broke for shore. 'Show me around your garden.'

Gibbings' lips became tight and thin. 'I don't think I should be doing that.'

Veronica touched him on the shoulder, glanced up at the castle, then back at John. 'I want to take a little interest in the work of a man who saved my life, I'm sure nobody will mind.'

Gibbings shook his head; there was an earnest expression on his face as his eyes flicked briefly up towards the castle dining room. 'Madam – Veronica, I don't know much about violins, but I know you're famous – and I want to keep this job. Right now your place is up there – please go back – now.'

It felt like a slap in the face to Veronica, but she saw the concern in his eyes. Again she touched his shoulder, thought she saw the trace of a smile. 'You take care, John Gibbings.'

Veronica returned to the castle, sought out Hambleton who directed her to the washroom. When she returned to the dining room Llewellyn and Dorothea were in subdued mood, but it was Dorothea who eyed her coldly. She lofted her head. 'We saw you shake his hand, I for one am surprised you did that. His hands are always filthy – a disgusting lack of hygiene.'

'He is a gardener, Dorothea, is he not?' Veronica said curtly. 'What would you expect? He labours into the evening...'

'On my account and I am grateful,' Llewellyn cut in, irritated both by Dorothea's causticity and his prized guest's support of a servant.

'I will hear no more of this.' He raised his glass to Veronica. 'We will drink wine, and I will toast your health.'

'And I shall retire,' Dorothea said with a touch of bitterness, sweeping out before another word could be uttered.

'You must not mind my sister,' Llewellyn said, his voice hushed as Hambleton cleared the table. 'She is strongly opinionated.' He clasped his hands together, leaned forward. 'Miss Day – Veronica if I may call you that – I would be greatly honoured by your continued presence at the castle tonight. In anticipation, I have had Hambleton prepare a room for you.'

Veronica frowned; Llewellyn noticed just the faintest of lines on her skin. 'I feel I am not altogether welcome…'

'Oh but Veronica you are – my sister means well but she is headstrong – please do not let her unfortunate comments dissuade you.'

Veronica nodded. 'I have enjoyed your company Mr. Llewellyn, and so to save you the inconvenience of returning me to the village this evening, I shall accept.'

Llewellyn tweaked his moustache. 'Shall we retire to the drawing room then Veronica? I am eager to learn more about your career.'

'Thank you Mr. Llewellyn, I am indebted to you. But I am growing weary. I should like to retire myself if you are not inconvenienced.'

'No Veronica, I am not inconvenienced, and please call me Thomas.' He leaned forward, pressed her hand between his palms. 'I will drive you home tomorrow morning before I return to London. You too, I gather, will shortly be leaving. Veronica, in the short time I've known you, you have greatly enriched my life. You are welcome here at any time. Please say you will return as my guest.'

Veronica gave a slow smile and Llewellyn felt its warmth spread through his body. 'I have a busy schedule, but will do all I can to enable it.'

Llewellyn released her hand. 'Hambleton will show you to your room.'

But as he bid Veronica Day goodnight and watched his butler escort her to an upstairs room, Llewellyn felt a deep yearning and rising disappointment that she could not see fit to spend the remainder of the evening with him.

***

Veronica lay in a comfortable four-poster bed listening to the sea breaking on the rocks below, so deeply in thought she couldn't sleep; she was thinking of John Gibbings, a man too wary of the castle's occupants to even take a short walk in the garden with her. Thomas Llewellyn seemed attentive, appreciative. Kind – surely he would pose no threat to John's employment. Only Dorothea seemed capable of doing that, her attitude towards him fell little short of open hostility, precisely why, she'd no idea. Her assertions that he was filthy were preposterous. But Dorothea wasn't the castle's mistress –

Llewellyn called the tune – though he was returning to London in the morning.

Left to her own devices, could Dorothea be vindictive enough to sack John?

She had one more day on the island before her brother arrived and they were to leave for Edinburgh. John Gibbings had saved her life, she'd given him her thanks but that didn't seem enough.

But what could she do to help?

Chapter Six

'I fear the weather's on the change.' Llewellyn glanced across at the gathering blanket of grey out to sea. 'Nonetheless, your visit has brightened our skies and will do so again when you return.'

Veronica said nothing, sitting tight-lipped in the trap as it left the castle grounds.

'You are quiet this morning, Veronica,' Llewellyn remarked with concern. 'I take it nothing has transpired to mar your stay?'

Veronica looked over her shoulder, they were beginning the descent onto the road to the village, but to the west the castle grounds were still visible.

'Thomas, would you mind stopping for a moment please.'

Llewellyn pulled the pony to a halt. 'What is it Veronica, what is the matter?'

'My apologies for delaying you,' Veronica said casually. 'I simply wanted one last look at your delightful grounds.'

'You should have asked earlier, I would have walked them with you.'

Veronica did not meet his eyes. 'You have a fine gardener do you not?'

'Indeed, we are privileged in that respect.'

'Then it would be a pity to lose him.'

Llewellyn shook his head. 'Lose him Veronica? I do not understand.'

'Your sister Dorothea has a very low opinion of him.'

'No, no, you misunderstand, as I explained Dorothea can be headstrong but she is a competent woman, she knows an asset when she sees one. Nonetheless, if it pleases you I will speak with her.'

Veronica exhaled, nodded. 'I do not seek to cause friction – only…'

'I know what drives you Veronica,' Llewellyn said quietly, leaning towards her.

'You do?'

'Of course: it is understandable concern. Gibbings was the man who saved your life, was he not?'

'He was.'

Llewellyn gathered up the reins and resumed the journey. 'My sister will make no rash decisions, I will ensure it. And you will honour us by returning to the island?'

Veronica smiled. 'I will.'

***

Llewellyn sat in the castle's drawing room sipping tea; he cast a glance at the grandfather clock and rang for his butler.

'Ah Hambleton, I shall require you to transport me to Berwick station in fifteen minutes, my luggage is packed and ready if you would oblige me by loading it.'

'I'll attend to it sir.'

Llewellyn watched Hambleton stride out in his dignified manner and then turned his attention to Dorothea.

'Yes, what is it?' She asked, without looking up from her paper.

'I trust there will be no discord while I'm away.'

'Meaning what?'

'Meaning Gibbings. His gardening is exemplary, our grounds are a great asset and we cannot afford to lose him.'

Dorothea billowed smoke into the air. 'He is uncouth, undisciplined. He has the wild look about him.'

'He was disciplined enough to pluck a woman from the sea…'

'Ah – I see brother.' Dorothea smiled triumphantly. 'Your violinist friend has wielded her influence. Did I not warn you against this approach?'

Llewellyn jumped to his feet, cocked a forefinger. 'I mean what I say Dorothea, do not dare to dismiss Gibbings.'

Dorothea narrowed her eyes, held his furious gaze. 'We shall see what we shall see – life is interesting, is it not?'

Llewellyn marched across to Dorothea and stood over her, placing his hands on the arms of the Regency chair. 'I will be back within two weeks, I expect no major alterations, remember that.'

Dorothea smirked and he stormed out red with rage; would she defy him and in so doing cause him to let down Veronica? Even Dorothea, he thought, would not venture that far.

***

Veronica strolled down from the abbey ruins to where the lifeboat was moored, arms crossed, hands on her shoulders for the morning was fresh.

There was a hint of blue breaking through the grey skies, a halo from the sun just beginning to appear. The shore was deserted, the red and black boat seemed neglected in its solitude but she knew the crew was just a klaxon call away.

She wondered how John Gibbings would fare, whether her words to Llewellyn would have any effect. An appraisal of John told her he was not without intuition or intelligence. Work on the island must surely be hard to find but he clearly didn't want to leave it. With his black curly hair and slightly brooding face he had something of the gypsy in him. She wondered whether he was a native of the island or if not, what had brought him here.

'Veronica dear, you look lost without your violin; life without music is nothing, one suspects.'

Dorothea's voice sliced through Veronica's thoughts, an unwelcome intrusion that triggered resentment.

'Since you approached me from behind,' Veronica said slowly turning, 'how can you see what I portray?'

'I do not need to see your face to read your mind – you will be glad to leave this island, it is not for you.'

Veronica stared into Dorothea's cold eyes and saw not a conversation but a threat. 'On the contrary, I feel a connection with this island, I am quite certain I shall return.'

Dorothea, at least two inches shorter was forced to raise her head to meet Veronica's gaze. 'Then I am compelled to be abrupt; you might be an accomplished violinist Miss Day but I sense something of the flirt in you – you are not welcome here – certainly not at the castle.'

'I believe that is for your brother to decide, the owner? Now please excuse me, I have no inclination to listen to your insults.'

Dorothea seemed unwilling to give ground so Veronica pushed past her heading towards the village. Dorothea's voice, frosty and sharp, followed her. 'You will do well to heed my words.'

The warning had been starkly delivered but Veronica was in no mood to heed it. Just why was Dorothea so vindictive? She felt renewed concern for John Gibbings in the face of such inexplicable hostility.
***

Dorothea Llewellyn watched Veronica Day all the way to the village, then turned and headed back to the castle.

But she wasn't heading for the castle itself, she was making for the walled garden on its western flank.

John Gibbings had been trimming verges surrounding the flower beds when he saw her approach, wearing a tight fitting full length white dress and matching hat. He lowered his shears. 'Good morning, Miss Llewellyn,' he said respectfully.

'Good morning Gibbings.' Dorothea waltzed slowly up to him, carried on by a yard or two and then stopped, angling her head towards him.

'You might be aware that Mr. Llewellyn has returned to his London business, thus the day to day running of castle affairs lies in my hands.'

'I have heard as much.'

'I have been of mind to cancel your employment forthwith,' she said, swinging up to him. 'I find you dishevelled, not to say filthy, particularly your hands; put down the shears, Gibbings.'

Gibbings laid them down beside azalea flower beds, and Dorothea looked up at him, taking the tips of his fingers in her hands. 'Ah look at them Gibbings, your fingernails are black, your fingers are encrusted in dirt.'

She let go of them, looked searchingly into his eyes. 'However, Mr. Llewellyn is of the foolish notion that you are of some value to the castle, therefore I am goodhearted enough to grant you a reprieve.'

'Thank…'

'On the understanding that you use the castle washroom regularly and leave it in a fit state.'

'I do so already Miss…'

'And that you report to me each morning before commencing work, so that I might assess your standard of hygiene. You understand?'

Gibbings gave a slow nod of the head.

'Good.' Dorothea began to walk away, stopped and without turning, said, 'One more thing, you are to make no contact with the musician Veronica Day, should she choose to return here.'

'There has been no contact,' Gibbings protested mildly, 'other than Miss Day thanking me.'

'Oh yes, for your brave deed. Noble indeed.' Dorothea swung round, eyes narrowing. 'It is my considered opinion that Miss Day would prove a disruptive influence if encouraged. I saw how close the two of you were standing – I have eyes Gibbings. Mr. Llewellyn might own the castle but in his absence I control affairs. You have been warned.'

She raised a forefinger towards his eyes. 'You are indebted to me Gibbings, do not be foolish enough to forget it.'

The gardener met her stare, retrieving his shears, before continuing his work in silence.

Chapter Seven

Llewellyn longed to see Veronica Day again. Even though but a few weeks had passed since he'd watched her brought ashore on the island, the thought she might return was ever on his mind.

She'd smitten him like never before; never before had he experienced the longing, the desire he felt now. He'd been a hardcore business man until her appearance; he'd had one or two relationships in his thirty plus years, but none that had endured. And Veronica Day, despite her beauty had no ties, he'd been informed thus by people who knew about such things.

Her effect on him had been such that his nights in London had filled with thoughts of her, playing the violin solely for him in candlelight on the castle's roof garden, her red hair fanning behind like a rich burgundy banner. And then afterwards he'd welcome her into his arms, curl them around her and draw her down, but that was where desire had turned to torment – torment caused by the longing to see her again – not knowing when that might be.

Llewellyn had spent the evening at a Berkeley Street private members club he was apt to visit on occasions, sitting in a plush, red leather chair, fingering through the pages of his newspaper routinely when he'd reached the arts and music section. There, beside a photo of Veronica was an account of her recent performances in Edinburgh. The newspaper reported that she had played to five packed houses in Edinburgh during a series of concerts and had received a standing ovation at each one. He read on to learn that from the Scottish Capital she was travelling south to York for more concerts.

He assumed she would travel by rail and thus pass close to the island, at a time when he was planning a few days return. Was it too soon to invite her back? If reason said yes, then his heart said no – and it was his heart, for the first time in his thirty plus years, that held sway.

It drummed at the thought of speaking with her, a sense of anticipation and yes, nervous apprehension.

But first he would need considerable good fortune, because Veronica had not left a forwarding address, promising instead to contact him when able to return.

He could only surmise that she had not yet left Edinburgh, and that she remained in one of the main hotels there.

Llewellyn got to his feet and made for the club foyer, engaging in a brief conversation with an official and tapping restlessly on the oak desk until a few moments later, the official returned with a list of hotel contact numbers. He made several calls without success, his hopes falling like a severed parachute as he approached the bottom of the list, whereupon he heard a gravelly voice say, 'Miss Veronica Day sir? She is indeed residing at the Arthur's Rock Hotel.'

Taking Llewellyn's name and number the porter promised to convey a message to the effect that she call him as soon as possible. Llewellyn hadn't wanted to alarm her but he did want to deliver his message personally, and thus thanking the porter he spent an anxious hour in the members lounge, eyes travelling uneasily between his paper and the ornate mantelpiece clock.

Eventually a blue-uniformed official came hustling in. 'Mr. Llewellyn, sir, a telephone call for you in reception – a Miss Day is on the line.'

Grabbing hold of the stem, 'Good evening Veronica,' Llewellyn called through the mouthpiece. 'I do hope I am not inconveniencing you…'

'Not at all Mr. Llewellyn – I do trust there is nothing wrong,' she broke in, sounding perplexed.

'No, no, nothing, I assure you – and call me Thomas please,' Llewellyn hastened, tweaking his moustache. 'Forgive me for the intrusion but I have been reading an account of your fine performances in my newspaper, and note that you will soon be following up with performances which will bring you close to the island.' Llewellyn coughed. 'I was wondering whether you might favour us with a return visit?'

'So soon?' Llewellyn heard Veronica draw breath and felt he'd been shot down by a bullet. 'I really cannot afford any time prior to my performances in York, I need to rehearse frequently you see.'

'I see…' Despondency weighed down on him.

'However, I shall have a week free once I've completed my concerts; I should be more than pleased to return to your castle. Can I suggest the first of July?'

Llewellyn smiled. 'You certainly can; that would be first rate.' Quickly his mood had lifted, life was happiness itself. He didn't bother to consider whether prior engagements might prohibit his return at this time. 'We shall finalize arrangements later; perhaps you would be kind enough to write to Hambleton, advising him of the time of your arrival. Either myself or Hambleton will then meet you at the station.'

'Why thank you Mr. Llewellyn, until the first of July then.'

Llewellyn replaced the telephone on the desk as the line went dead, collected his paper and marched out feeling as light as a feather. Veronica's answer was all he could have expected, more in fact.

He'd deliberately arranged that she contacted Hambleton, for an indefinable reason he knew he couldn't trust Dorothea one iota concerning Veronica.

The less she knew before her arrival, the better.

Back at his London residence, Llewellyn wasted little time contacting the castle via the newly installed telephone system. He was more than grateful that Hambleton answered and not Dorothea.

Chapter Eight

July 1st

Dorothea Llewellyn cast disapproving dark eyes around the castle entrance hall and then swept along a corridor beckoning the butler to follow her. 'Hambleton as you are aware, my brother returns this afternoon, you know how he dislikes slovenliness and the castle appears a trifle dingy. See what you can do to brighten it up. I would summon Gibbings but I have other duties for him.'

Hambleton gave a discreet sigh, weren't all castles dingy? Their original purpose demanded it, and just what "other duties" was Dorothea planning for Gibbings? After her now daily inspections of him, there seemed always to be a private task to hand. He watched her throw open a guest room door, raise her nose and sniff, then gaze down at a freshly made bed. 'I was going to suggest that you air the guest rooms, not that company is expected but for Mr. Llewellyn's benefit you understand. But this room has been freshly prepared, would you mind telling me why?'

Hambleton looked into eyes that burned not with curiosity but certain knowledge. Llewellyn had asked that Veronica's visit be kept secret, but he could oblige no longer…

'Well come on Hambleton, let's not dilly dally,' Dorothea said, hands thrust on hips. 'This was the room Miss Day slept in, was it not? Are you now informing me she is returning?' Dorothea's tone had risen a notch, her hooded eyes taken on their formidably hawkish look.

Hambleton raised a finger to his lips, trying to conceal his discomfort. 'Madam, that is so.'

She took a step closer, fiercely meeting his eyes. 'And why wasn't I informed of this?'

'I beg your pardon, Madam, but as Miss Day is Mr. Llewellyn's guest, I thought it unnecessary.'

Dorothea's complexion had a dark tinge to it, her angry eyes shooting rapidly to and fro as she screwed them. 'It is your responsibility, Hambleton, to see that I am informed of *all* developments relating to this castle – remember, you might be my brother's appointment Hambleton – but you are not indispensable – just when is this woman expected?'

'I am to collect her from the station at two pm.' Hambleton overcame a stammer, managing to keep his dignity in the face of Dorothea's ferocity.

'That will not be possible,' she snapped. 'I have already

instructed that you check the castle interior thoroughly prior to my brother's arrival.'

'I beg to differ Madam,' Hambleton said in his humblest tone, 'they are Mr. Llewellyn's instructions and cannot be overridden.'

From a sudden movement of Dorothea's right arm Hambleton thought she would strike him, but as he stepped back her forefinger quivered an inch from his nose, before speechless with anger she swung away, storming back down the hall.

A sound of boots on the flagstone floor drew her to a halt. The lean figure in dark overalls stood before her. 'Miss Llewellyn, sorry for my late arrival,' John Gibbings said, 'the lifeboat klaxon sounded – a false alarm, I…'

Dorothea raised a hand dismissively. 'I will overlook it on this occasion.' She searched his eyes. 'I take it you have been made aware?'

'Aware, Miss Llewellyn, aware of what?'

Dorothea snatched a look back at Hambleton. 'It seems that Miss Day is to make an unannounced return visit forthwith, unannounced to me at any rate…' she fixed her eyes on him again. 'Is that interest I see on your face?'

Gibbings shook his head emphatically. 'No Miss Llewellyn, just surprise that's all.'

'She distracts you from your duties at your peril,' Dorothea hissed, her jaw tightening.

'She will not distract me, Miss Llewellyn,' Gibbings said solemnly. 'I have no interest in her, other than my duties as a lifeboat man…'

'Enough…' Dorothea gave a sharp intake of breath. 'Come, show me your hands.' She took them in hers, turned them, applied some pressure – 'They look clean to me; before you endeavour to dirty them I have a task for you.'

Hambleton watched as Dorothea did an about turn, guided Gibbings along the hallway, passing him without a word. But Gibbings flashed him a look from his brown eyes, though its meaning if there was one, was hidden.

***

Hambleton arrived at the station to see steam from the locomotive waiting at the platform billow over the station roof. No sooner had he pulled the trap to a halt than Veronica Day, all leggy elegance in a flowing dress of pastel shades and fine lace trimmings, emerged through the exit, carrying her luggage in one hand and her violin case in the other.

She was attractive in the extreme and Hambleton knew his employer was fond of her. For his employer's sake he hoped the feeling was reciprocated, but Dorothea's thinly disguised hostility towards the violinist caused him concern. He did not trust Dorothea, his first look into her hard, dark eyes had bestowed in him wariness, but now he sensed she saw a threat in Veronica Day.

Precisely why, he couldn't comprehend. Perhaps she feared that a place in her brother's affections might prejudice her own position in the household, or could it be something to do with Dorothea's strange behaviour towards Gibbings? Unlikely as that might seem, Hambleton kept an open mind.

'Good afternoon, Miss Day, a pleasure to greet you.' Hambleton smiled as he slipped from the trap and collected her luggage. 'I take it your journey has not been too tiring?'

'Not at all, Mr. Hambleton, I am stronger than I look.' She returned his smile though it faded a little. 'Is Mr. Llewellyn indisposed?'

'No madam, he is due to arrive later this afternoon, he had hoped to have arrived sooner, however an important customer of the bank has booked a late appointment.'

'Ah.' She fell silent as Hambleton gathered the reins and the pony commenced its trot through the rolling Northumberland countryside. 'I'm certainly pleased the weather's picked up,' she said at length. 'Such a nice, fresh feel to the day don't you think, after all the morning rain. Far better conditions for your gardener, Gibbings aren't they? It must be awful for him in foul weather. How has he been faring?'

Hambleton fingered his throat, it felt cloyed, perhaps it was just summer pollen, but certain aspects of Veronica Day's visit did not bode well, there was an air of portent that made him tense – and just a short distance into the journey she'd hit on Gibbings.

'He seems well, madam,' Hambleton said uncomfortably. 'You understand that he spends much of his time on outside duties, therefore I do not see much of him.'

Hambleton coughed, something needed to be said before they reached the castle. 'However, I feel obliged to advise you that Miss

Llewellyn's behaviour has been a little erratic of late, therefore any welcome she might extend may seem somewhat strained.'

Veronica didn't respond immediately, but the long intake of breath and the fact that her face was suddenly turned from him suggested there was something on her mind.

'Miss Llewellyn has seemed indisposed towards me, though I do not feel I have done anything to sour her attitude,' Veronica said thoughtfully as Hambleton led the trap onto the three-mile causeway which connected the island to the mainland.

This was a subject that Hambleton did not want to be drawn into; it was part of the air of portent he thought was gathering. Whatever was influencing Dorothea's behaviour directly or indirectly involved the violinist, but her antics were certain to be curtailed by the arrival of her brother later that afternoon.

Or so Hambleton thought, because when he arrived back at the castle with Veronica he found that a surprise was waiting.

He had collected Veronica's luggage, followed her up the castle's steep, cobbled slope, quietly impressed with the ease and grace with which she negotiated what most found to be a difficult climb, when they passed Gibbings on the way down. Veronica moved across to greet him but there was just a hint of recognition beneath his long dark lashes as he hurried past.

'Hambleton…' Dorothea's sharp voice resounded around the church-nave-like entrance hall, and shortly afterwards she emerged from the passageway, cigarette holder between her fingers as she blasted a cloud of smoke and ash in their direction.

'Mr. Llewellyn has been further delayed Hambleton,' she said with the merest glance at Veronica. 'He telephoned a few moments ago, there is an obstruction on the line – his arrival at the station will be delayed by at least two hours.'

'The tide will be out,' Hambleton grimaced.

'I am well aware of what it means Hambleton; the causeway will not be negotiable until ten thirty this evening – however Mr. Llewellyn has decided not to impose on you at this hour, generously he has elected to book a hotel room in Berwick. You are to collect him at ten o'clock tomorrow morning from the Station Hotel.' She raised her head in an unsuccessful attempt to match Veronica's height and said stiffly, 'My brother sends his apologies for circumstances beyond his control; he trusts you will enjoy your evening.'

'I will escort you to your room, Miss Day,' Hambleton cut in, 'following which I will have Mrs. Simms consult with you on your dinner.'

'Following which I should like to take a walk to fully familiarise myself with the island,' Veronica said, her eyes engaging Dorothea's for several seconds.

'I see.' Dorothea rested her arm against one of the hall's stone pillars, blew smoke in Veronica's direction. 'It's your prerogative, though I should have thought you were well enough acquainted from your previous visit.' She leaned forward, whispered in Veronica's ear, 'Remember what I told you, my dear you are not welcome here.'

'Only in some quarters I suspect,' Veronica whispered back with a cool smile, watching Dorothea's face freeze over.

***

Dorothea's stance didn't so much worry Veronica as irritate her. She had been invited as Thomas Llewellyn's guest and as such her presence wasn't resented in all quarters – but why had John Gibbings all but refused to acknowledge her return – was it on account of some hold Dorothea held over him? Or was he normally so shy or rude? She decided not, he hadn't seemed it when he'd rescued her or when she'd first spoken with him in the garden, their conversation only becoming stunted when he'd gazed at the dining room window – and seen who – Dorothea?

And then there was Dorothea's offensive manner during their encounter on the shore, where she'd stopped little short of labelling her a flirt. But she'd bitten back her indignation and summoned her resolve. Dorothea wasn't going to dictate to her and she *was* going to address the problem with Gibbings.

She ate alone that evening, attended by Hambleton, who in contrast to Dorothea she found genial and affable. Looking out at the gardens, tranquil and colourful in the evening sun, she saw no sign of Gibbings, and thankfully Dorothea was either out or in her private rooms.

Veronica thanked Hambleton and excused herself, and after freshening up made her way down the castle slope, her long hair entwining itself around her neck in the breeze. Below, the sea was turquoise in the strong evening sunlight, and as she reached the bottom of the slope, turning towards the village she saw the lifeboat at its moorings along the shore, and a cluster of figures busying themselves around it.

From a distance it wasn't possible for Veronica to assess whether John Gibbings was amongst them, or even what the group's purpose was, but she willed that he be there and as she approached saw this was the case, making out his slim form amongst several washing down the hull.

She held back for fear of disturbing him, perching on a craggy rock behind the shingle from where she could see the crew going about their work, then looked in the opposite direction, towards the castle, sitting on its high mound of volcanic rock, and pictured Dorothea's brooding presence within. But she was a visitor – a guest of Mr. Llewellyn's and therefore in no position to confront Dorothea as well she might given differing circumstances – in any case to do so now might prejudice John Gibbings. If there was an opportunity to talk with him beyond Dorothea's prying eyes she would take it.

It was some thirty minutes before the crew disbanded, most headed in the direction of the village, but Gibbings, after bidding goodbye to another, began to amble in her direction, hands thrust in pockets, eyes on the shingle. He was almost upon her when he looked up, saw her sitting on the rock and froze.

'Hello John, such a nice evening I thought I'd take a stroll…'

'And watch me working on the lifeboat…'

Veronica chewed lightly on her bottom lip, stared into eyes that did not fully meet hers. 'That you presumed my attentions were solely for you could be deemed vanity.'

'Why are you here then?'

Veronica thought carefully, in truth her visit had much to do with him, but was it indignation, resentment she saw in his eyes – and if so why?

'At the invitation of Mr. Llewellyn – only he has been delayed, so here I am, sitting on this rock, admiring the peace and tranquillity of this island.'

'Then don't let me disturb you.'

'What makes you think you're disturbing me, won't you sit down? Room enough for two.' She patted the rock, smiling, aware there was a challenge in her eyes.

'I can't, the garden needs watering – the rainfall this morning weren't near enough.' He made to move on, his face was impassive but his eyes told a different story.

'Then I'll join you if you don't mind, I could do with the company. I feel somewhat isolated without Mr. Llewellyn's presence.'

'No, I don't need company,' his reply was rough, harsh, 'and I can't understand why you're taking this interest in me.'

'I've already told you that; because you saved my life…' her tone was a little stronger than she'd intended so she dropped it a touch, 'and because I think you've got a problem…'

'So you don't just play the violin – you're a clairvoyant,' Gibbings said as he walked away, the sudden sophistication of his speech both amusing and surprising her.

She watched him go, without another word, but she saw something else – from the castle window facing the village, high up, a shadow moved. Just a fleeting glimpse, but someone had been watching.

Chapter Nine

Llewellyn clambered into the trap and stretched out his legs. 'Spot on Hambleton, ten o'clock precisely; damned inconvenience yesterday I say, the wind bringing a tree down on the line like that.' He slapped a hand on the trap's side. 'So how are things at the castle – is Miss Day nicely settled in?'

Hambleton brushed a finger across his lip, taking the reins with his free hand. 'She arrived on time sir.'

'I see, fine, just fine.' Llewellyn tweaked his moustache, gave his butler a lengthy glance. 'You seem unusually reticent, Hambleton, is something the matter?'

'It may be nothing sir.'

'It is plainly something if it is causing you disquiet.' Llewellyn settled back in the trap, folded his arms. 'Is my sister proving bothersome?'

'Miss Llewellyn is at best, difficult sir.' Hambleton drew breath, sighed. 'She appears to have developed an unusual relationship with Gibbings.'

Llewellyn let out a high pitched laugh, at variance to his speaking voice. 'Relationship, Hambleton – oh come now.'

Hambleton shook his head, concentrated while he guided the pony out of Berwick into open countryside. 'I am not suggesting it is in any way physical you understand. However she has taken to giving him daily inspections as to his cleanliness…'

'That is not at all strange, she has the notion that he is untidy – I do not hold with it but…'

'Forgive me for interrupting sir, but there is more – she has taken to finding him odd jobs within the castle…'

'That is another of his duties.'

'They seem almost entirely to be within her private quarters, sir.' Hambleton fell silent, allowed his words to sink in.

Llewellyn took a deep breath of warm summer air and shrugged. 'Oh I am certain there is a simple explanation for that; my sister has a loathing for Gibbings which is quite beyond my comprehension. In fact it quite unsettled Miss Day on the last occasion. I had to go out of my way to rebuke her less she dismiss him. The castle is centuries old, Dorothea has a knack of finding faults, that is the explanation.'

'There is more sir.'

A twitch of amusement showed itself in Llewellyn's cheek. 'You are of an unsettled frame of mind this morning, what is it?'

'That I cannot say sir, Miss Llewellyn has a boisterous nature and that may be all, however Miss Day also displays an interest in Gibbings.'

The smile was back on Llewellyn's face. 'That is understandable Hambleton, he did after all save her life, she therefore worries for his welfare. It is nothing more than that.'

Onto the causeway and around the bend the castle came into sight, high on its rock. 'Ah,' Llewellyn gasped, 'what a welcoming sight that is, Hambleton.'

'Yes sir.' But Hambleton's features were grim.

***

'If you're looking for your guest, you're too late – she's out.' Dorothea turned her attention from the dining room window, where she'd been watching Gibbings gardening, and regarded Llewellyn through narrowed eyes.

'That's her choice, she's here as a guest after all.' Llewellyn shrugged, endeavouring to conceal his disappointment that Veronica hadn't been present to greet him. 'How are things Dorothea, I trust there are no problems to speak of?'

Dorothea waved a hand dismissively. 'Nothing I haven't been able to handle – I would have thought she'd have the courtesy to await your return before undertaking her expedition of the island,' she persisted, swinging up to him, arms crossed.

'Why do you take it upon yourself to be so vindictive?' Llewellyn suddenly snapped, receiving a triumphant smile from his sister.

'Oh dear, dear,' she patted his arm. 'More than a little touchy this morning, aren't we, Thomas?'

'On account of your behaviour, nothing more.' Llewellyn brushed down his blue blazer and white flannels, turning away from her. This wasn't the homecoming he'd expected.

'I beg your pardon – and what is wrong with my behaviour?' Llewellyn felt Dorothea's hand grasp his upper arm. 'Has somebody been complaining, and would that somebody be Hambleton?'

'Hambleton has said nothing,' Llewellyn lied, removing her hand from his arm; for the equilibrium of the castle he could not impart what his butler had told him. 'Purely my own observations, I know you well enough, Dorothea.'

'Not as well as you think it seems.' Dorothea's tone had lowered, her lips twisting into ugly shapes, she lofted her head back and black curls swung about her face. No sooner had he set foot in the place than she was becoming confrontational, but he had allowed her to goad him over Veronica's absence, though he retained enough composure to prevent her capitalizing on it.

He turned away with her taunts ringing in his ears and headed upstairs, out onto the roof garden, past the benches and table to the parapet, and then sweeping his eyes along the shoreline he saw her, a tall figure in a flowing green dress making her way jauntily towards the castle, pausing now and then to hurl a pebble into the sea.

Delighted to see her returning he dashed through the castle and down the slope, which she now approached looking windswept, slightly tanned and very healthy, her red hair fanned out by the wind. She greeted him with the broadest of smiles.

'I'm delighted to see you Veronica.' He took her hand and when she clutched it gently, let go. 'I'm so pleased you could come. I would have arrived yesterday but for a fallen tree on the main line.'

She swept her hair away from her eyes. 'Well you're here now and that's nice.' She glanced out to sea and then up at the skies. 'The weather's been kind to us after all that wind and rain. I was going for a walk around the island but I saw you and Mr. Hambleton in the trap.'

'Perhaps we can do so together?' Llewellyn suggested, with a tweak of his moustache. 'I hardly know the island myself, never having had the time.'

'Yes, let's.'

Llewellyn felt like a love-struck youngster, longing to take her hand but fearing to be so bold, so soon.

'Isn't it great to be at one with nature?' Veronica said cheerily as they headed back along the shoreline.

'Most certainly,' Llewellyn replied, nodding at a flock of birds foraging amongst the seaweed, 'they seem happy enough.'

'Turnstones,' Veronica smiled.

'I beg your pardon?'

'They're called Turnstones, they're distinguished by their short orange legs and small black bill – oh, and look at the baby gulls,' she pointed to a small group on the edge of the breakers, observed by their parents, splashing and tipping their tails. 'They're learning to swim. In a minute one of the bigger ones will stretch a foot out, tip them over – sink or swim technique, that's what it is.'

Llewellyn was impressed; he hadn't counted on getting a nature lesson. They stopped to watch the gulls; sure enough one of the parents toppled them over, one by one.

'You seem quite acquainted with nature,' Llewellyn remarked as they strolled away from the shore, heading towards the abbey ruins.

'That's down to my parents,' she said, 'principally my father; we spent long holidays on the coast when I was a child, he taught me a lot – he was a great enthusiast on wading birds...' she sighed, 'and then we moved to Vienna and everything changed.'

'In what way?' Llewellyn asked, offering a hand to assist Veronica as they climbed a steep bank.

'No, it's okay, I can manage.' She waved him away, climbed the bank easily and Llewellyn felt a momentary stab of resentment at her refusal to take his hand. 'My father was a professor, and took a post at the University of Vienna, and my mother became a music teacher in the city.'

Llewellyn noticed the smile had gone from Veronica's face. 'Would you like to rest? There is a garden adjacent to the abbey grounds...'

'Good heavens no, why, are you tiring?'

Llewellyn was taken aback. 'No, of course not – it's just that, well – you seem suddenly a trifle weary.'

'No, no,' Veronica said dismissively. 'It's just the thought of all those years in Vienna; although I received an outstanding education and learned the violin, I missed my childhood in this country.' Veronica turned her back, gazed out to sea and clapped her hands. 'Especially locations such as this – peaceful, remote, isolated.' She swung back to him. 'Come on, let's carry on inland, I'm turning melancholy.'

Llewellyn led her into a curving lane, its hedgerows adorned with hawthorn and elder. 'I've read about your years in Vienna, but I hadn't realised you were unhappy there.'

'I wouldn't say I was unhappy exactly, but it's not that I had a lot of option – more a case of having to. I must sound ungrateful...'

'No of course not,' Llewellyn was quick to shake his head. 'I undertook a career in banking, under my parents' guidance you understand – I cannot say however that I've felt any regret, or had the inclination to pursue anything else.'

'Then I'm happy for you.' Veronica broke off as a gaggle of geese flew low overhead. 'You have made a success of your career doing something you like.'

'As have you...'

'Yes, but at a cost.'

Llewellyn was going to question her reply but she gave him an inquiring glance and said, 'You say you read about my years in Vienna, where did you read it?'

Llewellyn swallowed heavily, in his desire to become familiarized with Veronica he had studied every classical music journal he could get his hands on, but he wasn't certain he should admit to it.

But as he was formulating his reply Veronica broke into his thoughts, pointing across to the castle grounds. 'That's your gardener out there, I believe – he does such a fine job on your gardens.'

'Yes, indeed he does. Shall we have a word with him?'

'Oh no, I wouldn't want to intrude on his work.'

'Nonsense, I'd intended to speak with him on my return and you, I know have a concern for his welfare, a concern that I fully appreciate.'

Veronica briefly lowered her eyes as Llewellyn opened the gate and led the way to where Gibbings was planting rose trees. 'Good morning Gibbings, a fine job you're doing...' he outstretched his arm, 'you remember Miss Day, no doubt, she was just expressing her admiration for your work.'

Gibbings afforded her a quick glance, broody, unsmiling.

'I try my best.'

'That's all I ask.' Llewellyn cupped a palm to his chin. 'You are well I take it, you look a trifle jaded...'

'Aye sir, I'm fine.' Gibbings tapped restlessly on the shaft of his spade. 'Everything's fine.'

'And Miss Llewellyn has treated you well?'

'Yes, sir.'

'Very well, keep up the good work.' Satisfied, Llewellyn turned to go, but Veronica remained still. 'Mr. Gibbings, I shall be holding a recital in the castle's roof gardens tomorrow evening, weather permitting...' she looked to Llewellyn who turned abruptly in surprise, 'with Mr. Llewellyn's permission of course. I would deem it a great honour if you would attend.' She glanced again at

Llewellyn. 'This invitation is naturally extended to your entire household.'

Gibbings' eyes widened. 'No, he protested, I can't…'

'Nonsense Gibbings,' Llewellyn interrupted sternly, glancing to Veronica. 'What a fine gesture, to refuse would be an act of rudeness and I do not tolerate incivility. You shall attend, as shall my sister, Hambleton and Mrs. Simms. Beforehand we will dine on the terrace.'

Gibbings opened his mouth to speak but clamped it shut without uttering a word, though his jaw was clenched and he was biting his lip.

Veronica gave him a smile and a nod, before joining Llewellyn in a walk back to the castle. 'Forgive me for not seeking your permission, she said quietly, 'but it was an impromptu decision, and I thought it would be nice for your household to be involved.'

'Indeed it would, what a noble gesture. We are so fortunate to have you as a guest.'

Llewellyn, smiling broadly, approached the castle, his pleasure growing. The presence of Veronica with her fine music on a lovely summer's evening would dissolve any disharmony that existed in his midst as surely as ice-cream melted on a hot day. Though he suspected that a lot of what he'd heard was a figment of his butler's overactive mind.

Chapter Ten

Dorothea looked up from her paper, a frown lining her forehead as the strains of Veronica's violin seemed to fill the castle, cascading down from her room. 'This place is becoming an incessant musical box,' she complained to Llewellyn from her armchair.

'Nonsense, Veronica needs frequent practice to maintain her exceptionally high standard,' Llewellyn said, raising his ears to the music as he reclined in a high backed leather chair. 'We are fortunate to be given the opportunity to listen to her music – indeed, I should inform you she will be holding a recital out on the roof garden tomorrow evening, I trust you will be gracious enough to attend; I expect the whole household to be present.'

Dorothea put the paper down, her lashes meeting repeatedly, before giving Llewellyn a disbelieving look. 'Hambleton I concede – Mrs Simms I confess to not knowing her musical inclinations. But as for Gibbings, you are not suggesting that the likes of him would be in the slightest interested…'

'The invitation was not mine Dorothea.' Llewellyn arced from his reclined state, placed his hands on his knees. 'It was extended by Veronica herself, most generously.'

'Oh such generosity Thomas,' Dorothea laughed incredulously. 'Have you not noticed her tendency to "call the tune" if you'll excuse the phrase. She seems to do as she pleases and that is not normal for a mature woman of her standing.'

'What pleases me Dorothea, is that you, Hambleton, Mrs. Simms and Gibbings do the lady the courtesy of attending her performance.' Llewellyn brushed his moustache roughly with the back of his hand. 'And I will thank you to keep your ill-conceived opinions to yourself.'

Dorothea gave a slow, bitter smile, 'Oh that you be stung by mere words, Thomas. Are you so star-struck that you cannot see the truth in them, or do you indeed do so and choose to shut your eyes and ears?'

'Your nonsense is the only thing that deafens my ears Dorothea and I will listen to it no longer.' Llewellyn sprung to his feet, made for the door, stopped as he grabbed the frame and turned; his voice low in contrast to the music from the violin, he said, 'I trust you will remember your civility at dinner this evening, for the sake of our guest.'

Dorothea rose and sauntered towards him, her long cream gown brushing the stone floor. 'Unfortunately I shall not be present. I have an engagement with an intermediary from the village. Someone needs to maintain supplies for the demand made on them by your unexpected guests.' Dorothea raised her head as she brushed past him, regarded him with wide eyes, 'Don't they?'

Llewellyn watched Dorothea approach the stone stairway with a familiar swing in her stride, but more pronounced on this occasion; he heard her steps as she climbed it, presumably to the next floor where she had two adjoining rooms, one serving as her office. He wondered momentarily what work Gibbings had undertaken in them then chastised himself for even reflecting on it.

Dorothea's powerful aura, her attitude, her haughty sarcasm, seemed to encompass him at times, and in times of his absence, seemingly the castle itself and those within it, and this within a few short months of taking possession of the place. He wondered ultimately whether she might engulf the whole island, and then shuddered at the thought.

For the first time that day he considered whether an impartial administrator might have proven a prudent investment whereby his sister could have remained in her Richmond home. But his business dealings had extended him beyond his ability to purchase the castle outright, and only Dorothea's intervention had made the acquisition possible. Hence she now held a stake, and control of castle affairs in his absence.

Upstairs the music had ceased, and fearing that in her present frame of mind Dorothea might provoke a confrontation with Veronica, Llewellyn ascended the steps to the upper floors, on the first of which Veronica's room lay. Her door was slightly ajar, he tapped twice without response and so, nudging it open a fraction he peered through. Veronica's violin sat on its stand, but of her there was no sign.

He ran up to the roof garden and from the shade of the open door, saw Veronica and his sister.

Veronica was relaxing against a green wrought-iron bench, with Dorothea, arms folded, prowling to and fro, her hawkish gaze angled towards the violinist. 'It was very generous of you to arrange to perform for the household's benefit, even those of us who do not wish to hear you.'

'My offer was made with all good intentions,' he heard Veronica calmly say. 'It was meant to convey my gratitude at being invited back. Miss Llewellyn, I wasn't the one who deemed it compulsory.'

'No indeed it was I.' Llewellyn had intended simply to eavesdrop but Dorothea's belligerence had gone a step too far. He was livid, lunging into the roof garden, his fists clenched so tightly they shook. He sensed that Dorothea knew it, because for once that arrogant stance had deserted her. There was nervousness in the way she stepped back.

'Thomas wait.' Veronica had moved with surprising speed across the bench, he felt her hand clasp his wrist with a gentle firmness. 'It's not what it seems. Dorothea's duties leave her tired, running the affairs of a building such as this, is, I suspect, no small order.' With her eyes firmly set on Dorothea, she said, 'I think you mistook what you saw as rudeness for frustration.'

Llewellyn took a huge breath as Veronica released his wrist, and swung away. He recalled Dorothea's agitation a few minutes earlier, over the evening visit she had to pay an intermediary, but he still couldn't excuse her behaviour -*"even those of us who do not wish to hear it."* Despite Veronica's intervention on her behalf Llewellyn struggled to interpret Dorothea's remark as anything other than rank rudeness.

'Thomas, might I suggest that tomorrow evening Miss Llewellyn relax in her own way,' Veronica said quietly, her hand upon his wrist. 'I shall be quite satisfied with the company of the remainder of your household.'

'Very well,' Llewellyn stammered, he had all but lost control of his reasoning; he needed space, time to regain his composure. Admirably, Veronica seemed to have lost none of hers.

***

Dorothea lofted her head, gave Veronica a stony glance as she followed her brother out.

She was smarting – had she of all people, played directly into another's hands? She'd lost face, for the first time she could recall; her brother had lost his temper as he occasionally did when pressured, but all the while Veronica Day had remained ice-cool. She'd out-manoeuvred her, and despite that placid composition, the woman knew it. That one fact released a message darting to her brain – she was not to be underestimated.

Back in her main room Dorothea stretched out on a Chesterfield sofa, a glass of Scotch whisky in her hand, fingers tapping restlessly on the glass while her eyes travelled frequently to the clock.

She had a visit to pay somebody shortly, but that somebody wasn't the intermediary she'd informed her brother of, neither was it business related; the recipient of her visit had crept his way into her mind and soul by some invisible, unguarded entrance she hadn't known existed until too late, by then he had taken root, governing her thoughts and actions so that all she saw was him, yes – and a lurking, ice-cool predator.

John Gibbings was loathsome – he was dirty, untidy, of undeniably low social standing and yet she desired him, needed his presence on an ever-increasing basis –

But he hadn't responded the way she'd have liked and so she'd found him regular jobs in the privacy of her rooms, until they were no longer enough. It was his full attention, his full, *physical* attention she wanted and nobody was going to stand in her way.

Veronica Day wasn't the quiet, introverted classical violinist she gave the impression of being, she *was* the lurking, ice-cool predator, the classic wolf in sheep's clothing; but John Gibbings didn't answer to Day, he answered to her, he was in her debt and at any time she could recall it, would do if he failed to comply with her demands. Though it wouldn't be necessary, because Gibbings, she was certain, would come to cherish her affections.

Dorothea coiled her hand tightly around the stem of her glass, swirled a mouthful of scotch and felt it glide warmly down her throat, before embarking on the short walk to John Gibbings' cottage.

***

Thomas Llewellyn had been embarrassed beyond measure by his loss of composure in the roof garden. In the past he'd occasionally allowed his temper to rule his actions and ended up regretting it. Only Veronica's calm response had prevented him exploding at his sister, but in losing his equilibrium had he diminished her respect for him? How did he stand in her eyes now?

For the past two hours he'd reflected on that, and whether to seek her out and apologise for the scene he'd helped create but he'd held back, determined to regain his full composure, to present himself in his true colours, that of a rational, well mannered and cordial man – someone capable and worthy of becoming her suitor.

Now he experienced a fizz of excitement as Veronica walked into the dining room where he stood waiting, the white dress she wore enhancing her tanned, unblemished skin, while a slim gold bracelet sparkled from her wrist.

He caught the fragrance of her perfume as she responded to his outstretched hand, taking a seat opposite, a hint of honeysuckle on a summer's evening. 'Veronica, it warms me to see you looking so lovely,' he said, seating himself in a plush red dining chair and leaning forward. 'I feel I must apologise for my inexcusable behaviour this afternoon.'

'Not at all Thomas.' She reached across, placing her hand on his, her long fingers enveloping it and sending a tingling thrill through him. 'You must not feel that; you misinterpreted the situation, that is all – you acted on my behalf and showed your true, good nature.'

He was glowing inside from the feel of her touch, so soft, and yet he'd so recently experienced the firmness of her restraining hold on him. 'My – my self-control deserted me. I felt that my sister was being insufferably rude.'

Veronica removed her hand from his, raised a glass of red wine to her lips, he felt her vibrant green eyes on his as she said, 'Your sister is what she is, Thomas, somewhat volatile, but I've told you it was all a misunderstanding – and please do not feel the need to intervene on my account. I am not easily alarmed or offended.'

Her voice was quiet and yet so clear, her composure seemed absolute, her beauty as the evening sunlight shone through the castle's Gothic windows exemplified in her hair, rich in vitality, its hue matching the reddening sunlight – he took in her broad, intelligent face and fine nose – Veronica Day had it all and Llewellyn was aroused.

He was ready to fire his big question, it seemed the perfect moment. 'I was wondering -' he began, but stopped short as he saw Hambleton enter the dining room bearing a tray containing dishes of smoked salmon. 'Thank you Hambleton.' He watched his butler carefully lay out their meals. 'I trust we shall enjoy this as much as we surely will Miss Day's violin recital tomorrow. Let us hope for a fine evening.'

'I'm sure it will be sir.' Hambleton glanced out of the window and saw a figure passing the walled garden, heading towards John Gibbings' cottage. 'For Mrs. Simms' benefit sir, might I enquire as to whether Miss Llewellyn will be requiring supper; she hasn't mentioned it you see…'

'I have no idea,' Llewellyn said edgily, the mere mention of his sister's name was becoming enough to irritate him. 'She has an appointment in the village with a supplier. If she had made no mention then Mrs. Simms may be released for the evening.'

'Very good sir.' Hambleton left the room and Llewellyn contemplated bringing up the subject uppermost on his mind until Veronica spoke between mouthfuls of salmon. 'This is excellent. Mrs. Simms is a splendid cook, in fact I must compliment you on your selection of staff, they are all first rate. I assume they were your appointments.'

'Such as they are – a very small staff you will have noticed. Hambleton is my own man; he accompanied me on my move here and elected to stay. Mrs. Simms is a native of the island and John Gibbings is our gardener – in truth I know little about him.' Llewellyn paused, looked out at the gardens, a spectacle of multi-coloured splendour – 'other than that he does a first class job…'

'I see. Then how did you come to appoint him?'

Llewellyn adjusted his black smoking jacket – his favourite; this evening it felt a little tight. Perhaps it was the food or perhaps simply that the conversation was taking a course other than his intended one – 'Well, in point of fact I didn't employ Gibbings directly; whilst I was surveying the castle with intention of purchase my sister undertook to examine the grounds, encountering Gibbings near the cottage he rents on the edge of our boundaries. Apparently, she had some reservations, but again there were good recommendations, thus we employed him.'

Veronica turned her head away, placed down her cutlery, cupping her chin with the tops of her hands. 'What kind of reservations?'

'I really don't know.' Llewellyn was finding it difficult to suppress his growing irritation.

The intricacies of Gibbings' appointment as gardener seemed an insignificant topic for conversation over dinner.

'Is the salmon not to your liking?'

She returned her attention to him. 'Indeed it is, but I habitually take small breaks for digestion purposes.' Her eyes remained on him, although her face was expressionless they seemed to be searching – the clear message was, she wasn't through with the subject.

'I see; most commendable. With regard to your question,' Llewellyn said through a mouthful of salmon, 'I can only surmise that my sister took objection to the condition of his hands, which she continues to insist are always filthy, though what would you expect of a gardener?' He paused, took a sip of red wine. 'She has a strange attitude towards him which caused Hambleton to comment, but we are talking of Dorothea here one must remember.'

'What kind of comment?'

Llewellyn looked into Veronica's widened green eyes; they seemed to melt his frustration. 'Apparently that she gives him regular odd jobs and daily inspections. Anyway, her obsession with cleanliness was probably the cause of any reticence,'

'Perhaps,' Veronica said quietly, resuming her meal.

'I beg your pardon?'

'Perhaps we shall never know, and perhaps we shall.'

Llewellyn shook his head and then searched for a change of subject. Veronica's pre-occupation with Gibbings' appointment had voided his mind for the moment of his intended course of conversation.

***

The door to the tiny stone built cottage lay open and so Dorothea didn't bother to knock, she didn't deem it necessary. She and her brother owned the castle and grounds after all, and that included the drab, unimposing dwelling she was now entering.

She blinked her eyes, adjusting to the gloom within, making out Gibbings' silhouette as he boiled water on a stove in the tiny kitchen beyond the drawing room.

'Miss Llewellyn...' sounding surprised he placed a kettle on the stove and came towards her, bare from the waist up, a towel slung over his left shoulder, his slim, well defined and tanned upper body glistening beneath a mop of dark curly hair. 'Anything I can do for you?'

'You do wash occasionally then?' Dorothea drew close, running the back of a forefinger slowly down the centre of his chest; she thought she saw a flicker of resentment in his eyes as his mouth tightened.

'Struck dumb are you?'

'Miss Llewellyn I...'

'Yes, there is something you can do for me.' She pushed past, brushing against his bare skin. 'After I've examined your quarters. Show me your bedroom.'

'If you care to look yourself, Miss...' Gibbings pushed open an adjoining door. 'I must attend to the lifeboat...'

'Do you not trust yourself in your own bedroom in my company Gibbings, is that it?'

She watched him clasp the back of his neck, shake his head. 'No, Miss.'

'Then step inside, it is not a request Gibbings.'

The room was sparse, a single bed, a worn oak wardrobe and an oil lamp atop a cabinet. A threadbare carpet covered the floor but Dorothea was not the least interested in the furnishing.

She entered the room and turned, Gibbings had halted barely inside the doorway. 'It seems that I am braver than you Gibbings, why – you seduce me here and I would be at your mercy – why, I'll make it easy, I'll come to you.'

Dorothea took two paces towards him, held his arms, her head craning towards his neck. 'No – Miss – please,' Gibbings thrust her away, 'don't be doing this.'

She breathed deeply, made to come again then checked herself. 'Very well, you have passed my test, but I am most displeased with the condition of this cottage, more regular inspections will be necessary.'

Dorothea swept past him to the door, turned, swallowed back her indignation. 'Should Veronica Day place any demands upon you, be certain not to concede to them. I remind you that your position here is by my own good grace. Was Mr. Llewellyn to learn of the true circumstances surrounding you then he would dismiss you forthwith.'

Gibbings lowered his gaze. 'Aye Miss Llewellyn.' He watched Dorothea stride along the path, head high, arms swinging, and then slammed the door shut.

Chapter Eleven

Dawn revealed a grey morning with a few yellow streaks on the horizon as the rising sun struggled to show. Llewellyn looked down from his room towards the harbour where the fishermen were preparing their nets, but his thoughts were concentrated on the evening that lay ahead. He hoped that nothing would arise to mar Veronica's recital; Dorothea's absence in the light of her recent behaviour would turn out to be a blessing and now the weather appeared the only factor that could adversely affect it. Over that matter he had no control. Over his sister disturbingly, he had increasingly little. It was an issue which needed to be addressed sooner rather than later, particularly in view of his plans for Veronica.

Veronica would be offered a permanent room at the castle, doubtless she would accept. He hadn't had the opportunity to expound to her the previous evening due to her curious preoccupation with Gibbings, but nonetheless he would do so first opportunity that morning. He yearned to enter into a permanent relationship with her. Never before had he experienced such heightened feelings for a woman, but he knew that time and familiarity must combine to enable it to happen.

He sat at his writing desk, spending some time on business correspondence he'd brought from London, finding it unusually difficult to concentrate, before ringing for Hambleton, eager to convey news of his decision.

'Ah Hambleton, come in, take a seat.' He gestured to a high-backed Queen-Anne chair across the room, then noticing his butler's air of surprise, 'I shall dispense with formality on this occasion, you have long been a confidant of mine. I wish to advise you of a decision I have made.'

'Decision sir?'

'I have decided to bestow upon Miss Day the offer of having her own room at the castle.'

'A permanent room, sir?'

'Why yes.' Llewellyn frowned at the incredulity in Hambleton's tone. 'Is there something which disturbs you about that?'

Hambleton drew a finger across his lips, an insignificant gesture perhaps, but long association with his butler told Llewellyn that the movement portrayed concern.

'Feel free to deliver your opinion, Hambleton,' Llewelyn prodded patiently.

'Sir, there could be considerable friction in such a move; there appears bad chemistry in certain quarters…'

'By which you are referring to my sister,' Llewellyn interrupted touchily. 'She will learn to desist with her unruly behaviour or pay the price.'

Hambleton shook his head, gave Llewellyn a sombre look. 'By chemistry sir, I am suggesting that more than one party is at play.'

Llewellyn twisted his lips, just what was Hambleton trying to say? 'And that suggestion is surely not that Miss Day is a contributing factor in this "bad chemistry"?'

Hambleton swallowed, pinching his chin between thumb and forefinger. 'Not wilfully, perhaps sir, but they are such contrasting personalities that I do feel conflict will arise, and as I have said, Gibbings is somehow at the…'

'Ah, Gibbings, yes,' Llewellyn glanced down at the pen he'd been rolling between his fingers, recalling Veronica's curiosity of the previous evening, and of Hambleton's account of Dorothea's strange behaviour towards him. But somehow it seemed too insignificant a matter to be wasting time on – the real culprit was Dorothea. Llewellyn waved his hand dismissively. 'Gibbings is of no serious account. It is my sister we need to keep account of, be sure that I will do so – and while I'm away, see that I am advised of any abnormal behaviour…'

'Forgive me for interrupting sir – but has Miss Llewellyn been informed of this development?'

'Good Lord no, I have yet to advise Miss Day, but I remind you that the say-so is mine, Hambleton, not my sister's.' Llewellyn gave the butler a long, reflective look. 'I have to say, that I am beginning to regret accepting her presence here. There has always been a sarcastic edge to her character; it seems of late to have developed a vindictive one.'

'As I see it sir, the purchase could not have been accomplished without her funds.'

Llewellyn shrugged. 'I could have explored other possibilities ,' he said, head bowed, and then raising his eyes to meet Hambleton, 'perhaps I still can.'

'I fear she will not be easily dislodged.' Hambleton rose to his feet. 'If I might suggest sir, perhaps you should begin by asking Miss

Day whether she would accept a room here; if she declines, it might greatly reduce any future altercations.'

'I very much doubt that,' Llewellyn snapped. Hambleton's words had arrived like a slap in the face; that he should even imply, as he appeared to be doing, that Veronica was in any way involved in this "bad chemistry," was outrageous. But he'd asked for an opinion and been given one he hadn't liked.

Llewellyn sighed, turned to the window. The skies had lifted, the sun had broken through and with it, raised his spirits. After breakfast he would treat Veronica to a ride in the trap, and he would announce his offer of a room in the castle.

***

'Oh but I have to practice my music if I am to entertain you to the best of my abilities.' Veronica placed her cup in the saucer and brushed the arms of the light yellow dress she wore.

'I thought that on such a refreshing morning a ride inland would be invigorating,' Llewellyn persisted, overcoming a pang of disappointment. 'Are you familiar with horses? I could let you chair the trap…'

Veronica gave an easy, relaxed smile. 'Familiar? Why I grew up with them. Horses were another of my father's passions – but I never let anything interfere with my objectives and my objective now is to ensure that I entertain you to the best of my abilities this evening. So I must decline your kind invitation, at least on this occasion.'

Llewellyn nodded, conceding unwillingly. 'Then before you leave, perhaps?'

'Providing you allow me to drive, I agree.'

Llewellyn marvelled at her abilities, not too many women could handle a pony and trap, certainly not Dorothea who had a dread of horses.

Llewellyn, pleased with her acceptance of his offer, delayed as it was, tweaked his moustache and felt the tension building within. 'Veronica,' he said leaning towards her, 'I want to make you an offer.'

He saw her expression change, become at once more serious. 'An offer?'

'Why, yes – you say you have a liking for the coast, you seem to have an affinity for the island, and your company here has been heavenly. I'd like to make you an offer of a room here, any time you wish – your own special room.'

Veronica chewed her lip, she looked uncertain, like the first time he'd encountered her on the shore. 'There are no strings,' Llewellyn said quietly.

'I don't know what to say, it is true that I find the island and the coast in general alluring, but your offer is too much. I cannot warrant…'

'But you *do* warrant it.' Llewellyn's hand was atop of hers. 'It is a pleasure to offer it.'

'And your sister, would she accept…'

'My sister is not the owner of this castle – I am,' Llewellyn said firmly, and aware of the bitterness in his voice abruptly moderated his tone. 'She oversees affairs while I am away. That is all.'

'Well it is a most generous offer which I shall consider.' Veronica rose to her feet. 'It would be nice to have such a place to stay as this, from time to time.'

Llewellyn watched her stride out of the room, tall, elegant, composed. She hadn't said yes to his offer, but there was a suggestion she would accept. And Llewellyn was a step closer to his ultimate desire.

***

Dorothea spent the morning perusing the castle's record books. Management of castle affairs was no great strain on her resources and a couple of hours a day was enough to keep matters in order. But the strains of Veronica's violin were an unwanted background accessory and a constant reminder of an unwanted guest her brother foolishly doted on. She could see it in his eyes, the way he looked at her, but Veronica Day hadn't returned to the castle for him, any more than her concert that evening was arranged on the household's behalf.

Someone else held her interest, perhaps even fancy, and that someone was John Gibbings.

Dorothea pulled back her chair, strolled to an oak cabinet beside the window, then poured a double measure of Scotch and lit a cigarette. John Gibbings was in her pocket, she had him at her mercy and he knew it, she could read into those fine eyes. The violinist might have beauty on her side but in a few days she would be gone, and once she saw she couldn't sway him she would never return. She could afford to miss out on the concert that night, the devious woman had got her way but it would produce nothing.

Dorothea gulped down the whisky, poured another, John Gibbings would come to her in the end of his own accord, and she would get some reward for settling on this island.

She'd been bored in London, her social life had become stale and the same old rounds bored her. When Thomas had proposed the castle, having seen its sale advertised in a national newspaper, it seemed the perfect adventure and she'd provided the money to back Thomas' purchase.

But the island was small, few people inhabited it and events happened so slowly they scarcely happened at all. Nothing excited her apart from John Gibbings. He had a wild side he was struggling to contain and that wildness was as challenging as it was appealing. Moreover she was certain that in a short while she would appeal to him.

Life had its rewards and her duty here as administrator of the castle would see that she got that reward through him – once Veronica Day and her brother were out of the way.

Dorothea blew smoke rings into the air, poured a final glass of scotch and allowed herself a smile.

All she needed was patience.

Chapter Twelve

Llewellyn got his wish. The fine weather held, with the evening sun beginning to sink behind the castle ramparts, leaving the roof garden bathed in a deep golden glow, while a soft, warm breeze rustled amongst the tubs of pansies.

Prior to Veronica's recital, Mrs. Simms had prepared a seafood salad and now she, Hambleton, Veronica and Gibbings were seated around the garden's oval table listening to an enthusiastic Llewellyn. 'It is indeed a pleasure to be able to listen to the music of a beautiful lady, in such a setting as this.'

'Why thank you.' Veronica smiled, cleared her plate and gently brushed her white dress. 'I am pleased that the weather is fine.' She locked eyes with Gibbings. 'Are you familiar with the violin, John?'

Gibbings shook his head. 'No I am not,' he said, his expression surly.

'Well now, with all the work you do I doubt that you'd have time for music. After my recital I could let you take a closer look, perhaps let you play on it.'

'No I don't think so,' Gibbings said dismissively, but Veronica appeared not to have heard. She cocked her head at Llewellyn. 'Would that be alright, Thomas?' she asked quietly.

Llewellyn raised his brows, he couldn't see how Gibbings would be remotely interested in Veronica's violin, indeed why she'd invited him in the first place, but she was giving the distinct impression that refusal would disappoint her and he wasn't having that –

'If Miss Day wants you to try playing her violin then I would deem it rude should you refuse.' Gibbings reddened, his eyes didn't meet hers but he accepted and Veronica slapped the table. 'Good then it's settled, a little private lesson for you once the performance is finished – and please all of you, I insist you call me Veronica.'

Mrs. Simms cleared the table, assisted by Veronica who waved aside any protests. During their absence from the roof garden Llewellyn turned to Gibbings. 'Well you are honoured, young man,' he said without concealing his surprise, 'to be offered what amounts to a lesson by a celebrated violinist – and you were going to refuse…'

'I think he was just simply taken aback,' Hambleton said, intervening on Gibbings' behalf, 'as we all were.'

'Indeed.' Llewellyn swallowed, glanced at Hambleton and then back to Gibbings. 'Miss Day – Veronica, shows a market interest in your welfare, you are most fortunate in that respect.'

'I do nothing to encourage it, sir.'

'Indeed, that is plainly evident,' Llewellyn grunted. 'You show a distinct lack of courtesy in your approach towards her.'

'I think the lad feels a little, shall we say, out of place,' Hambleton said again. 'Miss Veronica exudes the kind of presence one doesn't meet on a daily basis.'

'Hambleton I'm certain the young man can speak for himself,' Llewellyn remarked showing a little irritation. 'Nonetheless I feel there is truth in what you say.'

He broke off as Mrs. Simms came through the door, followed by Veronica carrying her violin and bow; she took up a position at the far end of the roof garden which pleased Llewellyn, for what was left of the sunlight reflected there on her hair, providing it with the rich red tint that he loved.

She played for an hour, the base of the violin tucked neatly under her chin, while the bow glided effortlessly across the strings and the music both gentle and vibrant carried over the roof garden, blending with the soothing tumble of the sea.

When she had finished, Llewellyn, deeply captivated conducted a generous round of applause, before, reluctantly guiding the others away, he left Veronica in the company of Gibbings.

'Well John,' she said quietly when they were alone, 'I finally get the chance to speak with you, I'm sure you're not that enthusiastic about playing the violin…'

'No madam.'

'No Veronica,' she said sternly.

'No Veronica.'

'Is that resentment I read in you?'

The same height as Gibbings, she met him full in the eye and when he didn't reply, said, 'Are you being manipulated, John Gibbings?'

She saw him visibly tense, his jaw tighten, his face colour.

'Madam?'

'Veronica…'

'I beg your pardon, Veronica?'

'You heard what I said. The sea isn't that noisy today,' she waited patiently, legs and arms crossed, eyes unwavering. 'Look, it couldn't be more obvious if it were written across your chest in large letters.'

There was defiance, perhaps anger visible in his dark eyes but she remained steadfast. 'What hold has Dorothea got over you John?'

'You're impossible,' he muttered beneath his breath.

'No – but I could be,' she leaned close, her hair brushing his shoulder, 'now are you going to open up?'

'Not now – not here,' his eyes darted to and fro, and then settled on her. 'Christ, why did I save you from the sea?'

'Then where?'

'I don't know – you can't help anyway.'

'Give me the chance to repay what you did for me.' She took a look round the garden, checked they were alone and grabbed his shoulders with both hands. 'Give me that chance.'

He lowered his eyes, then flicked his long lashes up at her. 'Tomorrow morning early – sunrise – the abbey grounds – though what good it'll do…'

'Finally he concedes.' Veronica stooped down, collected the violin and bow, shoved them into his hands. 'Now I don't care what kind of row you make with this, but for the benefit of the others inside, try and play it.'

Gibbings exhaled deeply, gave her a look bordering on a scowl, laid the violin clumsily against his cheek and the bow grated across the strings. Veronica pressed her hands against her ears and she saw John Gibbings break into his first real smile.

***

Hambleton heard the echo of heels, the swish of stiff dress fabric and instantly knew Dorothea was approaching the hallway. He sighed, managing a polite smile as she hurried through.

'Hambleton, did you enjoy the virtuoso performance this evening?'

Bolting the door, turning back towards Dorothea Hambleton said, 'Quite splendid Madam.'

'Indeed,' Dorothea clasped her hands together. 'I also heard the most awful grinding sound, it made my teeth judder.'

'Gibbings, Madam.'

'Gibbings?'

'I believe Miss Veronica offered him the use of her violin…'

'Absurd – quite absurd – as if Gibbings would be interested in such an instrument.'

'No Madam.' Hambleton took a step forward. 'If you'll excuse me…'

'Were you all offered the opportunity to "fiddle" with her violin?'

Hambleton baulked, drew a finger across his lip. 'As far as I know the offer was restricted to Gibbings.'

'What do you *mean* as far as you know?' Dorothea cried. 'Hambleton of *course* you know.'

'The offer was not extended elsewhere.'

'How cosy…' Dorothea narrowed her hooded eyes. 'As if it wasn't to be expected.'

'If there is nothing further Madam ?'

Dorothea stepped across, blocking Hambleton's path into the passageway. 'You are aware that Mr. Llewellyn dotes on Miss Day, Hambleton?'

'He – he displays a fondness Madam – I presume that is why he invited her back.'

'Hambleton,' Dorothea said, her voice lowered, 'would you not now concede that the woman is not all she seems, that her interest in Gibbings is other than normal and that her effect on the castle is disruptive? Is it not my brother we should be concerned for? Be sure she shares no concern for him.'

'I…'

'Hambleton – Hambleton – oh, there you are.' Llewellyn swept into the hall, ignoring his sister. 'I was looking for Veronica, she remained on the roof with Gibbings – I was seeking to ensure she has not been locked out.'

'Miss Veronica has retired to her room sir.' Hambleton sidestepped Llewellyn and Dorothea, readily taking the opportunity to extricate himself from her presence. 'And now if you will excuse me?'

'Certainly, Hambleton.'

Dorothea watched the butler recede along the passage, turning to her brother with a glint in her eye. 'And she did not think to seek you out – to wish you goodnight?'

'I have suffered enough of your presence for one day, sister,' Llewellyn uttered through barely parted teeth, before turning on his heels and following Hambleton along the passageway.

Dorothea noted his aggravated stance, placed a hand beneath her chin, knew her words had found a weak spot in her brother's disposition towards Veronica and vowed to capitalise on it.

And Hambleton was not only her brother's butler but also his ally. She was getting through, he was having his doubts, she could tell in his manner. Veronica Day's association with the island would be short lived, of that she had no doubt.

Chapter Thirteen

Veronica left her room shortly after sunrise, quietly making her way down to the entrance hall where she found the main doorway bolted. She was about to draw the bolt back when she heard footsteps behind. 'Allow me Miss Veronica, it is a trifle stiff.' She watched the silver-haired figure of Hambleton emerge from the shadows, eyebrows raised as he drew back the bolt. 'You are an early riser this morning.'

Preferring to have left the castle unnoticed Veronica masked any embarrassment behind a smile. 'I habitually rise early Mr. Hambleton, normally I do not like to disturb the household but the gulls and the sea have enticed me into taking an early walk.' His fixed, quizzical smile as he opened the door seemed intended as encouragement to elaborate, but she said simply, 'Do you never sleep, Mr. Hambleton?'

'About as much as you, it seems Miss Veronica; do enjoy your walk...'

'Thank you, I shall.' She skipped down the castle slope with the distinct feeling that he hadn't closed the door, but it wouldn't matter if he had, with the views the castle afforded he could chart her course for some way if he had a mind to.

She knew now why Gibbings had chosen the priory, its vast ruins provided privacy even from the castle's all-seeing eyes – and now as she approached from a rough pathway running between the coarse grass, she'd no idea whether Gibbings would be there – whether in the cold light of day he'd backtrack on his decision. She'd broken some ice last evening but achieving it had been hard work.

Veronica climbed a low stone wall on the perimeter of the priory grounds and saw the figure lurking between the cloisters close to the monastery walls. The gloom produced by the brooding arches in the early light obscured its identity until Gibbings stepped forward, hands deep in the pockets of his trousers, shoulders hunched with the chill of the morning.

'Sunrise I said,' he called across. 'Sun's been up an hour or more.'

'Has it really?' She crossed her arms, stared him in the eye before scouring the heavens. 'I don't see much sun.'

'You're not funny Veronica,' Gibbings scowled, then pointing to the stone wall, 'and you climb like a boy – there's a gate the ladies use...'

She cocked her head at him, narrowed her eyes. 'If you knew me better, John Gibbings, you'd know how much of a lady I am – now then – you have something to tell me, such as what hold the dark witch of the castle has got over you.'

He turned away. 'I don't know that I can say.'

'Oh yes you can,' she said, her voice raised above the cry of the gulls, then gently clasping his shoulder, 'I haven't made this journey to pay my respect to the departed monks.'

He shook his head. 'I don't know you well at all – and you seem different now to when you talk to the castle folk – I can't take no chances, if you tell Mr. Llewellyn…'

'If I tell him what?'

Gibbings gritted his teeth. 'One moment you're refined and posh like – the next you're kind of saucy. I'd like to know the real you before I say things…'

'John, this *is* the real me, the one you see before you now – the one the dark witch thinks is something of a flirt.'

'No – does she?'

Veronica laughed at his intrigued smile. 'She does, she told me so the last time I was here, warned me off practically.'

'But you came back; for Mr. Llewellyn?'

'Perhaps – who knows?' She skipped around him, her long dress swirling around her legs, then stopped; placing both hands on his shoulders she drew close and whispered in his ear. 'Or perhaps for you John Gibbings – after all, you are quite good looking and I am a flirt…'

She saw a flare in his eyes, resentment – he didn't know how to take her. She quickly withdrew her hands, thrusting them on her hips. 'Right, let's get serious, I'm here because I want to help, John – here in a windswept, deserted monastery at Lord knows what time in the morning, now please tell me.'

He led her through an archway, into a recess which housed a wooden bench. As they sat he said, 'I was caught in bed with a woman in the cottage I rent from Mr. Llewellyn.'

'Is that all?'

She saw the incredulity on his face and added, 'Well, sex is hardly a new concept.'

'You're mocking me,' he glared. 'I'm going – I'm not sitting here.'

'John, please stay -' her hand was on his arm, he pulled but she resisted. 'It's just that it hardly seems a crime...'

'Not to you, perhaps, but here – on this island – damn.' He sat back down, thrust his chin into the cup of his hand and met her eyes. 'Look, the dark witch as you call her walked in on us the day they bought the castle – she threw Rose out, called me a disgusting wretch and made it clear Mr. Llewellyn would dismiss me straight away if he knew about it – well he would, he's fair but he don't have time for things like that.'

'You mean immoral behaviour.'

Gibbings lowered his eyes. 'Aye.'

'So why didn't the dark witch just tell him and be done with it?'

Gibbings threw his hands in the air. 'She's a strange woman, she acts like she hates me but I reckon she's not that sure – she keeps giving me looks – as if she owns me. She started doing weird things like inspecting my hands, finding me jobs to do in her quarters that hardly needed doing, now she's getting randy like – she came into the cottage the night before last like she wanted sex – I had to force her away.' Gibbings thumped his fist into the palm of his hand. ' I nearly lost my temper – but it's getting to the point where if I don't do what she wants she'll push me that hard I'll have to get tough. And what happens then eh? I'll lose my job.'

Veronica leaned towards him. 'It sounds like a love-hate complex kind of a thing. If she's attracted to you, why not give her what she wants? Life might be easier for you.'

Gibbings' jaw clenched. 'I don't desire her, how could you suggest such a thing?'

'But she found you in bed with Rose, so she might be thinking, why not me? Is or was Rose special, John Gibbings?'

'Is that important?'

Veronica shook her head. 'Not to me, but I sense you have more to tell – no, no...' she raised her hand, 'we'll not dwell on that now, can you not find work elsewhere, is your job that important?'

'It's all I know, gardening, odd jobs – apart from manning the lifeboat of course, but I'm not happy at sea.'

Veronica lifted her brows. 'I would have thought...'

But Gibbings was on his feet, 'I've talked enough and I've work to do; besides Miss Llewellyn will be really mad if she knows I've been talking to you. Like I say there's nothing you can do – nothing anyone can do until the dark witch goes over the top and I get the sack.'

'I'm going to try to help you John,' Veronica said, extending her hand and grasping his. 'I won't pretend at the moment that I know how but I promise you I'm going to try.'

Gibbings nodded and went on his way. Veronica watched him go, his predicament under Dorothea's auspices was severe but she didn't understand why he had to endure it. Why was he so dependent on the job? There had to be something he could find, if not on the island then inland. But as long as he was in this position she'd vowed to help, and now making her way back to the castle she was hardly aware of the lashing rain.

How could she deal with Dorothea, solve Gibbings' problem and yet retain the respect of the household when Dorothea was hell bent on ruining that respect?

Veronica climbed the castle slope to find Dorothea waiting in the hall. 'Why Miss Day, you are drenched – what on earth possessed you to journey out in conditions such as these – and without so much as a coat?'

But it wasn't really a question, Dorothea knew there was more to it than a walk in the rain, the set of her sharp features told Veronica that.

'It really isn't a problem, Dorothea.' Veronica brushed Dorothea's shoulder, stopped a pace away from her. 'But I must get out of these wet clothes.' She swept her fingers across the top of her dress and rainwater splashed into Dorothea's face. Dorothea squinted as it struck her eyes, coughed as she breathed in the droplets. Veronica placed her hand to her mouth. 'Oh I am so sorry, how careless of me – it is, as you say, very wet out there.'

Dorothea twitched with anger, her eyes wide, darker than ever. Veronica expected a lash from her hand but the movement was curtailed. 'Whatever you're plotting here Miss Day, it won't work you know – you are foolish crossing swords with me. I always have my way – you will not be returning to the castle a third time, mark my words.'

'We shall see whether your spells are strong enough to prevent it,' Veronica whispered in Dorothea's ear, provoking renewed animosity. 'Why, I think you'd quite like to strike me, wouldn't you?'

'Grant me with more intelligence than to resort to such an action in the face of your insults.' Dorothea managed a bitter smile. 'In two days time you will be gone, never to return. That is my response and my victory.'

'I prefer not to talk in terms of victory Miss Llewellyn, but in terms of what is moral, and immoral.'

'Just what are you inferring?'

Veronica smiled, chewed her lip. 'I'll leave you to dwell on the answer to that, you most certainly know it.'

Chapter Fourteen

'It was gracious – most gracious of you to devote your time to familiarising Gibbings with the violin,' Llewellyn said with the trace of a smile, 'though the infernal noise I heard which must surely have derived from his playing prompts me to suggest your good intentions were wasted.'

'Let us simply say he tried – come in, won't you, Thomas?' Veronica had barely bathed and changed before Llewellyn had knocked on her door.

'If it is convenient.' Llewellyn followed her through looking uncomfortable. 'It is not generally my custom to enter ladies' rooms. I merely came to request your company at breakfast.'

'You were invited, Thomas. I shall make myself presentable and then we will breakfast together.'

'Presentable?' Llewellyn protested. 'Oh come now Veronica, you are never *less* than presentable.'

'Thomas,' Veronica began, ignoring the intended compliment, 'I must tell you, I fear I may have provoked further animosity in your sister.'

'Oh.' Llewellyn brushed his moustache and then gave a lop-sided smile. 'That is hardly difficult to achieve – when did you encounter…'

'I'd been for an early morning walk,' Veronica said, examining herself in the mirror. Satisfied, she swung back to face him. 'Rather foolishly as it turned out, you see I got soaked and encountering Dorothea in the hall, I accidentally splashed her with rainwater from my coat. Needless to say she was not happy and did not accept my apology. Thomas,' Veronica outstretched an arm, easing him closer, 'she has some kind of misguided conception that I am a troublemaker, a bad influence; I am here as your guest, and can assure you this is not the case.'

'Good Lord no.' Llewellyn clasped Veronica's arms. 'I will hear of no such accusation – I will put an end to such behaviour forthwith!'

Llewellyn, his lips twisted in anger turned to the door, but Veronica, as she had out on the terrace stretched out an arm and held him back. 'No, Thomas, please do not admonish her on my account, I seek only to reassure you of my good intentions in the face of such accusations. Your understanding of that is all I desire…'

Llewellyn took a deep breath, adjusted his yellow waistcoat. 'Very well Veronica. Your generosity is as always, overwhelming, though I will not have you upset in any way – please tell me, have you put thought to my offer of a permanent room here?'

'No.' Veronica shook her head. 'Not fully Thomas. I will advise you before I leave, have no doubt of that.'

'I urge…'

'Thomas, there are but two days remaining before I depart the island, once I have considered fully I will advise you.' She looked out the window and sighed. 'I was wondering whether we might journey out this morning in your trap.'

Llewellyn threw out his hands, 'But it is a wild morning…'

'I am not afraid of a little rain, unless such a prospect disturbs you?'

'Indeed not.' Llewellyn rocked on his heels, clasping his hands together. 'I am only too happy to oblige. Your welfare is my only concern.'

'I am deeply touched.' Veronica stepped forward, took his hand between hers, breaking away as he brought his head forward. 'Come, let us hope for a peaceful breakfast.'

***

Dorothea was nowhere to be seen at breakfast that morning and Llewellyn was grateful for that. That she could perceive Veronica conceiving some kind of plot was outrageous and beyond his comprehension. Only Veronica's firm intervention had prevented him storming into Dorothea's quarters demanding she make full apology. It was the second time in as many days that she had prevented him creating a scene and it struck him for the first time that she must possess considerable strength to restrain his weight with a single arm and with such apparent ease.

Entering the gallery en route to his room he encountered Hambleton carefully dusting the paintings. 'Hambleton, Miss Veronica has requested a ride in the trap; we shall be gone for much of the morning.'

Hambleton paused from his task, raising his brows and gesturing through the window towards the sea. 'The conditions are somewhat inclement…'

'Yes, I am aware of that,' Llewellyn snapped impatiently. 'However it is what Miss Veronica requests.'

Hambleton traced a forefinger across his upper lip. 'She is

certainly one for the conditions sir, why only this morning…'

'Yes, I know Hambleton, Miss Veronica informed me she'd taken an early walk.'

'I believe she had an appointment sir…'

Llewellyn narrowed his eyes, 'An appointment? What are you talking about?

'Hambleton, please elaborate…'

'A pre-arranged meeting, sir.'

Llewellyn clenched his jaw. 'Please spare me a dictionary definition, Hambleton – I was merely expressing surprise at such an unlikely occurrence; who might she have been seeing at such an unlikely hour?' He widened his brows, waiting with exaggerated patience for enlightenment.

'There is only one name which springs to mind, that of Gibbings sir.'

Llewellyn shook his head. 'I fail to see what could possibly transpire to induce such an early morning event. What brings you to such a conclusion – not that it is the slightest business of ours…'

Hambleton outstretched his hands. 'As you know sir, I am a habitually early riser; I was simply going about my business when I encountered Miss Veronica just after dawn. Shortly afterwards, while drawing the curtains in the gallery I noticed her walking towards the priory grounds, a direction I saw Gibbings returning from some twenty minutes later. I naturally drew the conclusion they had cause to meet.'

'There is nothing natural about it, Hambleton; it appears you have engaged in a deliberate act of spying,' then noticing his butler's rare look of indignation, he added, 'why should you surmise such a clandestine meeting should take place?'

Hambleton shrugged, said quietly, 'I have no idea sir; all I can say is that whilst closing the castle windows last evening I heard hushed conversation between Gibbings and Miss Veronica that I was unable to distinguish the nature of. I only know she shares an interest in Gibbings as does your sister. I believe it my duty sir, to advise you that developments are afoot which are not healthy to the smooth running of the castle, or indeed, your good self. It is my belief that you should reconsider your invitation to Miss Veronica, of a room here.'

Llewellyn raised a finger to Hambleton in a rare show of

incivility. 'I will have an end to this preposterous warmongering and indeed, spying. You appear to be in collusion with my sister over Miss Veronica, for what purpose I do not know.' Through grating teeth he hissed, 'My offer is not retractable, you will do well to remember as much.'

Llewellyn marched to his room, seething. Slamming the door he breathed heavily, struggling to control his anger. Just what had possessed Hambleton to side with Dorothea, and then to develop his own ridiculous assumption that Veronica had some desire towards Gibbings? That was what he seemed to be implying and such a suggestion was as absurd as it was unthinkable.

Nonetheless, at the back of his mind just the tiniest grain of doubt had lodged. The previous evening Veronica had offered Gibbings instruction on the violin, an offer that required them to be alone. According to Hambleton, hushed conversation had ensued, could that have led to an early morning meeting, and had Hambleton heard more than he was saying?

Could Dorothea be right? Was Veronica's presence here not on account of him, did she have other desires or motives?

Almost certainly not. The delightful Miss Day enjoyed his company; he could sense it. He would probe most sensitively during their trap ride for confirmation of that.

***

Veronica, waiting in the hallway, heard the echoing step of Llewellyn as he approached along the passage, then noticing his heated expression she asked, 'Is anything the matter Thomas? You appear somewhat flushed.'

'No, certainly not.' Llewellyn stopped beside her, fastened his raincoat and raised his large umbrella. 'I forgot this, that is all. I thought we might need protection from the rain.'

'I think not, Thomas.' Veronica ran her eyes quickly over his face, then gestured through the open doorway. 'The rain has stopped and the sun is breaking through, surprising how the weather changes so quickly in the north east, is it not?'

'It certainly is.' Llewellyn led the way down the slope, to the pony and trap that Hambleton had tethered to the railings. 'The island will not be the same without you,' he said, guiding the trap onto the road, 'though I leave but a day after you, your company will be sorely missed.'

'As will yours, Thomas.' She felt his eyes linger as she stared towards the priory, its brooding arches drawing closer.

'Truthfully, will you miss me Veronica?'

Disturbed by the question Veronica ran her teeth along her upper lip; seeds of doubt were developing in his mind, planted no doubt by Dorothea or Hambleton, perhaps both. They needed eradicating.

'I shall miss you Thomas, as I shall miss this island, why do you seek to question me?'

Llewellyn coughed, raising a hand from the reins and tweaking his moustache. 'I...' he swallowed, she heard him sigh... 'there seems to be some foolish notion within the castle – I cannot mention the source from which it derives – that you are involved in some kind of scheming – that it involves Gibbings...'

'Huh!' Veronica threw her head back and laughed. 'Preposterous, now who shall we suppose is behind this? Your sister we have spoken of – therefore I deduce Hambleton as the likely cause of such mischief – is he not? Whatever brings him to such a conclusion?'

'It matters not, my dear Veronica.' Llewellyn pulled the pony to a halt. 'It is my earnest wish that you become a frequent visitor to the castle; I pay such vindictive notions no heed...'

Yet you were concerned enough to mention it. Veronica turned her head away, bit her lip, looked back at him. 'It seems I have enemies here, people who doubt my good intentions, under such circumstances I doubt that I can accept...'

'I swear to you Veronica,' Llewellyn grabbed her hands, 'that I have put a stop to such hostile accusations.'

Veronica shook her head, raised it towards the sky. 'It seems that at the very least I have brought disharmony to the castle.'

'No – I implore you, do not let that thought influence your reasoning.' Llewellyn's grip on her hand tightened. 'It is my sister who is the main source of disunity. I am sorely regretting her presence. Her departure would dispel the gloom that has descended over this place.'

Veronica slowly removed her hands from his grasp. 'Would such an event be possible?'

Llewellyn puffed his cheeks. 'Difficult. She is co-owner of the castle, she provided me with the necessary funds to secure its purchase. Her stake is small in comparison to mine, but without it I could not have achieved its acquisition.' He cupped his chin, 'Nonetheless, there might be a way…'

'Oh?'

'I have business associates, wealthy ones, who might possibly fund me if I were to approach them. I fear my sister is restless here and would readily agree to relinquish her share for appropriate compensation – would such a prospect enable you to consider my offer favourably?'

Veronica smiled, looked out to sea. 'I feel I am close to a decision already, Thomas – might I take control of the trap?'

Chapter Fifteen

Dorothea watched from the gallery as Llewellyn led the pony & trap onto the track at the bottom of the slope. It had stopped raining and the sun had broken through. That was a pity for she would loved to have seen the oh – so – elegant - and refined Miss Day receive another soaking. The fact that she had deliberately splashed rain from a soaked coat into her face was enraging, but she had amassed all her self control and drawn back from the confrontation the woman had seemed set on provoking. That she'd had the nerve and stupidity to attempt such a thing was galling in itself, she could only suppose it to be a pathetic attempt to get her to incur her brother's wrath, thus undermining her position in the castle. If so it had failed dismally, and she'd come out all the stronger for it; she might have been out-manoeuvred during the scene on the terrace but she'd evened the score by her admirable display of self-control. All she needed now was to patiently wait out the next couple of days, until Veronica Day's departure.

For once Hambleton would be her ally in persuading Thomas that this woman must never return, that she was a disruptive, even malicious influence, far from the perfect woman her brother supposed her to be. She pressed her hands onto the sill, leaning closer to the window; Thomas had drawn the trap to a halt and appeared to be in intense conversation with Day. He'd taken her hands in his and for a moment Dorothea had misgivings. Had this boring island turned him into a hopeless romantic? She couldn't understand how Llewellyn had become so besotted with the woman. He'd never been so lovelorn in the past. But it had only been fleeting, in a moment she'd extracted her hands or he'd released his grip, she wasn't sure which, and shortly afterwards the journey was resumed.

What had occurred to cause him to draw the trap to a halt? She shook her head; it wasn't a question worth dwelling on. There were more pressing matters.

Passing Veronica's room she pushed the door open, her violin sat on its stand, the bow alongside. There was an urge, almost irresistible to smash it to pieces; it wasn't hers anyway, Thomas had foolishly bought it, so the satisfaction, quite apart from a response from her brother that Veronica would gleefully appreciate, was muted.

She passed through the castle hall and onto the slope; Gibbings was on his way up it, a broody look in his dark eyes. 'Ah Gibbings, I was coming in search of you, my window latch is stiff, it requires attention, but first show me your hands.'

He was slow to present them for her inspection and she thought she saw annoyance in his eyes. 'Don't hold back on me Gibbings,' Dorothea said quietly. 'My brother returns to London shortly, if I am dissatisfied with your manner I am at liberty to dispense with your services.'

She took his slowly extended hands and turned them palm upward, pressing on his fingertips, her face close to his. 'Clean enough,' she whispered through pouted lips. 'This evening I need to inspect our property, expect me at seven.'

'Gibbings shook his head. 'Lifeboat duty Miss Llewellyn.'

Dorothea wafted a hand. 'Then I shall attend at nine – now come and adjust this infernal latch.'

***

Veronica reached her room and saw at once the door had been pushed open. She inspected her belongings, none had been touched. She sighed, supposing it could have been the wind, the castle got draughty when the breeze was strong.

Washing her hair free of the salt and grit that their lengthy trap ride had bestowed on it, she recalled the events of the day. Thomas had conceded control of the reins to her, full of admiration for the way she handled them. They'd crossed the causeway onto the mainland and journeyed through the countryside to Berwick, where they'd enjoyed a meal at a hotel before returning shortly before the tide cut the causeway off.

Thomas had asked much about her musical career but it was part of her life she was reluctant to elaborate on. In truth much of it had been forced on her – she'd been conditioned to becoming a concert violinist, when her love was for the open spaces and expansive skies and shorelines of the north-east.

Similarly, she had no real interest in the growing world of banking, though she'd thought to engage Thomas in polite conversation in that respect.

Could he really reach agreement with his clients and buy Dorothea out? She thought at once of John Gibbings, some of his problems would be solved were she to return to London. Some, for she was certain Dorothea was not his only problem, something else lay beneath, deeply rooted; finding out what that something was, remained uppermost in her mind.

Thomas had been reserved at first, one glance had been enough for her to determine as much. Hambleton's influence no doubt; unlike Dorothea his words carried weight. But what had Hambleton said that had planted doubt in Thomas' mind? Had he overheard her talking to John on the terrace?

Or had he seen something? She'd often had the feeling that someone had been watching her from behind those Gothic windows, putting it down to Dorothea – but why not Hambleton? He conducted himself with civility but his quiet, watchful eyes travelled everywhere. Mrs. Simms could be ruled out, she didn't have the run of the castle that Hambleton had.

If there was discord between Dorothea and Hambleton it didn't extend as far as her. Both of them were likely to conspire against her. Well so be it, that wouldn't alter her decision to take up Thomas' kind offer one iota.

Veronica towelled her hair dry, took up the violin and began to practice.

***

It was late in the afternoon when Veronica finished practicing. She went up to the roof garden and stared out to sea, drawing in the moist, salty air, aware of Hambleton's presence in the background as he emptied an ashtray containing Dorothea's cigarette butts.

'Does my presence here disturb you Mr. Hambleton?' she asked, her back to him.

'I beg your pardon, Miss Veronica?'

Veronica slowly turned her head. 'My presence here, I asked if it disturbed you…'

'Why no, Miss Veronica.'

'I feel you are not quite telling the truth.' Veronica took several paces towards him, arms crossed, watching his throat tighten. 'You are concerned that John Gibbings and I are involved in some kind of underhand conduct.'

A muscle twitched in Hambleton's cheek as he shook his head. 'I would never go so far…'

'You may not go so far as an outright accusation Mr. Hambleton, but you have drawn that conclusion, or one very close to it. I can inform you your suspicions are unfounded.' Seeing the butler's discomfort, she added, 'Do not think that Mr. Llewellyn has betrayed your confidence, my own intuition as much as anything else causes me to form this opinion. I have nothing but respect for your employer Mr. Hambleton, there is nothing underhand in progress, rest assured of that.'

Hambleton coughed, placed his fist to his mouth, Veronica reached out and touched him as he brought it down. 'I do not seek to make an enemy of you, I fear I already have one in Miss Llewellyn and one is quite enough, thank you.' Veronica left the roof garden with that, leaving him to ponder her words.

In a little over an hour she would be dining with Llewellyn, but in the meantime the afternoon was bright and warm, and she would walk alone.

Wavelets hissed and sucked on the shore, the fragrance of meadow-sweet filled her nostrils blending with the smell of rotting sea-weed; here, away from crowded concert halls she bathed in the glory of clean air and space. Despite the tension in the castle, she would return as often as she could. For this would be her passport to the joys of nature.

Veronica turned inland, negotiating the grassy mound around the volcanic rock that supported the castle; at its summit she could look down on the garden and doing so now caught sight of Gibbings, busily freeing the garden of spent summer plants.

Fearful that he'd react to Dorothea's torments physically she needed a word with him, armed now with at least a modicum of hope that Thomas might just be able to arrange her departure.

'It's not good for you to be here,' he glowered on her approach.

'I came to offer you advice,' she said, unruffled by his manner.

'I don't need advice,' he turned his back to her, bending his lean frame into the fork.

'Hear me out,' she said, lowering her tone.

Gibbings exhaled heavily, thrusting his fork deep into the soil, then hands on hips, 'Make it quick, Miss Llewellyn has the eyes of a hawk...'

'And the looks of one,' Veronica said, tongue in cheek, noticing a flash of amusement lighten his face, 'has the dark witch bothered you today?'

The cloud returned. 'She pesters me every day and I've told you,

you won't make things any easier by interfering.'

'Who said anything about interfering? It's your problem not mine, but I can help and you'll find me more amenable if you drop your resentful tone.'

'So what's the advice?' He finally met her eyes.

'No matter how much she bothers you, do not show aggression; I sense you are capable of it.'

'Easy for you to say,' Gibbings snarled, 'she's carrying out her so-called cottage inspection this evening – but that's not the reason she's coming.'

'I can guess that. Just show patience and trust me,' Veronica said calmly, undaunted by his intransigence. 'If we are lucky the dark witch might have outstayed her welcome at the castle.'

Gibbings frowned. 'You mean she's leaving?'

'I said if we're lucky. I cannot divulge any more than that but I am hopeful – and then at least *one* of your problems will be solved, John Gibbings. There are more, aren't there?'

For a split second his eyes were a little misty, but he blinked and they were their normal unreadable selves. She raised a finger as she turned her back. 'Restrain yourself, John, that's all I ask.'

'I'll try,' she heard him say, 'and thank you.'

She turned at that, gave him a long, lingering smile that he returned, then she glanced upwards, to the dining room window, from where a figure moved sharply back.

Chapter Sixteen

Dorothea ate dinner in her quarters, preferring to avoid the company of the obnoxious Veronica, and her own foolishly doting brother. She poured a generous measure of Scotch, glancing up as Hambleton placed the salad dish before her. 'I feel we have a common bond for once, Hambleton,' she said, her head lofted towards him.

'Madam?'

'Come now Hambleton, your brows are raised in bewilderment when you know full well to what I refer.'

'If the subject is Miss Veronica, I have no wish to become embroiled in the matter,' Hambleton replied blandly.

Dorothea sniffed, took a gulp of whisky and regarded him with her hooded eyes. 'You do not approve of her presence in the castle; you are not your normal, imperturbable self.'

'I feel it might be unwise, Madam, to attempt to influence Mr. Llewellyn in respect of Miss Day.'

Dorothea sat back, interlocking her fingers, ignoring her evening meal. 'By your lowered eyes, Hambleton, do I detect that you have tried?'

Hambleton exhaled through his nose. 'I thought it my position to express concern – I simply feel that Mr. Llewellyn has a yearning for Miss Day that she does not carry for him.'

'Because she has a fancy for Gibbings.'

Hambleton shifted uncomfortably. 'I cannot go down that path…'

'Nonetheless your expression betrays you; we must combine at once to convince Thomas of his folly.'

'I fear we are wasting our time…'

'What causes you such pessimism?'

'To put further pressure on Mr. Llewellyn would only incur his wrath,' Hambleton answered, ignoring her question. 'If that is all Madam, I have other duties to attend to.'

'Ah, by that I assume you mean my brother and that woman.' Dorothea picked at her salad. 'You find my brother a good and considerate employer, do you not? I am not finished with this, Hambleton, we will speak later.'

'Madam.' Hambleton left the room, closing the door quietly behind him.

***

The sun was sinking, crimson clouds streaking across its melon surface. The evening had turned breezy and showery, another squall buffeting Dorothea as she reached Gibbings' cottage.

Thrice she thumped the door with her fist, aggravation mounting with each knock – was he deliberately making her wait? Large drops of rain began to fall on her shawl before she heard the latch being pulled back and the door creak open.

'I'll thank you to attend the door with more urgency.' Pushing past him she glanced around the drawing room, throwing her dark shawl onto the couch and taking a quick look at the kitchen, before thrusting open his bedroom door. 'Step inside Gibbings,' she said, casting her eyes around the room.

'I'm alright here,' he said flatly.

'You'll do as I say.' Suddenly her glare was upon him, a warning etched in the furrows of her brows. 'I might consider the condition of this cottage to be adequate or I might provide my brother with a damning report, coupling it with an account of your licentious behaviour with that wench – now step inside while I judge.'

The moment Gibbings stepped through her arms wrapped around him, swinging him round. She dropped her right hand down to his crotch, her fingers forming a claw which clamped firmly on his testicles. He uttered a curse, pushing her away and breaking her hold but she simply laughed as she fell back, grabbing his arm with her hands, the momentum forcing him down on the bed on top of her.

'Why there is fight in you Gibbings, I like that in a man, a bit of excitement in this dull, boring place.' She squeezed her arms around his neck. 'Am I not attractive? A better proposition to the serving wench you lured here?'

'There was no luring,' Gibbings said bitterly, and then placing his hands on the bed to pull himself away. 'I swear I'll…'

'You'll do what? Think carefully about what you say, your actions, your future…'

'I have no future.' Gibbings broke her hold, thrust her arms on the pillow and scowled down, just as the klaxon boomed from the harbour.

'No future?' Dorothea narrowed her eyes. 'Please me Gibbings and your future could be bright, antagonise me and you could well be right.'

'It's you who antagonise me.' Gibbings bit his lip, hauled himself himself up. 'The klaxon's sounding, I got to go…'

'Yes, that's right Gibbings, rescue your distressed little souls while you dream of Veronica...'

'I don't dream of Veronica,' Gibbings yelled. Dorothea caught the flash of anger in his eyes and smiled. 'Do you not? Well that is just as well, for she will not be returning to this castle, mark my words.'

She watched her words hit home; Gibbings' haste was disturbed for just a moment before he made for the harbour.

Her smile turned to a glower, Veronica Day, damn her, was the centre of attraction for Gibbings, no matter what he protested. With the finality of her words sinking in, he might just yield to a little pressure.

***

Veronica ran a tissue across her lips and took a sip of white wine. 'The lobster was excellent Thomas; you must compliment Mrs. Simms.'

'Most certainly.' Llewellyn raised his goblet, regarded her thoughtfully. 'You look particularly radiant this evening, my dear, how that shade of dress compliments your hair.'

'Why thank you,' Veronica swilled her glass, placed it down. 'I've come to a decision Thomas...'

'Oh?' She watched his eyebrows rise, his complexion colour a little.

'I would be more than happy to accept your kind offer of a room here.'

'Why Veronica, that is *wonderful* news.' Llewellyn slapped his hand on the table, then reached out and took her hands in his.

'I take it my acceptance will not cause additional animosity?'

'Not in the least, I am sure any complications can be resolved.' He looked up on Hambleton's approach. 'Ah Hambleton, another bottle of wine to celebrate Miss Veronica's acceptance of a room here.'

'Certainly sir, I'll uncork one now.'

Veronica studied Hambleton upon his return, there was a twitch in his cheek and his brow had furrowed, 'I shall try not to place any undue demands on you Mr. Hambleton, I'm sure we'll get along famously.'

'Famously indeed,' Llewellyn answered for him, clapping his hands. 'Now then, a glass for you too.'

'No sir, thank you kindly, but I have a slight headache. If there is nothing further?'

'Veronica?' Llewellyn asked, then watching her shake her head he said, 'No thank you Hambleton, that will be all.'

With a curt bow of his head, Hambleton left the dining room.

Veronica sighed, curled her hand around the wine glass. 'I do hope Thomas, that my presence here, although infrequent, will not be too much of a strain upon your resources…'

'Of course not, Veronica.'

'I thought that Hambleton appeared somewhat withdrawn…'

Llewellyn smiled, though there seemed tension beneath. 'My dear Veronica, Hambleton has confessed to being "under the weather," as they say – it is nothing more than that.'

'In which case, I have no worries.'

'Indeed not,' Llewellyn leaned forward, 'and I trust your visits here will not be too infrequent, you are the smiling face of this castle. Your presence here will be cherished. Veronica…'

'Thomas, I feel the wine going to my head. A breath of fresh air will do me good, following which I should like to retire. Would you mind if I bid you goodnight?'

'Why no – goodnight my dear.' But Llewellyn's face registered surprise and a certain disappointment as Veronica left his company.

Upstairs, standing in the roof garden she heard the klaxon sound, noticed how choppy the sea had become. She thought of the lifeboat, thought of Gibbings, of how he had saved her from the sea that night – and then minutes later she caught sight of him, running towards the mooring in the gathering dusk, she sighed, then raised a smile.

Chapter Seventeen

Llewellyn made up his mind the moment Veronica left the dining room to get it over with. Dorothea had to be told of her acceptance of a permanent room at the castle. Bracing himself for a stern encounter he stiffened, before marching upstairs to her quarters.

She wasn't in, or otherwise wasn't answering his knock, and with a sense of anti-climax he continued towards his own room.

'Were you wanting me, Thomas?' Dorothea's sharp voice penetrated the silence only his own footsteps intruded. 'Yes,' he said, coming to an abrupt halt. 'I've something to tell you…'

'Have you now.' She raised her head, fixing him with her dark eyes. 'Can it wait? I'm rather tired.'

Llewellyn took in her appearance, the shawl covering her dark dress was ruffled and her complexion was coloured. 'You do seem a trifle windswept, however I'd prefer it didn't wait, shall we go inside?'

'Oh very well.' Dorothea pushed open the door, walked through to the annexe she used as an office, slumped down on the couch, hand on head. 'But get straight to the point; I'm not in the best frame of mind.'

'Are you ever?' Llewellyn ignored Dorothea's glare, stared down at his interlocked fingers then back to her. 'I made Veronica the offer of a permanent room here.'

'You did what?'

'I think you heard what I said.' Llewellyn watched his sister's eyes reduce to slits, saw her look of disbelief.

'Oh my God.' She sprung off the couch, flounced to the window, arms thrust across her chest and then swung to face him. 'What inspired such an act of crass stupidity, your craving for her I…'

'Keep your voice down, Dorothea.'

'Don't dare address me in that tone.' Dorothea's breath whistled through her teeth. 'I cannot believe your obsession for her Thomas.' She turned her back on him, placed her hands on the window ledge. 'No doubt she's accepted.'

'As a matter of fact she has. Look try to see reason…'

'There is no reason in this, only pure lunacy.' Dorothea glowered at him over her shoulder. 'How often can I expect her infernal presence?'

'Whenever her time allows,' Llewellyn said, grinding his teeth.

'Do not think I will make her welcome, Thomas.'

'I do not expect you to become friends, that would only be wishful thinking. I only ask that you accommodate her.'

'Huh, do I have a choice?' Dorothea snarled. 'Time will see you regret the stupidity of this decision, now please leave my room.'

'With pleasure.' Llewellyn turned and strode out, passed through the gallery to his room, more determined than ever to effect a deal with his associates that would un-tie the hold Dorothea had on the castle. With Veronica's presence and Dorothea's absence, what a pleasant place it would become.

***

Dorothea rose early, poured herself a whisky to calm her shattered nerves, lit a cigarette and rang the bell for Hambleton; there was still a chance that her brother could be persuaded out of his foolish fascination for Veronica Day.

'Hambleton come in, close the door,' she said pacing the floor in her dark robe. 'I've told you I have not finished with the matter of my brother's foolish indulgence of this – this musician. I suspect you know Mr. Llewellyn has provided her with a permanent room here?'

Hambleton ran a finger beneath his nose. 'Not officially Madam, I overheard them speaking.'

'Absolute lunacy.' Dorothea bellowed smoke towards the ceiling. 'But there is still something we – you can do to rescue the situation.'

'I fail to see what that can be Madam…'

'You are displeased with this situation and do not deny it.' Looking directly into Hambleton's eyes she added, 'You can offer to resign.'

Hambleton's breath caught in his throat; he winced. 'Madam, I simply couldn't do that.'

'Couldn't you Hambleton, couldn't you really?' Dorothea held her cigarette holder away from her mouth, stared at him with unblinking eyes. 'You are his right-hand man, Hambleton, someone he could not afford – would not be expecting to lose. Once he appreciates how great your concern is – that it has come to this, he will finally see sense.'

Hambleton took a deep breath, shook his head slowly. 'If I tender my resignation madam, and Mr. Llewellyn accepts, I will have lost both my livelihood and a cherished position here.'

'He will not accept and he *will* see sense.'

'I very much doubt that any cause of action will deter Mr. Llewellyn in terms of Miss Veronica.'

'Do not dismiss the issue out of hand, Hambleton.' Dorothea twiddled the holder between her fingers, then drew on the cigarette, expelling a ring of smoke towards the window. 'Think about it Hambleton. It is a means to an end.'

***

Dorothea's words seemed to buzz around Hambleton's head like an angry bluebottle that wouldn't go away.

For all her deviousness she had a point which tugged at his conscience. Thomas Llewellyn had been a caring employer and Veronica Day, whether knowingly or by chance had seemed to place a blindfold over his rationality. But using his resignation as blackmail to induce a change of direction was against his principles, and yet, his misgivings concerning Veronica Day's presence demanded that he at least gave it thought.

And thought, whether logical or not, won the day. Llewellyn's habitual early morning call for tea in his room was met with apprehension and tension as Hambleton duly obliged.

Llewellyn had his back to the door, gazing out at the wide panorama of sky and shoreline that the view from his room afforded. 'Ah, Hambleton,' he said over his shoulder, 'as punctual as ever, fine morning is it not? After the storms of last night – Miss Veronica's last day for a while should at least be pleasant.'

Hambleton sombrely placed the silver tray on the table, running his fingers across his upper lip. 'If I might have a word, sir.'

Llewellyn raised his brows. 'Why certainly Hambleton, you seem a trifle harassed, is something the matter, is…'

'Forgive me for interrupting sir,' Hambleton hung his head, 'but I must say my piece and then tender my resignation.'

Llewellyn squinted in a fleeting gesture of disbelief. 'Would you kindly explain yourself, resignation?'

Hambleton sighed. 'Sir, for a while now I have harboured reservations concerning the situation in this castle, it has come to the point whereupon I feel I can no longer be of service here.'

'What nonsense are you speaking?'

Hambleton felt fluid solidify in his throat. 'I have previously spoken of my reservations sir; I have considered the matter comprehensively and feel I have no choice…'

'Hambleton, you have long been a pillar of support to me,' Llewellyn said, tugging at the lapels of his dressing gown. 'This is the work of my sister – I urge you to reconsider ...'

'No, with all due respect you are making a mistake by inviting the young lady to become part of this establishment; I do not indulge as a rule in the behaviour of Miss Llewellyn, however on this occasion I feel she is right. My position here is compromised to the extent that I must offer my resignation.'

Llewellyn shook his head, let out a heavy sigh. 'You would terminate an association of more than a decade on account of Miss Veronica's association here?'

'She does not have your interests at heart, sir.'

'Damn you Hambleton.' Llewellyn flapped his hand wildly. 'You have no right to assume such a thing – Miss Veronica is a fine, upstanding woman and on no account will I have her good intentions slandered.' He poured his tea, the cup rattling in its saucer. 'Nonetheless, you will be sorely missed. I shall see that you are supplied with first class references. You will have the courtesy to continue service until I appoint a replacement?'

'Yes sir.' Hambleton swallowed heavily, his – their gamble had fallen flat. Had he succumbed to Dorothea's influence or were his doubts genuine? He was no longer certain but it made no difference now, he faced a situation that before the week had commenced, he wouldn't have considered possible.

***

Veronica Day sat cross legged on a grassy mound some distance from the castle, her long green dress tucked around her thighs; she was watching and listening to the waves lap ashore. She was contemplating an imminent return to the Capital, where she would perform a series of concerts. She no longer relished the prospect of playing before crowded venues, indeed, if she ever had at all. Veronica felt at home with the environment she was in now, though the atmosphere within the castle was turning distinctly chilly. But there was fascination and purpose here for her, when all said and done –

Footsteps on pebbles suddenly alerting her to the fact that she wasn't alone, Veronica jerked her head round to find John Gibbings climbing the mound.

'Veronica...'

'Well, this is a surprise, it is normally I who seek you out...' she patted the ground beside her. 'Hardly luxury seating I'm afraid.'

'I'm not used to luxury,' he said scornfully, 'unlike you.'

Veronica looked out to sea, returning her eyes to him slowly. 'Your opinion of me leaves something to be desired. I am uncomfortable with luxury, that's a paradox, is it not? In time John, perhaps you'll realise as much.'

'There isn't time, you'll be leaving tomorrow and you won't be coming back.'

'Won't I?' Veronica smiled, turned her head to the wind, lifted her face and let it rustle through her hair. 'Now I wonder where you heard that – no, don't tell me I can guess.'

'Well it's true, isn't it?'

Veronica placed her elbows on knees, fists beneath her chin and gazed out to sea. 'Have you ever wondered John, what lies beyond the horizon?'

When there was no answer she looked at him, saw his eyes flash, his lips part, revealing white teeth. 'You're mocking me – do you get some kind of kick out of it?' He was edgy, turning to go.

'John stay; come, sit down. If I were not returning I would have sought you out and told you so. The dark witch is incorrect, but you are not worried about her prying eyes?'

'If you mock, then she torments,' he snapped angrily, rifling a hand through his black, curly hair. 'I have had enough of her ways; she is pushing me to the limit...'

'Self control John.' Veronica clamped her hand on his wrist, tightened it. 'For just a while longer, trust me.'

Some of the anger went from his eyes; he went to speak then buttoned his lips. 'That's better,' she said, 'thought is better that impulsive action.'

'You have firm hands.'

'You sound surprised at that, I suspect your perception of me is totally inaccurate. Let us hope that time will change it, and that in time you will open up to me, and tell me what your problems really are.' She saw him shuffle uncomfortably, controlled an urge to push him further as they sat for a while in silence, listening to the waves lap ashore.

Gibbings got to his feet at length, brushed the cheeks of his trousers. 'I must be going; I've work to do.'

'So soon?' Veronica reached up, tapping his hand lightly, 'Answer me one question…'

Gibbings screwed his nose. 'What?'

'Oh John, really – your face loses some of its attraction when you do that.' She saw him blush, smiled faintly then added, 'Why did you seek me out today. You didn't come across me by chance, did you?'

She saw that look of resentment conceal his embarrassment again and then said, 'It does not matter, John, you don't have to…'

'I was afraid you weren't coming back,' he blurted. 'I saw you leaving the castle and followed. I wanted to know…'

'Is it that important?'

But Veronica's question was so quiet that it might have been engulfed by the waves as he strode away without answering.

She watched him go, then cupping a hand beneath her chin, she stared out to sea.

***

Dorothea reached out, grabbed Hambleton's hand as he passed her room, pulling him inside. She could tell by his forlorn expression that the gamble had failed.

'Well?'

Hambleton inhaled, meeting her eyes only briefly. 'It is as I feared. Mr. Llewellyn cannot be pressured into a change of direction; therefore I have been forced to tender my resignation.'

'Curse my stupid brother and that scheming woman.' Dorothea turned her back on Hambleton, arms crossed, fingers tapping rapidly on elbows. 'You were not forceful enough, Hambleton, did you abandon your position so readily?'

'I fear no amount of force would prove sufficient in this instance,' Hambleton replied gravely.

'With due respect you have succeeded to no greater effect than I.'

Dorothea waved him away indignantly, kicking the door shut before lighting a cigarette and pouring a double whisky. The double measures she'd drunk at breakfast had blurred her mind, and a solution to the problem of Veronica Day seemed far from hand. With her anger breaking new boundaries she marched into the annexe, dragged the chair from under her desk and flung herself down on it, whisky in one hand and cigarette in the other.

Two double measures of drink later her temper broke completely.

Charging out of her rooms, she rampaged along the corridor, flinging open Veronica's door with such force it rebounded against the wall of her room and slammed shut.

Veronica wasn't there but the vibration echoed around the castle walls, drawing angry shouts from Llewellyn as he came running up the stairs. 'My God, woman, what has got into you – have you taken *entire* leave of your senses?'

'Can't you see?' She turned on him, veins in her neck taut against her skin, voice hoarse from the strain on her cords. 'It's that fancy trollop you've invited into this castle that's blinding you from reason. Get her out of here before I do it myself.'

'Oh...' She recoiled, her hand clawing her right cheek, where Llewellyn had struck it with his hand – 'You are drunk,' he said savagely, perspiration glistening his forehead. 'That's the real problem here. You need sobering up.'

Dorothea, her face twisting in fury swung a hand, but Llewellyn caught both wrists, hurling her in a circle that was broken only as her back struck the wall. It knocked the breath from her and she doubled up, coughing violently.

But Llewellyn wasn't finished. Pulling her roughly by the arm he dragged Dorothea through to her room, flinging her down on the four-poster bed. He stood over her pointing breathlessly, 'The only saving grace for you – is that Veronica wasn't here to witness such abominable drunken behaviour – God help you if she had been.'

Dorothea raised her head, her body swelling and sinking through her dark robes. 'To hell with you,' she coughed, before eyes wide with horror she saw and felt Llewellyn's hand deliver a stinging blow, followed by another.

Hambleton had heard the screams; he came hurrying along the hallway at the moment Llewellyn slammed Dorothea's door shut.

'It's alright,' Llewellyn panted, palm of his hand raised. 'The excitement is over; my sister has been enticed into a little rest.'

'Sir, I heard blows, and then screams – are you certain ...'

'It is nothing for you to worry about,' Llewellyn persisted, composing himself. 'My sister simply suffered a bout of hysterics, the matter is disposed of now.'

Nothing to worry about. Hambleton returned to his downstairs room, Llewellyn's reassurance repeating continually in his mind.

What he'd heard amidst the screams was brutal slapping of hand on skin. He was appalled that whatever provocation his respected employer had undergone, he was able to effect such savage retribution on his only sister. Surely, even Dorothea didn't deserve that.

But the incident had provided Hambleton with food for thought. Because a short while ago he'd tendered his resignation with deep regrets; now he'd knowledge of another side of Thomas Llewellyn. One that chilled him to the core.

***

'Why Veronica my dear, I was becoming concerned for your whereabouts – you appear to have been gone for much of the day.'

Veronica met Llewellyn's enquiring gaze with apparent unconcern. 'Since this is my penultimate day here, I thought to explore as much of this wonderful island as I could – I trust I have not aggrieved you?'

'Of course not, Veronica dear.' Llewellyn tweaked his moustache, then clasped his hands tightly together. 'It is purely that I had envisaged more of your company, on this, your last full day here.'

Veronica touched him lightly on the arm. 'But we shall enjoy each other's company at dinner, Thomas, and then shortly, very shortly, I shall return.'

Llewellyn felt warmth rekindled in his veins. 'Might I ask how soon that will be?'

Veronica gave a sideways smile, not quite meeting his eyes. 'Well that depends on my itinerary – whether any additional concerts have been added – of which on account of my stay here I am not aware.'

'I see,' Llewellyn said, not completely satisfied. 'Ah, Hambleton, I have been meaning to speak with you.' He led the butler out into the entrance hall, saying quietly, 'I shall attend personally to my sister's requirements this evening; you understand I am concerned for her current state of mind.'

'Sir…'

Llewellyn met Hambleton's grim face with a prolonged stare, then proceeded back to the drawing room where Veronica sat. 'Hambleton will serve our dinner shortly my dear,' he paused… 'Veronica – I wonder, since this will be our last evening together for a while, whether I might ask a favour of you?'

'Which is?'

'That you perform for me this evening, a personal rendition in the gallery would put a splendid cap on my memories of your stay here.'

'Since you have been such a perfect host I fail to see how I can refuse.'

Llewellyn clutched Veronica's arm tightly. 'Please do not regard me as a host, Veronica, but as a friend – a very close friend.'

***

Veronica gave a personal rendition that evening. Her violin, sometimes melancholy, sometimes vibrant, other times sweet, elevated Llewellyn to unprecedented levels of rapture. And above it all, her beautiful form, lovely strong boned face, crowned by her fanned red hair became a vision of excellence, even when he closed his eyes.

He applauded until his palms stung and then reluctantly he bade her goodnight, conceding that she had a long journey to undertake the following day and needed a well-earned rest.

***

On the morning of her departure Veronica awoke, expecting and prepared for a battle of words with Dorothea, but of her there was no sign; surprised and somewhat disappointed at missing out on a battle of wits Veronica shrugged it off, leaving the castle driven by Llewellyn in his trap, and in possession of a letter slipped into her hand by Hambleton in the entrance hall.

She slipped the unopened envelope into her pocket, believing it to be an attempt to dissuade her from returning, Hambleton hardly being an advocate of her presence there.

As the pony trotted onto the road leading through the village she caught sight of a slim, lithe figure standing on the same grassy mound he'd occupied with her the day before, one hand raised in a wave.

She couldn't help but smile back, returning his wave. Llewellyn followed her eye, but Gibbings had slipped down the other side of the mound, heading back towards the garden.

As their journey to Berwick station progressed, Llewellyn heaped praise upon her, ranging from her musical qualities to her looks. But his was a voice in the background – for her thoughts were with Gibbings – her thoughts and worries – worries about how he would react in her absence to Dorothea's provocation.

They persisted long after her farewell to Llewellyn, sealed by both with a kiss on the cheek, and words from him that she couldn't recall – persisted in fact until well into her train journey, when she remembered the letter from Hambleton. It read:

My dear Miss Veronica,
You will know of course that I am not wholly in favour of your prolonged presence here at the Castle, but in explaining why, I shall endeavour to be honest.

Put simply, my belief is that Mr. Llewellyn has developed intense feelings for you that I do not believe you hold for him, which can only lead, I feel, to severe trauma for an employer I respect and admire.

However my reason for writing to you derives from an event which occurred yesterday. A severe incident which revealed an aspect of Mr. Llewellyn's character that hitherto I had no knowledge of.

I cannot go into great detail except to say that at times of great pressure I now believe that Mr. Llewellyn is capable of developing a violent disposition.

I stress this only to warn you, that should your feelings not match his, which in my opinion amounts to an obsession, then you may be in risk of physical harm.

This letter, I hasten to assure you, is written purely out of concern for your welfare.

Sincerely,
Alfred Hambleton

Veronica looked out over the ever-changing countryside, folded the letter carefully, slipping it into her pocket.

Whether or not Thomas had an obsession for her, this wasn't a brazen attempt by an interfering butler to block her return. Hambleton's letter had been written out of genuine concern, of that she had no doubt. Something had happened during her absence the previous day and it would explain the non-appearance of Dorothea. She'd intervened previously to prevent a clash between Thomas and his sister, but this time she'd been absent and God only knew what had happened.

Veronica took a deep breath, let it out gently. John Gibbings, Thomas Llewellyn, Dorothea, perhaps Hambleton also; all such perplexing, in some ways vulnerable people – and she drawn in amongst them on account of a shipwreck – and now committed to being so.

Hambleton had warned of danger, she'd like to think that Thomas didn't present one, but in any case she wasn't frightened or deterred.

She had a cause to fight for.

Chapter Eighteen

'And that gentlemen, seals it...'

Sitting in the lounge of his Berkeley Square private members club, entertaining his two special guests, Byron Rothman and Edward Reynolds, Llewellyn slapped the arm of his favourite red leather chair, delighted to have completed the deal that would free him of Dorothea's presence at the castle. The one hundred thousand pounds he'd raised from them in exchange for a ten per cent increase in dividends on their investments was more than enough to pay her off. With things as they were, he failed to see how she could refuse.

His over-riding desire was to return to a castle, along with Veronica, which was free of Dorothea's influence. Though now so elated was he with the outcome that an idea sprung to mind and developed with the swiftness of blood through veins. 'Gentlemen, in return for your generosity, I wish to bestow upon you an invitation to join me in a visit to my castle when I next return there – be it for the duration of a weekend – there you will meet my delightful Veronica – Veronica *Day* no less.' He leaned forward, seeing the surprise register on their faces. 'Yes, *the* Veronica Day.'

'You are a quiet one, Llewellyn.' The ginger haired, boyish looking Rothman cast a glance at the bemused Reynolds alongside and smiled. 'So she is your...'

'Not exactly...' Llewellyn cut in, anticipating Rothman's remark, then looking down and twiddling his thumbs, 'though I must say the matter has crossed my mind...' then switching back to his invitation, 'I extend the invitation of course, to your good lady wives.'

Rothman stretched out in his chair, a cigarette protruding from the forefingers of his right hand. 'You forget Llewellyn,' he said with a coy smile, 'that I am unmarried...'

Llewellyn coloured rapidly, fingered his neck. 'Forgive me Rothman, for my ignorance.'

'Pay it no heed.' Rothman's smile lingered as he enjoyed Llewellyn's embarrassment.

'I will travel alone,' Reynolds cut in, slapping his knee and rising, 'so that Rothman here doesn't feel out on a limb, so to speak. Mary will not mind at all.' He adjusted his spectacles. 'Now business is completed I'm afraid I must rush. Mary might excuse my absence for a weekend, but if I am but an hour late home, there is concern.'

'I too must be going, party to attend, old chap.' Rothman stood, dusted his dapper white suit.

'Then do not let me detain either of you,' Llewellyn said, rising to shake the hands of both, before re-seating himself and contemplating a future, consisting of Veronica, himself, and a castle.

***

Hambleton hadn't decided on his future, he'd agreed to stay on at the castle until Llewellyn's return with a newly appointed butler. In fact, he was reluctant to leave the island; it wasn't merely his affection for it but his growing unease that events surrounding the castle could easily get out of hand. The ingredients were there – Dorothea's scheming had backfired, not only at his own expense but hers also – at the hands of Llewellyn who had recently displayed a side to his character hitherto un-witnessed.

And Veronica Day, beautiful but enigmatic in his eyes, was the central element in this; Llewellyn's rising desire for her was as obvious as it was disturbing. She was as cool as he was hot, perhaps even calculating. From what he'd seen she wasn't capable of returning his feelings because hers led another path, towards John Gibbings, an arcane character himself.

With Veronica's acceptance of a room at the castle, her obvious regard for Gibbings, Dorothea's animosity and Llewellyn's propensity towards violence, a powder keg was developing, and the fuse had already been lit.

Hambleton felt a peculiar allegiance and yet he couldn't determine to which character that allegiance was anchored – perhaps it was his sense of duty, despite his soon to be terminated employment, that was the over-riding factor.

Standing now at the castle entrance, his eyes cast below, he saw one of those characters pass along the beach. It was John Gibbings, his expression as surly as ever. Their eyes met and Gibbings slowed before making an about turn and striding up the slope towards Hambleton.

Hambleton acknowledged his approach. 'John, are you well?'

'Aye – as can be expected.'

Hambleton nodded. Here was a man of few words, he hadn't expected much by way of reply. He wondered what had caused him to divert from his chosen track.

'Miss Llewellyn, she all right?' Gibbings asked at length.

Hambleton sighed, not wanting to divulge too much; he knew Gibbings resented the attention Dorothea was bestowing on him, wondered why he'd asked. Since Llewellyn's assault Dorothea had been uncharacteristically quiet, remaining in her room for much of the time, it was something he thought that Gibbings would appreciate.

He looked up; Gibbings' eyes were fixed on him, unblinking, unreadable. 'She has been unwell of late.'

'What's up with her then?'

'I would have thought you would appreciate the peace.' Hambleton gazed out to sea, concealing his surprise at Gibbings' persistence; he weighed how much he was prepared to divulge, his concerns needed sharing, even if that someone was Gibbings.

'You are aware I am leaving Gibbings?'

'Not heard anything,' Gibbings shrugged. 'It don't answer my question.'

'Perhaps it might do when I enlighten you.' Hambleton tilted his head towards the heavens. 'All does not bode well here, and you, I fear, are a major player in events.'

'Quit talking riddles,' Gibbings snapped. 'I only asked about Miss Llewellyn.'

'Miss Llewellyn received facial injuries inflicted I believe, by the hand of her brother.'

Drawing a finger across his lip, Hambleton continued, 'I also believe there to be some association between Miss Veronica and yourself. Given Mr. Llewellyn's apparent obsession with her, I fear for her welfare if his feelings are not returned – and…'

'There is *no* association.' Gibbings tensed, leaned towards Hambleton. 'I've gone out of my way to prevent…'

'Nonetheless, at least on her part there is something – I have witnessed…'

'You have witnessed Veronica's concern for me, nothing more – I would do nothing to put her at risk.'

Hambleton drew back at the vehemence of Gibbings' reply. 'I merely sought to…'

'How bad are Miss Llewellyn's injuries?'

'They are healing – almost healed, though I feel her ego has been damaged.'

Gibbings sniffed, drew in a breath. 'If that's the extent of it, then it's not such a bad thing.'

A facial nerve twitched, Hambleton was surprised to say the least, but he wouldn't betray himself with a smile – this was no smiling matter.

***

Llewellyn had been reading a morning paper when the phone in his London mews home rang. He lifted the receiver to be greeted by Veronica's voice and immediately adrenalin surged through his body like hot breath.

Down the crackling line he heard her say, 'Thomas, I trust you are well?'

'Indeed my dear, and your good self?'

'Fine Thomas. I am calling to advise you that my current series of concerts is completed and I intend to return to the castle at the weekend – with your kind permission, of course.'

'Of course, my dear, of course. I shall look forward to joining you; will you be travelling by train?'

'Yes, I arrive in Berwick on Friday; my train is scheduled to arrive at four pm.'

Llewellyn's grip on the phone tightened. 'I shall return tomorrow with my new butler, Dawson, who will be replacing Hambleton. Good fellow Dawson, you'll like him…'

'Thomas, please do not feel you need to make the effort on my account.' Veronica's voice had dropped a touch, and Llewellyn felt a prick of resentment that she could even think he might not want to join her. 'Not at all, my dear,' he answered hurriedly. 'By a strange quirk of fate I had already decided upon taking a long weekend break at the castle. I will be at Berwick to greet you.'

'Thank you Thomas, most kind. I look forward to seeing you.'

Llewellyn heard the phone click, mopped his brow; two days' hence was short notice but in truth he'd covered every eventuality, such was his desire to be re-united with Veronica again. He'd been disappointed that he hadn't heard from her for two weeks, he'd provided her with his contact details prior to their departure, though due to the mobile nature of her profession, she hadn't been able to supply him with hers.

Now he knew of her return however, he was wasting no time in hatching his plans; he began by contacting his business associates, Rothman and Reynolds, apologising for the late nature of his invitation, but nonetheless procuring acceptance from both. They would join Veronica and himself on the Saturday morning, travelling by one of those new-fangled automobiles Rothman had recently purchased.

At lunchtime he made the short journey to Regent Street, purchasing the all-important ring he intended placing on Veronica's finger, on Saturday evening during their meal. The moment couldn't come soon enough – and then the icing on the cake – the one hundred thousand pound offer to Dorothea, her monies returned in full, plus an additional twenty per cent dividend on her investment – an invitation to leave that she wouldn't be able to refuse, leaving Veronica and himself free to enjoy the fineries of the castle.

Llewellyn gently removed the glittering sapphire from its gold case, examined it between forefinger and thumb; pure perfection, suitable only for the love of his life. It seemed to him, right then, that his world couldn't get any better.

Chapter Nineteen

Llewellyn took the trap to Berwick having left Hambleton to familiarise his new butler, Dawson, with the castle.

He was in a state of euphoria; everything was set fair and it was a perfect summer's afternoon, there wasn't a single cloud in the sky.

His heart pumping like the steam engine soon to pull in, he arrived at the station a full thirty minutes early. As it transpired he had to wait an hour, the train having been delayed by operational difficulties, before finally the sight of grey smoke filled his eyes and clogged his nostrils, and the growing thunder of the locomotive as it ground into the station.

And then there she was – the first to alight from the carriages, a treat to his eyes as he stood by the exit, all leggy elegance with her yellow dress swirling in the breeze, the afternoon sunlight enhancing her rich red hair.

But his excitement was dampened by the absence of the familiar violin case he had bought for her. Her right hand carried luggage, and that was all.

'My dear Veronica, how wonderful to see you, and as always, looking so lovely.' He strode forward, taking her free hand, pulling her towards him and kissing her cheek.

'Why thank you Thomas, it is nice to be back, I can smell the sea air already.'

'From ten miles in? I doubt that,' as his smile became a frown, he asked, 'your violin Veronica, surely you haven't left it behind?'

'I feel rather drained as far as my music goes, Thomas; I have trusted it to the care of my brother in Gloucester. A few days without it will not go amiss.'

'But your practicing…'

'I can make it up Thomas,' Veronica said dismissively as Llewellyn guided her through the exit to the trap. He grunted. 'It is simply that I have invited some important guests to stay this weekend, I had envisaged you playing for them…'

'I am sorry, Thomas, I had not realised,' Veronica said tiredly.

'It is not your fault Veronica, I failed to mention it.' Llewellyn leaned his head closer to hers. 'I have other news,' he whispered.

'Then please do enlighten me, Thomas,' Veronica prompted, turning her head towards the countryside.

'I have secured a business transaction.' Llewellyn held his hands high, clapped them joyfully before taking the reins. 'My two guests who will be joining us tomorrow are our passport to ridding the castle of Dorothea's overbearing presence. It is soon to be ours alone.'

'Why Thomas,' Veronica swung to face him, her face brightening as she patted his arm, 'that is *marvellous* news – but are you certain she will accept?'

'I am offering an additional twenty per cent by way of dividend, given her present frame of mind I doubt that she will refuse.'

Veronica nodded, turned away again, staring silently at the rising hills.

'Is something the matter, Veronica? I thought you'd be delighted by my news.'

'Indeed I am Thomas, indeed I am...' but Veronica Day said nothing further.

'I assume you are returning on Monday?' Llewellyn inquired at length.

'A few days longer perhaps, I feel a longer break may do me good, if that is acceptable to you.'

'Why of course it is, my dear,' Llewellyn answered, his eyebrows widening in surprise. 'I of course have arranged to return, but my new butler Dawson will attend to your needs.'

Veronica lowered her eyes, let out the slightest of sighs.
***

Hambleton closed the door to the kitchen, acknowledging Mrs. Simms, and then glancing at the square shouldered, thick set Dawson. 'Well that is about it as far as the castle goes – for the most part it is quite routine, particularly when Mr. Llewellyn is away...'

'I will not be as permanent a fixture of the castle as you appear to be,' Dawson said as though his throat were laced in sandpaper, then locking his unfriendly eyes on Hambleton, 'I am to accompany him wherever he requires me – a full time servant here seems unnecessary.'

'Indeed, perhaps it is.' Hambleton straightened his tie. 'But when Mr. Llewellyn undertook the purchase of the castle, he needed a permanent presence...' Hambleton had been about to continue, to mention that Llewellyn doubted Dorothea enough to have a trusted servant provide a counter-balance. He had indeed provided a similar service to that required of Dawson up until the time of purchase; but a look into his replacement's hard face troubled him, told him that his words would be wasted. With its broken nose and square chin there was a pugnacious look about the fellow, his features suggested not a trace of gentility; his general presence added fuel to Hambleton's suspicions that here was a man employed to follow his master's every instruction without question or thought, and if so this was a worrying change in his former employer's stance – an indication of Llewellyn's changing personality perhaps?

Hambleton wondered briefly from where Llewellyn had secured his services, this fellow had the look of a pugilist about him, and a voice to match. Hambleton preferred not to dwell on the subject, but still it was an effort to drag his thoughts away, until an unlikely source came to his aid.

Dorothea came marching into the hall, head high, directly into their path, cigarette holder in hand, with her ego seemingly restored. 'Ah Hambleton,' she glanced at Dawson then dismissively back to the former butler, 'it is good to know that you are still around.'

'For a few moments, Madam, no more, my suitcases are packed and I depart within the hour.' He held a hand out towards his replacement. 'Dawson here will address your needs.'

'I see.' Dorothea's voice was seemingly flat with disappointment, and without so much as a glance at Dawson, she asked, 'And to where do you go?'

'I have secured lodgings on the island, Madam, for the time being.' Looking firmly into Dawson's eyes he added, 'I have no great wish to return swiftly from whence I came. Now if you would excuse me, Madam, I must be leaving. My best wishes to you, and indeed to you, Dawson.'

With that, Hambleton made for his room, and his possessions. Without a word Dorothea followed him along the corridor, leaving Dawson alone in the hall, his eyes fixed on them both.

Chapter Twenty

'Your baggage madam...'

'I can manage thank you.' Veronica ran her eyes briefly over the large man's granite-like face, taking in a big extended right hand which seemed unwilling to retract. 'You are Mr. Dawson I assume.'

'I am.' Dawson finally placed his arm by his side, his expression deadpan.

'I see, well thank you Mr. Dawson, but I require very little assistance as you will no doubt learn.'

'Madam.' Dawson managed a smile, or perhaps a scowl, Veronica couldn't be certain, before marching back up the slope.

'You were a trifle short, my dear, not like you at all,' Llewellyn said edgily. 'Dawson is new to the post, after all.'

Veronica lifted her case from the trap in a single, fluent motion. 'My first impressions suggest him to be overbearing, if not somewhat menacing.'

Llewellyn gave a lop-sided smile. 'As I say, he is a fine man – do not let it disturb you.'

'Oh he does not disturb me Thomas,' Veronica said, aware that Llewellyn was struggling to match her stride up the slope. 'I merely wonder what possessed you to employ him.' She smiled, tapped him gently with her free hand, 'Come, I mean no malice towards him, providing of course we remain at separate ends of the castle...' she laughed at his expression. 'Thomas, learn to know when I am joking...'

'You really should have allowed Dawson to carry your suitcase,' Llewellyn stressed upon reaching the castle entrance.

'Do I look fatigued?' she paused, looking calmly into his eyes.

'No, my dear, you do not.' Llewellyn tweaked his moustache. 'But such behaviour is not ladylike.'

Veronica met his eyes for several seconds. 'This lady, Thomas, does what she likes.' She watched his jaw tighten and when he didn't reply said, 'I must freshen up, and then if you do not mind I wish to take a walk...'

He angled his head, frowned, 'Alone?'

'Only for a short while Thomas, I have concluded a harrowing set of concerts and wish to unwind. I do so in my own company though I mean no disrespect to you. You will have my presence, should you require it, for the remainder of the day.'

'Of course, I adore your company my dear, please do as you wish, and then honour me with your company prior to dinner.'

Veronica climbed the stairs to her room, placed her suitcase on the bed and stared thoughtfully out to sea.

***

Dorothea heard the pony's hooves on the path below. Crossing to the window she saw her brother was back, together with the woman he'd grown so stupidly fond of. She saw the loathsome new butler Dawson stick out a stubby hand, and then what looked like a rejection from the red-headed woman. The sound of her voice, so composed, jarred her nerves. The sound of his, filled her with hate.

'Go on my love-lorn brother, make a fool of yourself over that woman...' she whispered, 'see if I wasn't right all along, and I shall be here to watch your poor heart suffer.' Dorothea laughed bitterly, slammed the window shut, and crossing to the table raised a scotch in her hand, swirled it and gulped.

With the beating he'd given her, any influence had waned; any influence she held in the castle had dwindled. Her advances towards Gibbings had fallen flat and facial bruising had combined with her vanity to dissuade her from pursuing him further. Now she had neither the authority nor the inclination to entice him.

Her only consolation now, on this desolate island, was in watching her brother's demise – she would sit back, relax and tolerate; enjoy the ending in the knowledge that it would come.

***

Veronica skipped down the slope, felt the warm afternoon breeze rustle through her hair and tilted her face towards the sun. Much as she loved the castle, she preferred to be out, rather than in, particularly on such a day as this.

And it was only a small white lie she'd handed Thomas; she did need time to herself, time in the open, prior to later formalities.

What she hadn't told him was of her desire to see Gibbings, if only to ensure that he hadn't fallen foul of Dorothea's antics which had threatened to tumble out of control. She'd caught neither sight nor sound of the woman in the short time she'd been back, but that counted for little on this island.

She was climbing the rocky mound at the castle's base to give herself a better view of the gardens where he worked, when she saw him – she waved, caught his eye straight away and clambering down, made her way across to the garden gate where he stood, a slight smile lightening his frown. He came forward to greet her, brushing the sweat from his forehead with the back of his hand. 'How are you, John, a little hot and bothered? Has the dark witch been tormenting you?'

Gibbings shook his curly head. 'No, actually – I've hardly seen a thing of her since – Mr. Llewellyn…'

'Yes, John, well at least that nasty business has produced one positive element; I've been worried, I can tell you…'

'Worrying again on my account,' Gibbings said, his frown deepening. 'I don't understand…'

'I am not easy to understand John; so do not try too hard – sometimes things are better off left that way.' Veronica leaned back against the gate, brushed her long hair back from her ears and glanced at him from over her shoulder; then raising her brows she asked, 'Would you care to walk with me?'

He looked reticent, then screwing his eyes as he glanced up at the castle windows, 'I'm not sure I should – I should be working and I don't trust them up there. I can't afford to be losing my job…' he glanced down at his hands and Veronica followed the line of his eyes. 'All this talk about you having grubby hands, they seem quite clean to me considering what you do.'

He returned his gaze to her. 'There – there's something I need to ask you…'

'Well take a break, walk with me John.' Veronica levered herself from the gate. 'And ask away.'

'I can't be long, but I need to know,' Gibbings began, undoing the gate latch and leading her into a field of long coarse grass, separated by a thin dirt track they could barely negotiate side by side.

'He starts a question but does not finish it,' Veronica chided, waving away tiny green insects that rose from the grass as they brushed it.

'There you go again…'

'John, just tell me what you want to know, plainly something is bothering you…' Veronica stopped, thrust her hands on hips, turning sideways, 'or do I need to shake it out of you?'

'I'd like to see you try.'

Veronica slapped a hand to her mouth. 'Oh my word, there *is* some fight in you.'

Gibbings gave an exasperated smile, sighing before stiffening. 'I want to know how you feel about Mr. Llewellyn.'

'How I feel? Well that's a strange question, John...'

'I mean are you and him going to...' Gibbings trailed off.

'Oh I see.' Veronica crossed her arms, glanced down at the waves of grass and bit her lip. She returned her attention to him only slowly. 'I'm not sure I want to answer questions like that – particularly when you choose to keep your innermost secrets from me...'

'They are not your concern.'

'Everyone needs a shoulder, mine are broad – or haven't you noticed?'

Gibbings hung his head. 'I have noticed; I have noticed many things about you...'

'Sounds intriguing.'

'Listen Veronica.' He grabbed her hand in a tight grip. 'Mr. Llewellyn's got a vicious streak, he seems alright on the surface, but I been speaking to Mr. Hambleton – he's worried you might come to harm – like Miss Llewellyn has, only worse?'

'Can I have my hand back, please John?' Veronica slipped her hand from his grasp, allowing a faint smile at his embarrassment. 'I can take care of myself, I assure you.'

'But Miss Veronica, if you can't return his feelings you should leave the island for your own safety.'

'Veronica, John, just plain Veronica.' She looked sternly into his eyes. 'Only I cannot do that John, can I?' She turned and walked slowly back towards the castle, willing his barriers to break down.

'I...'

'Yes John?' she stopped, crooking her head towards him. 'Let me help you, tell me what vexes you so.'

He shook his head slowly, dark curls tumbling over his brow.

Veronica sighed, nodded, resumed her walk, heading back to the castle. 'Then when you are ready, John Gibbings, come to me...'

'How long will you stay?'

Veronica heard the question, but no answer broke the afternoon air.

***

Llewellyn stared out of the drawing room window, his heart suddenly beating heavier against his chest walls. He sighed and turned upon hearing Dorothea's footsteps. 'Ah Dorothea, I have seen so little of you since my return, that I haven't been able to advise you that I have invited guests for the weekend. I would be grateful if you would keep your tantrums in check, at least for the duration of their visit.'

Dorothea crossed to the window, her eyes sweeping the gardens below, allowing herself a smile. 'Do not worry Thomas; I will be the portrait of civility, despite your manhandling of me.'

Llewellyn's jaw tightened, a vein pulsated in his neck. 'You provoked me beyond reason, your behaviour was intolerable.'

'As was yours Thomas.' She tapped his arm, 'Oh do look, here comes Veronica, fresh from a cosy chat with Gibbings no doubt; my, and so soon after arriving back.' She looked Llewellyn slowly up and down, smirking at his obvious discomfort. 'And who are these guests might I ask? Is their significance such that they should encroach upon your valuable time with the woman?'

Llewellyn clenched his fists, bellowed air from his lungs. 'I see your sarcasm hasn't diminished in the slightest.'

'I have good cause to scoff if you ask me.'

Dorothea marched away, leaving him livid at her insolence. But he'd been pre-occupied with the scene below and despite his irritation he returned his gaze to it, following Veronica until she disappeared from sight, heading in all likelihood for the slope, and the castle entrance.

Needlessly adjusting his tweed jacket, Llewellyn paced through to the hall, tensely awaiting her arrival, aware of rising adrenalin within and breathing deeply to combat it. The light tread of her steps echoed through the cavernous hall and a slender shadow spread along the floor as Veronica walked in.

Llewellyn allowed her to progress several paces into the hall before emerging from behind one of the stone pillars. Her path blocked, Veronica halted, placing a hand to her chest. 'Why, Thomas, you gave me such a fright …'

'I apologise my dear, I intended no such thing – I was merely passing through the hall when I heard your steps. How did you enjoy your walk? You certainly were not long…'

'I feel it would have been inconsiderate of me to have stayed out longer. You requested my presence Thomas and you shall have it.'

'And how is our gardener, Gibbings?' Llewellyn motioned jerkily towards the window.

Veronica crossed her arms, shrugged and frowned. 'He fares well I believe. Why do you ask? Thomas, you seem a little – flushed...'

'Not at all my dear.' Llewellyn tweaked his moustache, and without meeting her eyes, 'I merely ask, having observed you in the grounds. You appear to have become friends.'

'Ah,' Veronica ran her tongue along her bottom teeth, then smiled. 'I would hardly call it friendship. I came across him as I was passing the gardens; we caught each other's eyes. He asked after my welfare and I returned his interest.'

'How civil of you, Veronica. Gibbings is indeed fortunate to have someone so concerned.' Llewellyn, struggling to keep his voice level swallowed heavily, he wanted to go further but narrowly resisted. There had been something in their proximity, something in her bearing which caused him to reflect again on Hambleton's words – and on Dorothea's, damn her. These instances of their meeting might well be fleeting, but they were becoming many – how could Veronica deny there wasn't some form of friendship, however ridiculous it might seem.

'Thomas, are you certain nothing is troubling you?'

'No my dear.' Llewellyn wrenched himself out of his melancholy mood. 'I feel a trifle warm; I need to change into something cooler. Will you join me for afternoon tea?'

Veronica produced her delightful smile which so enthralled him. 'Of course Thomas, I shall look forward to it. I need to refresh, please allow me a short while.'

'Naturally.'

Llewellyn watched Veronica climb the stone steps, full of poise and elegance, her light green dress swirling around her calves. Such was his admiration that his doubts dissipated like mist in strong sunlight. What harm had there been in a little polite conversation, even if they were at opposite ends of the social spectrum?

But it was more than a change of clothes that Llewellyn required as he reached his room. He needed a long bath to relieve the tension that had unexpectedly surged within.

Chapter Twenty One

Veronica strolled along the shingle, drawing her pastel shawl closer around her body in the fresh morning breeze. The castle lay behind her, high on its base of volcanic rock; there was the feeling that somewhere within its walls someone watched. The discomfort was there and growing though she did her best to negate it.

As charming as Thomas had been throughout their meal the previous evening, his earlier behaviour had been strange to say the least. He had obviously been unsettled, and the fact he'd witnessed her earlier encounter with Gibbings was obvious.

Gibbings' concern for her was evident, and in a way unexpected; born of Hambleton's observations, she suspected, more than anything else.

Her number one priority remained to return the favour Gibbings had bestowed on her when he'd rescued her from the sea, to help him the way he'd helped her. Frustratingly she'd a notion he'd come close yesterday to unloading his problems – and now the temptation was there to seek him out again.

But she'd formed the opinion that Thomas' unusual behaviour stemmed from the fact that in his eyes, Gibbings was allowing her to distract him from his work. Not so long ago she'd singled out Dorothea as a threat to his employment, now if she were not careful that threat might come from Thomas himself. Any further conversations with Gibbings, therefore, would need more appropriate timing and be discreet.

Veronica's thoughts were interrupted by a deep drone, the sound familiar to her owing to her association with the Capital and other major cities. She turned to witness the approach of a shining silver automobile, which she assumed to be a hitherto unprecedented sight on the island.

She stood back from the rough road to allow them passage and as they passed slowly by she saw the man in the driver's seat incline towards her, raising his hat as he did so to reveal a crop of reddish-brown hair; nodding acknowledgement he smiled, his eyes remaining on her for some few yards, while his passenger's gaze remained steadfastly set ahead.

The vehicle continued onto the wide path at the forefront of the castle grounds, drawing to a halt at the head of the castle approach. Veronica suspected Thomas' benefactors had arrived and sure enough she saw Thomas emerge from the castle entrance the moment they pulled up, advancing swiftly down the slope to welcome them.

No sooner had he greeted them than he became aware of her presence, craning his head in her direction and waving her over.

'Veronica,' he called enthusiastically, and smiling broadly, 'the two gentlemen I spoke to you of ; come be introduced to my friends, Mr. Byron Rothman and Mr. Edward Reynolds.'

Veronica felt Rothman's blue eyes on her immediately; lively, almost dancing. She took in his thin lips and boyish countenance which creased into an easy smile. 'Byron Rothman. So you are the delectable Miss Day. I am a great admirer of your music madam; it is indeed an honour to meet with you in the flesh.' He took a step forward, taking her hand in his and kissing her palm softly.

'Thank you indeed Mr. Rothman, I am flattered.' She turned to his companion. 'Mr. Reynolds, good morning to you.'

'Madam.' Reynolds, a portly man wearing tweeds, with a blotchy complexion and brown moustache less neatly trimmed than his host's, acknowledged her with a brief downward motion of his head.

Llewellyn turned his attention to the car. 'A fine automobile,' he enthused.

'A Rolls-Royce Silver Ghost,' Rothman informed. 'Brand spanking new; six cylinder engine no less – reputed to be the finest motor car in the world,' he added proudly…'and what finer day to journey out in it.' He spread his hands towards the skies, gaze returning to Veronica, who shook her head. 'If you would excuse me I feel rather tired,' she said, regarding each in turn, 'but please do not let me deter you from enjoying a ride in this fine vehicle – but perhaps before you leave, Mr. Rothman…'

'Absolutely…' the disappointment on Rothman's face passed like a cloud from the sun, as Veronica glanced up to see the hulking figure of Dawson descending the slope.

'Ah, there you are, Dawson,' Llewellyn said flatly, and then turning to his guests, 'refreshments await you gentlemen, following which I will acquaint you with the castle – and then I look forward to our trip out.'

Dawson gathered Rothman and Reynolds' suitcases, carrying one in each hand with one tucked beneath each arm, while Llewellyn took a long look at Veronica. 'Are you certain you will not be joining us, my dear? If you like I can postpone our trip until…'

'No Thomas, I do not wish to deny you the opportunity of a ride on a fine morning such as this; please join your friends and do not think me unsociable.'

'We surely do not,' Rothman stated readily while Llewellyn remained silent. 'Come Llewellyn, let us enter this fine castle of yours.'

Llewellyn looked back at Veronica uncertainly, but her eyes were cast along the shoreline towards the harbour, from where the klaxon sounded urgently on the morning air.

***

Veronica, relaxing in a high-backed armchair by her room window, opened her eyes at the sound of voices below and heard Rothman's smooth, light-hearted banter and the more sober tones of his companion, Reynolds. There followed the sound of an automobile being started up.

Rising and stretching she looked out to see Llewellyn and his two guests sitting in the open top vehicle, which was pulling out onto the rough road to the village.

Leaving her room she climbed out onto the roof garden, watching the motor car proceeding along the road at a sedate speed, before turning her attention to the sparkling sea, slightly choppy in the strong, warm southerly breeze.

On the horizon a boat appeared, its shape gradually becoming more distinct, and then she heard steps behind her, recognising their familiar rhythm.

Veronica stiffened, her eyes remaining on the vessel as she felt Dorothea's whisky laced breath on her neck. 'So our hero returns, the *true* object of your desire,' she said, her voice falling to a whisper.

'He is not the object of my desire.' Veronica crossed her arms, turning to face Dorothea, staring down into her eyes.

'Some might believe you but I am not so naïve. I would have thought the gentleman with the nice automobile affords a better proposition than the wretched Gibbings.'

'You continue to misjudge my intentions, or indeed affections,' Veronica said coolly. 'I am becoming rather tired of your wit. I can see what induced Thomas into a rage.' Veronica sighed, was about to apologise for her impetuous remark, but Dorothea's hand, suddenly clenched on her shoulder was about to banish the gesture from her mind.

'Just the slightest push my dear, would send you plummeting below. I have always thought that having three foot railings around this garden was insufficient. You just toppled over, who would know otherwise?'

Veronica had no time to assess whether Dorothea was serious; in an instant she grabbed the woman's arms, swinging her round; Dorothea lashed with her foot, her shoe catching Veronica's shin, but to no avail. Her arms subdued in an intensifying grip, her temper drained along with her energy. But Veronica did not let go, not until Dorothea, exhausted by her struggling, crumbled completely, and then hands on her shoulders, forcing the defeated woman to her knees, she said, 'Be grateful my patience is stronger than Thomas'.

***

Veronica returned to her room, not so much shaken by her experience, but by the question posed by Dorothea's actions – had that been a deliberate attempt to kill her? Had Dorothea been so angered by her remark that she would have carried through with a push? Dorothea could have pushed without warning and sent her plunging below, but she'd delayed and therein lay the problem. But the threat in itself had been enough to force her to use her strength if only to restrain the woman – at the very least it had been a disturbing development, making it easier to understand, if not endorse the action Thomas had taken.

The lifeboat was preparing to moor now; Thomas and his friends would likely be gone for some time, and Dorothea would either return to her bottle or sleep off its effects.

If Veronica had been feeling tired before, she certainly wasn't now, she had an hour or two to herself and she would spend it walking and talking with Gibbings if at all possible. Apart from getting to the source of his predicament it struck her that he was the only person she could discuss her experience with.

***

Gibbings looked tired as he clambered from the boat, a slight pallor marring his normal tanned features, as, buttoning his white shirt, he trod across the pebbles to her.

'You look tired John,' Veronica said, aware of stating the obvious.

'Aye – you would if you'd just plucked three folks from rough water.'

'What happened?' she asked, walking ahead of him, picking her way through a hillock of tufted grass.

'A ketch went over.' |He sighed. 'Sea's rough, but not *that* rough – poor sailing if you ask me.

'What you doing here anyway?' he asked, now alongside her.

She shrugged. 'I fancied a little company…'

'Can't provide it now, Veronica – have to be getting back.' He strode ahead. 'Mr. Llewellyn's been giving me queer looks lately. I've been seeing his face at the window – staring – like he's checking on me and letting me know it.'

'It's alright John, he isn't there.' Veronica clasped his arm and drew him back. 'He has two guests, Mr. Rothman and Mr. Reynolds; I think these are the two men who have provided the money that allows Mr. Llewellyn to buy the dark witch out. They drove out in Mr. Rothman's auto mobile.'

'Buy her out?' Gibbings squinted.

'Yes, if all goes well she should be leaving, one less problem for you to worry about…' Veronica gave him a long, expectant gaze.

'How come you didn't join him in this - this automobile ride?'

'I wasn't invited,' she lied. 'Walk with me a while.'

'I shouldn't really…'

'John, will you stop worrying – the afternoon is bright and warm, the gardens are a wonderland of colour thanks to you – you can well afford a break. Mr. Llewellyn would be a fool to dismiss you and he certainly isn't that. And as for my part I do not think it at all a good idea that I encounter Dorothea again, this afternoon.'

'Miss Llewellyn – what's happened?'

Veronica exhaled, led Gibbings through a narrow sandy path between banks of lengthy grass and gorse, and down to join a lane bordered by low stone walls.

'There was an altercation out on the balcony – the roof garden.'

'An altercation?'

'A row, John…'

'I know what an altercation is,' Gibbings said with an edge to his voice.

Veronica bit her lip, looked him in the eye. 'I'm sorry John – I didn't mean to…'

'I'm not as dumb as I look, however much…' to Veronica's

surprise Gibbings stopped in mid-sentence, breaking into a smile, putting an end to her embarrassment.

'John, what is causing you such amusement?' she asked through half-open eyes.

'The look on your face.'

'Am I so abject?'

'Abject?' Gibbings looked bemused, she saw him redden. 'No' he said looking down... 'so pretty.'

Veronica's shoe found a pothole in the roughly surfaced lane, she stumbled sideways and spontaneously Gibbings' arms clasped around her, just like they had when he'd raised her from the sea. 'Why John, I can manage,' she laughed. A gentle push in the chest and he'd freed his hold, though her eyes remained locked steadfastly on his.

Gibbings swallowed, raked a hand through his dark hair. 'Tell me about this – altercation,' he said, resuming their walk.

Veronica folded her arms beneath her chest, eyes on the uneven road beneath but not seeing, 'I was standing by the railings looking out to sea. I heard Dorothea's footsteps – we had words. I said something I probably shouldn't have and then she pressed her hand to my shoulder. She uttered a thinly veiled threat; just a push and I would have been down on the rocks. I couldn't take the chance and forced her round – my hands on her arms. She went into a frenzy and lashed at my skin.' Veronica paused, pulled up the hem of her light blue dress. 'There – a bruise nothing more, but I did what was necessary to contain her until her temper was exhausted.' Veronica lashed her foot at a large stone, sent it flying into the fields. 'Stupid woman, I could have tossed her into the sea.'

She glanced at Gibbings, eyes moist with anger, teeth clenched – 'Now the fury comes out – better now than then.'

Veronica saw Gibbings' surprise, no shock – at the sudden change in her. 'You see John, I needed to be free of anger, to let it escape – I needed somebody to confide to – just as you do now. Tell me what's wrong with you John – I can help...'

'No – I can't, you're a woman...'

'How observant,' she said acidly.

'Look, I didn't mean to belittle you.' He clawed at his forehead. 'It's not what I meant; a man should stand on his own feet, and shoulder his own burdens...'

'So woman is not equal to man, in that I am not worthy to be aware of your problems?'

'No, no, *no.*' Gibbings held a hand high, then let it fall, placing both on his hips with a sigh – a look into his eyes told her he was defeated, she'd finally broken through his barrier.

'You're impossible – okay – I...'

And then a drone, a sound unmistakable to Veronica's ears, almost certainly the only motor vehicle on the island advancing towards them somewhere along the winding lane. Veronica knew Gibbings' employment would be endangered if he was seen out here, and in her company, and she too would risk Llewellyn's displeasure.

Their eyes met, they both had the same instinctive thought. Gibbings was first over the wall, extending a hand for Veronica to join him and though she didn't require it, she took his hand anyway. And then both crouched behind the wall as the vehicle whined up the ascending lane and slowly passed them.

'We need to get back.' Gibbings tone was urgent. 'If we cut across country we can beat them – they'll find it slow, bumpy going along the road...' he glanced at her despairingly, 'only it'll mean running and I'll leave you behind.'

'You speak nonsense, John.' Veronica's eyes flashed defiantly, she was eager for the challenge.

They ran the quarter mile flat out, occasionally needing to hurdle dry stone walls, tramping down the long grass as they went. Gibbings was amazed she could keep up, amazed at the smooth way she dealt with the undulating ground, and where their ways split he saw her shoot an audacious smile.

Back in her room, Veronica's breathing had returned to normal as she heard the Rolls-Royce draw up. She sighed, flung her head on the pillow and gazed at the ceiling. So close, so close to breaking John Gibbings down. Soon now, she'd achieve it.

Chapter Twenty Two

'How clumsy of me.' Rothman glanced at Veronica and smiled as he mopped drops of spilt tea from his jersey. 'So, Miss Day – I take it I may address you as "Veronica?" and as Veronica nodded and returned his smile, 'you must be quite taken by this island to accept permanent accommodation here.'

'I am indeed, Mr. Rothman, but then I do admit to a fondness for the North East…'

'Oh…' Rothman's brows rose fleetingly, 'call me Byron, please.'

Rothman looked across at his portly companion, Reynolds, a quiet smile crossing his smooth features. 'I must say, I would find spending any appreciable time here excruciatingly boring – wouldn't you Edward? Nothing to do all day but stare at the sea – which always looks the same to me.'

Rothman placed his cup in the saucer, lowering the china to the table. 'But you obviously have a close friendship with Llewellyn which changes the picture somewhat.'

'That aside, I find this to be a tranquil, pleasant island,' Veronica countered. 'A little experience of nature cannot but broaden our horizons, unlikely as it might seem to some.' Veronica had lowered her eyes, but now she raised them towards his companion. 'Isn't that so, Mr. Reynolds?'

'Most certainly it is,' the man in the brown tweed suit answered readily. 'Not everyone enjoys the hustle of the city.'

Rothman raised an amused smile, apparently undaunted by the combined rejection of his philosophy. 'Nevertheless, I would have thought that the beautiful lady here does have a preference for – shall we say – the brighter lights?'

'Then you would have thought wrongly.' But Veronica's next intended words were cut short by the appearance of Llewellyn. 'Ah Llewellyn, can we count on your sister's presence at dinner?' Rothman inquired, his brows raised.

'I have no word from her; I would deem it unlikely.'

Reynolds drew on his long pipe, smoke funnelling into the air. 'I feel that might be a blessing. She seems somewhat cantankerous.'

'I fear she is somewhat incapacitated.' The dryness of Veronica's remark drew attention from all three. 'I only mean, she seemed unwell.'

'Meaning she is heavily indulged in alcohol,' Llewellyn said, with undisguised bitterness. 'I take it you have had the misfortune to encounter her, my dear?'

'Only briefly, Thomas,' Veronica bit her lip as a deterrent to elaborate. Llewellyn seemed to sense her unease. 'Do not worry my dear, soon we will be free of the shadows she casts upon us, and then you and I can be content within the stout walls of this castle.'

'How nice, how very cosy…' Rothman's eyes focused keenly on Veronica as he spread out his hands. 'You make it seem, Llewellyn, as if your very existence revolves around this place. Surely your business necessitates a substantial amount of your time?'

Veronica noticed the slight twist in Rothman's lips. She saw Thomas stiffen and thought herself that Rothman had a point and he was obviously enjoying making it.

Llewellyn coughed, put a fist to his mouth and then ran a forefinger across his lips. 'My dear,' he began, his gaze on her becoming at once more earnest and intense, 'I had intended to announce my proposal over dinner but Rothman, I feel, has struck a chord.'

Only a distant clatter of cutlery disturbed the silence as Llewellyn, fingers trembling slightly, placed his hand inside his inner jacket pocket –

Veronica frowned, awareness dawning before his words came: 'My life has been transformed since we met – I wish to ask for your hand in marriage,' he said quietly, and unfastening the ring from its box, continued, 'I ask you to receive this ring, thereby confirming your acceptance of my proposal.'

"I cannot accept and yet I dare not reject…"
totally unexpected and unwanted, Veronica fought back the horror that seemed to have created a gaping hole in her stomach, grasping the tender threads of her composure – aware both of Llewellyn's willing gaze and Rothman's almost mocking smile, she answered calmly, 'Why Thomas, what a wonderful gesture.' She hung her head, looking at him through raised eyes. 'But I feel it is too soon.' She watched his expression cloud and added, 'Though given time I feel it might be favourable.'

'I see.' Llewellyn drew in breath, stiffened, examining the ring as if its significance had diminished, the intensity in his eyes giving way to a bland mist – 'How much time do you consider reasonable, Veronica?'

Veronica examined her interlocked fingers, finally regarding him earnestly. 'Until I am able to return your feelings, Thomas; I need to be able to do that to honour your gracious proposal.'

Rothman leaned forward, studying her with his blue eyes. 'I can see that the lady cares for you very much,' he said, a goblet of champagne poised beneath his lower lip. 'I can read it in her eyes – it is a noble deliberation she makes, mark my words.'

'Of course.' Llewellyn's eyes widened and regained some lustre.

"*Rothman you are enjoying my discomfort -"* the words were on Veronica's lips but she held them back – the stark fact was that he was compromising her and knew it.

Llewellyn had been placated, chiefly by Rothman – but Veronica retired that evening, disturbed because Rothman was turning out to be a complication she could well do without.

***

But Llewellyn had retained his faith and devotion to Veronica; he had Rothman to thank for that. Now, as he stared out at another fine morning, he contemplated his second main proposal – his proposal to Dorothea.

Dorothea would leave, and Veronica would accept given time - and his dream would become reality.

***

'Am I permitted a stroll in the garden, Mr…?' Rothman, already bored inside the castle's austere walls and determining that the only spark of interest was the beautiful woman who had become Llewellyn's intended, (he allowed himself a smile at that) had wandered into the castle's walled gardens and had encountered the gardener hoeing between rhododendrons.

'My name is Gibbings; aye – if you're a guest,' Gibbings added dubiously, not recognising the newcomer.

'I am indeed.' Rothman gazed around, taking in the colourful plants; he wasn't a great lover of horticulture but to his untrained eye the beds seemed well enough tended. 'Your master invited me along to be witness, it seems, to his marriage proposal,' Rothman said airily. 'I cannot think of another reason why he should invite me along to this godforsaken place, but well done er – Gibbings; a myriad of colour, quite glorious.'

'Marriage proposal?' Gibbings' mouth fell open as he cocked his head; he rammed the hoe into the ground. Did she accept?'

'Not as yet.' Rothman had been surprised by the question. He'd been speaking almost to himself, but as he continued his stroll through the gardens and considered it, he found himself doubting that she ever would. Then what was her association with this place? Somehow the pieces didn't seem to fit – and she'd been embarrassed by his inkling of that – he knew it.

***

Dorothea's approaching footsteps echoed along the corridor, filling Llewellyn with eager anticipation – the moment had arrived, the moment he'd bestow upon her the offer she couldn't refuse.

Soon he'd be free of her meddling, her interference, *and* her infernal drink-ridden, smoke-infested breath.

'Well Thomas, what is it?' she asked, pushing open the door, regarding him with quick moving pupils – 'my but you're looking pleased with yourself this morning – has the pretty violinist been pleasuring you?'

Llewellyn glared up at his sister from behind his walnut desk, attired today in a full-length peach shaded, frilled frock, which emphasised her slightly rotund figure rather than enhancing it.

'Sit down, sister.' Llewellyn stretched out a hand, indicating the high, wing backed Queen Anne chair which stood to the right of his desk. Steepling his fingers beneath his chin he watched her slowly oblige, her eyes narrowing.

'I have for some time suspected that you have been unhappy here – quite apart from your normal hysteria – I therefore have a proposal for you to consider…'

'A proposal, Thomas?' Dorothea inhaled on her cigarette, blew smoke into the air. 'What proposals could you possibly make that would…'

'A proposal that will free you from the confines of this castle and this island,' Llewellyn said enthusiastically, leaning forward, elbows on his desk. 'Dorothea, I will return your outlay in this castle, together with twenty per cent interest, in appreciation of your time and trouble…'

'Time and trouble? You mock me brother.' Llewellyn watched Dorothea's eyes darken, saw her face harden further, her jaw set tight – felt his own stomach knot as he waited for her reply – realising by the very set of her features that she would reject and not knowing why – at least until she spoke.

'You think your meagre offer will rid you of my presence?' Dorothea raised her chin, looked down at him through her hooded eyes, giving a dismissive sweep of her arm. 'Do you take me for a fool? I have no intention of leaving. Your offer is derisory, I refuse it.'

Llewellyn began to burn. He could scarcely control his indignation, his anger, his disbelief.

'Damn you Dorothea,' he stormed, pounding a fist on his desk. 'You do this to spite me, I *demand* that you accept.'

'I will not accept,' Dorothea said through gritted teeth, veins taut in her neck. 'I will cherish the memory of your humiliation at that woman's hands. I will remain and revel in your torment.'

'You continue to poor scorn on Veronica's good name.' Llewellyn thrust his hands against the desk, levered himself up and began pacing the floor. 'I have proposed marriage to Veronica,' he began, clasping his hands behind his back. 'There is no longer a place for you here, you *must* see reason.'

'And has she accepted?' Dorothea asked, her eyes narrowing to slits.

'Not yet, she merely requested time to prepare her way towards accepting my proposal,' Llewellyn snapped impatiently, his irritation reaching fever pitch at her outright refusal of his offer.

'Huh, we shall see which way the goose flies.' She gave him a lopsided, mocking smile, rose from her chair and then sauntered to the door.

'Be warned, Dorothea, I will no longer tolerate your presence in this castle,' Llewellyn had moved hurriedly towards Dorothea, within striking distance of her. She turned about swiftly, a defiant smile lingering on her face, her chin thrust high towards him. 'Go on Thomas; strike me if it relieves your frustration. But the marks will be there for your friends to witness and they will hear my screams – and still,' she said, her index finger pointing towards him, 'it will not free you from my presence.'

Llewellyn flung his hand out, but merely to slam the door in her face, and with such force it resounded throughout the castle.
***

Veronica glanced at the skies, the early blue had given way to cumulus, and the wind was rising. She could hear its dull pounding on the thick, sea facing walls of her room, seemingly in competition with the crashing waves below.

Sighing, she slipped out of her room. Apart from the muffled roar of the elements, the castle was so quiet it might have been deserted, except that was from one bone-jarring door slam some ten minutes past; though she supposed Thomas, his new butler Dawson, Dorothea, his guests Rothman and Reynolds, and presumably Mrs. Simms the cook to be inside its walls.

As far as Rothman was concerned she had been wrong, and the sight of the flamboyant figure with short ginger hair unlatching the garden gate caused her a certain unease.

She'd embarked on an early morning walk which wasn't altogether routine; the delicate situation she had so unexpectedly found herself in could not remain unresolved for long – now was the time for John Gibbings to speak out and declare his problems. In her heart of hearts she couldn't marry Thomas Llewellyn, he was a good man but her feelings would never ascend to the heights required to allow her to accept his proposal – and in fairness to Thomas, she'd need to make that plain sooner than later.

'Why Mr. Rothman,' Veronica forced a brief smile, 'you surprise me with your interest in the *great* outside. I would have imagined you to be far too disinterested in this island to want to take a closer look at it.'

'Ah, a breath of fresh air never did anyone any harm.' Rothman raised his nostrils high and took a deep breath, letting it out only slowly. 'Ah, how refreshing.' He looked across at Veronica, she could feel his eyes examining her. 'What I wonder, dear lady, is your purpose on this island – what I wonder is your *real* purpose?'

'I do not feel I know you at all well, Mr. Rothman, to be revealing my innermost feelings.' Veronica hitched her long violet dress and unnecessarily unlatched the gate to the garden intending their brief conversation to be terminated, but Rothman caught it as it swung back and followed her through.

'It is unnatural, Veronica – this romantic association between yourself and Llewellyn – you are as different as – forgive me for using the old adage – how would you say, chalk and cheese?'

'Something else takes your fancy does it not? I wonder what it can be?'

Over by the far wall Veronica caught sight of Gibbings hoeing. The gardener turned to meet her eye and even from a distance she could tell his face was sullen.

Rothman was quick to notice the eye contact between them. 'Ah, surely not,' he said, his lips creasing into a smile.

Just as rapidly Veronica transferred her gaze to the inquisitor. 'He is the gardener, I know little of him. He keeps a low profile. I find the peace here fills my lungs, clears my head. There is nothing more to it than that.'

'There is something dear lady.' Rothman touched the side of a nostril. 'I have a nose for this type of thing. Nevertheless I shall leave you to your own devices.' Rothman sighed as he turned towards the castle. 'You have summed me up as well as I have you. I feel I grow tired already of this island. I look forward to returning to London tomorrow.'

'And I will wish you good riddance,' Veronica whispered beneath her breath, watching Rothman in his red jersey and faun trousers, track back towards the castle.

She waited until he'd disappeared from view, quickly casting her eyes over the castle windows – and satisfied nobody watched, swung back to face Gibbings and then began heading towards him.

***

Llewellyn remained in a state of high agitation. Things weren't going the way he'd planned, not at all. Dorothea had rejected his offer outright and now she had the nerve to sit opposite him in the drawing room, a gloating expression on her heavily made-up face, that made him want to leap up and knock the smugness from her. With Reynolds deeply engrossed in his morning paper, Llewellyn had been about to seize the chance to seek out Veronica's company, when Rothman slipped through the open door, his eyes maintaining their seemingly perpetual twinkling brightness.

'Dorothea.' He greeted her with a cheerful smile, receiving merely a brief nod and lowering of her lashes in return, then glancing at Reynolds, 'Oh, my good man, as studious of politics as ever.' He selected a high-backed chair close to Llewellyn and leaned across confidentially. 'I fear you have competition Llewellyn, in the very unlikely form of the gardener chap – Gibbings, is it?'

'What?' Llewellyn's eyes widened in astonishment and then his forehead creased into a frown as he tried to comprehend his friend's words.

'Precisely what I have been trying to tell him all along,' Dorothea cut in, hooded eyes half open, 'but my foolish brother is so besotted he refutes as preposterous what clearly lies before his eyes.'

Llewellyn tapped the arm of his chair impatiently, red blotches blemishing his complexion he questioned in a slightly higher tone than usual, 'And how, my dear Rothman, do you draw this conclusion?'

'Merely from my own perceptions, dear fellow, though they are seldom wrong.' He waved the palm of his hand airily. ' She chooses to deny it of course, but...'

'You have interrogated her on the subject?' Llewellyn said crossly, both hands gripping the arms of his chair as he arced forward.

'She was bound for him, I merely observed what passed between their eyes – cross to the window, see what you will see...'

Llewellyn wanted to appear nonchalant, but his anxiety and irritation let him down. Quickly on his feet, he marched across to the window. Veronica's hand was on Gibbings' arm. He saw Gibbings shrug it off and from his vantage point in the castle watched Veronica turn, cast her eyes in his direction and hands clasping elbows, walk swiftly away.

***

'John, we must talk – urgently.'

Gibbings shrugged, glared. 'What for? You have what you came for, Veronica – a share in the castle, a wealthy man to support you – rich friends like the man with the posh new motor car I saw you walking with – what can you want with the likes of me? I saw the way he looked at me, and how you wouldn't meet my eyes.'

Veronica tossed her head vehemently. 'It is not what you think, John...'

She saw the downturn of his lips. 'You are marrying Mr. Llewellyn. Don't try to deny it. Your only interest in me was to make him jealous – to hurry him into making a proposal.'

'John, that's nonsense – I...'

Veronica stretched a hand to Gibbings' shoulder but he shrugged her off. 'Go back to your friends, I won't be seen talking to you.'

Gibbings abruptly turned his back on her, resumed hoeing with a vengeance. Veronica gritted her teeth, fighting back the urge to force him to face her.

Suddenly the clouds shrouding the sun seemed much darker than they were. Veronica hunched her shoulders and folded her arms as she felt a sudden chill, and then raising her eyes towards the castle saw Thomas Llewellyn, face almost against its Gothic windows; his expression at that distance was unreadable but she could almost feel the portent.

She tried – she'd tried to assist the man who'd saved her life but he hadn't let her and now fed with the news of Thomas' proposal, she suspected by Rothman, he'd misinterpreted utterly, shutting her out.

But faced with a marriage proposal she knew she'd ultimately reject and an alienated John Gibbings she seemed powerless to help, the prospect of a return to her concert routine didn't seem as uninviting as it had so recently. Moreover, Thomas' fluctuating mood swings of late were causing concern, and yet despite that a new resolve fuelled her. She would not give up on her quest. She needed to ponder, to get things straight with Gibbings. She didn't blame him for misinterpreting the situation just as she was gaining his trust.

A few days longer, she determined, and then if she hadn't succeeded, Veronica would leave the island for good.

***

Llewellyn made an immense effort to restrain himself, recalling the previous occasion, when following Veronica's chance encounter with Gibbings he'd almost snapped. This time he would be more reserved, more in control of his emotions.

Too many coincidental meetings – he'd been loathe to listen to Dorothea, even Hambleton, but now following Rothman's similar comments – a man who had proved to be so astute – he could no longer deny that Gibbings wielded an adverse influence over her. It had to be eradicated – she had to be protected. He would see to it.

He was conscious of Dorothea's scornful gaze following his every step as with an overly casual stride he left the drawing room bound for the hall. There he busied himself, carrying out a needless inspection of its ornaments and walnut furniture, examining them for the slightest layer of dust, even though he'd observed Dawson polishing some two hours previously, expecting at any moment to hear Veronica's light tread on the flagstone tiles.

By her direction, Llewellyn was certain she'd been returning to the castle. Now as apprehension grew he re-ran the scene he'd witnessed through the drawing room window.

Veronica's hand on Gibbings' shoulder, Gibbings shrugging her off. But it wasn't what it seemed. They were all wrong in that respect. Gibbings was a malign influence, a decent gardener perhaps, but a rogue behind his gypsy-like good looks. He had obviously plagued Veronica ever since he'd returned from the sea – played upon it, pursued her whenever she'd taken a stroll. She'd obviously been trying to pacify him when he'd watched them, but he'd resented her efforts; what if he'd followed his show of petulance by pursuing her?

Chapter Twenty Three

Veronica perched on a bench in the priory cloisters, the broad mediaeval arches shielding her from rain which drove down amidst squally gusts. She sat with forearms on thighs, face down reflectively, her long red hair swept around by a wind approaching gale force. It was a posture which troubled Hambleton the moment he laid eyes on her; the normally vibrant woman seemed a wearied, troubled soul, so deep in her own thoughts she'd seemed unaware of his approach. He found his own misgivings rising to the surface. 'Why Miss Veronica, it is a pleasure to see you, though preferably not looking so perturbed.'

'Mr. Hambleton...' her eyes widened in surprise. 'I thought you would have left the island once ...'

'Permit me to interrupt, but I find matters too troublesome to allow imminent departure.' He raised a hand, glancing at the skies. 'It has turned into an unfavourable day, would you mind if I joined you in shelter?'

'Why, not at all.' Veronica regarded him through her shrewd, narrowed green eyes. 'It is a pleasure to see you though it appears we both have our problems.' Clasping her hands together she added, 'Let us see if we can share them.'

'Veronica, I fear our two problems are one,' Hambleton said sombrely, taking a seat on the bench beside her. 'I could not leave sensing you were in danger...'

Veronica gave a lop-sided smile. 'Danger, oh come on now, we've been through this before.'

'In all honesty Veronica, can you say you are completely comfortable in Llewellyn's presence?'

Veronica shrugged. 'There is a considerable difference between not feeling completely comfortable and feeling vulnerable.'

Hambleton followed the gulls looping lazily through the air before turning to Veronica. 'He is a volatile man, much like the weather but becoming increasingly so – I have seen it in his eyes – and he has a yearning that you do not share.'

Veronica twisted her palms together. 'Do you think I do not understand as much? Last evening he made a proposal of marriage that I cannot accept, but that does not make him dangerous.'

Hambleton grunted. 'Your words are of no surprise, but have you told him outright of your rejection?'

Veronica hesitated. 'I cannot as yet, I need time; I need to help...'

'Gibbings is a closed book,' Hambleton interrupted with a shake of the head. 'It is a dangerous game you play – every moment you spend within the castle walls deepens Llewellyn's obsessions and still you will never be able to help Gibbings. In your own interest you should leave the island forthwith.'

Veronica hung her head, then raised it slowly to meet Hambleton's gaze. 'I have given myself three days, no longer.'

'Then you acknowledge the danger?'

'I acknowledge only the insecurity,' she replied calmly.

Hambleton got to his feet. 'Then I pray for your welfare. I shall be staying at the inn for the time being. Please do not hesitate to visit me there.'

***

Dorothea had seen what Llewellyn had missed in his eagerness to confront Veronica in the hall. She had watched Gibbings ram his hoe into the ground with force and then leaning into the gale trudge back towards the cottage.

Envisaging the first thorn driven into her brother's flesh Dorothea downed a double measure of whisky and then draping her coat around her body headed out into an increasingly angry summer afternoon.

Through rain-blurred vision she saw Gibbings reach his cottage and then disappear behind its thick, dark door.

Gibbings was angry, she hadn't needed to be within earshot. His body posture spoke for him and she knew why – pretty Miss Musician had got so far under his skin she could almost feel the swell of his vital parts.

How she loathed the woman, but not half as much as she'd come to loathe her brother – so he thought he could dispense with her so easily – in so doing he had insulted her intelligence, even the physical blows he'd inflicted on her couldn't have ignited greater indignation.

She reached the door, knocked; even through the thick cottage walls she could hear his rapid footsteps on the panelled wooden floor.

'What do you want?' he asked brusquely.

'You should have listened to Veronica, not drove her away...' Dorothea lifted her face imperiously, lowered her eyes. 'Are you going to deny me entry to my property?'

'You speak in Veronica's defence, it's not like you Dorothea. I'm in no mood for your antics.'

'Do not be flippant,' she said, brushing past him as he reluctantly stepped aside. 'I saw you push Veronica away; I asked why you did it.'

'No crime in it,' he said indignantly, and then as Dorothea widened her eyes, 'you know full well, you've come to gloat.'

'All I know full well,' Dorothea retorted, taking several strides into the cottage and turning to face him, 'is that Veronica has no intention of marrying my brother. If she was trying to converse with you, for whatever reason, you would have done well to have listened.' Dorothea blew smoke into the small sitting room, analysed his expression. 'You are intrigued Gibbings, you give yourself away too easily.'

'You say this and yet you despise Veronica.' Gibbings swept hair from his brow, his free hand on the rim of the open door, fingers tapping restlessly on the woodwork. 'You're playing your games, Dorothea – Veronica is not...'

'You appear to be hesitating, Gibbings, Veronica is not what? Does she not have your working class roots, Gibbings? Do you think she worries about that?'

'She walks and talks with the man with the red hair, the posh new motor car...' Gibbings said bitterly. 'The reason she visits this castle is to see your brother – and she has been given a room at the castle. Veronica exists in loftier circles; she does not worry about the likes of me.'

'Huh! What nonsense you talk. Wash out the salt and the red mist that clouds your eyes, Gibbings, before it is too late – not only for your own sake but hers also.'

Dorothea waltzed slowly to the door, placing her face close to his. 'Use your imagination dear man, my brother grows ever more obsessed with a woman who has no feelings for him, though he imagines she has. When he finally realises the truth God only knows what might happen.'

Gibbings removed his hand from the door frame, screwed his eyes. 'Why are you taking time to tell me this? What's in it for you?'

'That's my concern,' Dorothea said, swinging past him, and then touching his cheek with a forefinger, 'consider your poor conscience if you stand idly by. Go to her, Gibbings.'

John Gibbings stood in silence, watching Dorothea stroll serenely back to the castle.

***

'Ah Dawson,' Llewellyn tweaked his moustache, stared at the heavily built butler. 'Miss Day is currently out. Please advise me the moment she returns.'

'Of course, sir,' Dawson bowed.

'Good.' Llewellyn wrapped his fingers around the arm of his chair. 'And as for your duties this coming week, your instructions are to remain at the castle pending my return, during which time I have a task for you of the utmost importance.'

'Sir?' The butler's heavy black eyebrows rose as he watched his employer place a cup carefully in its saucer and wipe his lips with a handkerchief he drew from his top pocket. 'You are to dispose of the services of the gardener, Gibbings; his activities of late have been leading him to neglect his duties. You are to allow a few days following my departure in the morning. This will enable you to observe his unsatisfactory conduct.'

'And if the gardener, Gibbings,' behaviour is not unsatisfactory, what then?'

Llewellyn placed his elbows on the table, interlocked his fingers, regarded Dawson fixedly. 'Get my meaning Dawson, you *will* find it unsatisfactory. Do you understand?'

'Perfectly, sir.'

'Good,' then as Dawson bent low to recover the silver tea service, 'furthermore, you will then ensure that Miss Veronica is 'protected' from any nuisances he might cause her. Am I understood on that point?'

'Fully, sir.'

'And understand you are to take any steps you deem appropriate to prevent that happening.'

Llewellyn held Dawson's gaze for several seconds, receiving acknowledgement from the big butler.

He stood up, thrust hands in pockets and stared out to sea; he could eliminate Gibbings, appoint another gardener, but Dorothea's continued presence caused him considerable concern. Dorothea would do all she could to disturb his happiness with Veronica. It could not happen. His sister had to go one way or another. Llewellyn cupped a hand beneath his chin and mused.

***

'Would you say Llewellyn seems somewhat on edge? Not at all his normal self?' Rothman eased back in his chair, crossed his legs and looked sideways at Reynolds.

'His usual self? Not at all old chap, not at all. In fact he's been quite evasive, makes you wonder why we were invited.'

Rothman smiled knowingly. 'So he could show off his intended bride to be; I think he has some romantic vision – first he buys a castle, now he envisages the beautiful Veronica as his queen...' Rothman spread his hand. 'I fear it is only a dream; castles in the sand Reynolds, nothing more.'

'You speak lightly of such a serious matter.' Reynolds drew on his pipe. 'If what you say is true, will you enjoy watching the saga unfold?'

'Pah,' Rothman responded dismissively. 'I have no time for such things. I undertook the journey out of mild interest, I am less than impressed with this isolated island, and, Reynolds, I must ask a question...' Rothman drew forward in his seat, fixing his eyes keenly on his friend, 'would you regard our investment safe considering Llewellyn's current pre-occupation with creating his own Utopia?'

Reynolds' mouth dropped open; he caught his pipe before it could hit the occasional table. 'God, Rothman, you are not suggesting that Llewellyn is in any way – shall I say – losing it?'

Rothman glanced down, though his eyes remained on Reynolds; there was unusual severity in his features marked by the thin network of lines on his forehead. 'Llewellyn cannot see further than this island at the moment and what it contains. If it comes to a point where he cannot fulfil his obligations then our investment will be in peril.'

'But Llewellyn returns to London tomorrow, so surely his interest and resolve must still exist.'

Rothman smiled, little more than a chink in his cheek. 'And if Veronica remains on this island, how long do you suppose he will stay there?'

'Is she remaining?'

Rothman nodded. 'My intuition tells me she will; she has unresolved business.'

'Unresolved business?'

'Look around this place Reynolds, use your eyes – see what

rumbles beneath the solid foundations.'

'You talk in riddles Rothman.'

'Pay me no attention;' Rothman glanced at his watch. 'In a few hours we will be leaving this, as you call it, saga. I am grateful for that.'

Chapter Twenty Four

Llewellyn had sat in his room, restlessly scanning the shoreline and the coastal track leading from the village for a sign of Veronica. With the wind buffeting the castle walls and whistling around its turrets it was inconceivable that she could remain exposed to the elements and not nestled safely inside. But the fact that she should be so, he attributed to Gibbings, though he contented himself in part with the knowledge that any further attempts to impose upon her goodwill would be curtailed by his dismissal.

He started at the sound of heavy footsteps along the corridor and an equally heavy fist upon the door. 'Miss Day has returned sir,' the square jawed Dawson announced in his gravelly voice. 'She proceeded straight to her room.'

Llewellyn leapt up; it seemed that his nerves had received a stab at their core. 'Thank you Dawson,' he said adjusting his tie, his fingers trembling. He felt a heat incongruous with the unseasonably cool draught that filtered through the window frames. He followed Dawson out with a speed that almost caught the butler's heels; such was his desire to speak with her.

Because Gibbings had been pestering her, she had been upset and taken a lengthy walk; that had been the true reason for her absence. He needed to see that she was calm now, to re-assure her if necessary.

He rattled three quick blows on her door with his knuckle and as she pulled it open he thought that despite her prolonged exposure to the elements, she looked wonderfully unruffled.

'Veronica, please excuse my intrusion. I was most concerned for your welfare.'

He saw her flick a finger through that delightfully fine red hair. 'Oh, Thomas, why is that?'

Llewellyn drew back at the last moment from revealing the true source of his reasoning. 'I feel that this island is inhospitable in such inclement weather. I was concerned that you should fall foul to...'

'Thomas, forgive me for interrupting, but please understand that I am quite capable of withstanding the elements – in fact, I thrive on them.'

'That does not prevent me from being concerned,' Llewellyn stated more severely than he'd intended, then forcing a wan smile, 'would you care to take tea with me in the drawing room? I intend seeking the company of Reynolds and Rothman; they are returning to London shortly.'

Veronica appeared to hesitate before nodding her assent. 'Why – yes of course, it would be rude of me not to pay my respects to them before they depart.'

'I would hope most earnestly that you derive some pleasure in sharing my company,' Llewellyn said anxiously.

'Why, yes, of course Thomas, – of course.' Veronica quickly took his right hand between hers, 'Forgive me for not making that clear, I was merely responding to your comments concerning your visitors.'

'Thank you my dear.' Llewellyn appeased, afforded her a generous smile. 'I shall be in the drawing room, looking forward to enjoying your company.'

'I will join you shortly, Thomas.'

Veronica closed the door behind Llewellyn, took a brush to her hair, examining it in the mirror – for a moment, it wasn't her own image she saw but Rothman's, and for a reason – Rothman was the elegant, modern young gentleman, but he was more than that, he was mischievous, egotistic and she knew she would be under his scrutiny during the time she was in his company. Thomas had said his departure was imminent; if so, that was a blessing. Rothman tested her composure to the limit and he knew it.

He was sitting by the window when she went down, head inclined towards the garden. She wondered whether it was a hint of things to come and soon found out.

'Ah Veronica, you grace us with your presence, such a foul afternoon has befallen us – I feel quite sorry for that poor gardener chap, don't you? Out in all weathers...'

'I dare say he is used to it.' Veronica avoided his eyes, but failed to prevent hers straying through the windows towards the gardens.

'Do not fret, Veronica, he is not in attendance. Though I'll vouch it will not be long...'

'Veronica does *not* fret,' Llewellyn snapped, the veins taut in his neck, lips curved in a snarl as he glared at Rothman, then breathing deeply, his tone dropping as his gaze switched to Veronica, 'She has no worries within these walls. Is that not true my dear?'

'Why should I have, Thomas?' She met Llewellyn's unsteady eyes as calmly as she could, 'You are an excellent host...'

'Surely more than a host, Veronica,' Llewellyn's eyes widened, 'for you are my intended...'

'I understand Thomas,' Veronica said, placing a hand on his shoulder and kissing his cheek, and with a glance at the gloating Rothman, 'but we are here to bid our guests bon voyage, a fine journey home.'

'Why thank you Veronica.' Rothman glanced at Reynolds, 'And I take it Llewellyn, that you intend to return to London tomorrow as planned.'

'Naturally.' Llewellyn poured Veronica tea and handed it to her, the cup rattling in its saucer. 'Why do you question me?'

'No particular reason,' Rothman said softly, gazing around, listening to the wind booming against the castle walls, and returning his attention to Veronica. 'But tell me, dear lady, what keeps you here? In these conditions you would be worthy of a decoration should you continue your stay.'

'I need respite from my hectic schedules. Were you a musician Mr. Rothman, you would understand my meaning.' Veronica raised her cup, sipped from it and gave Rothman a challenging look. 'I intend remaining here a little longer.'

'I see.' There was a glint in Rothman's eye which cooled as he turned to Llewellyn. 'And does that meet with your approval?'

'Miss Day – Veronica – is a resident in this castle; she is entitled to remain here as long as she wants. Why, she need never return to the mainland again, if that is her wish.'

'That is most certainly not my wish, Thomas.' Veronica being unable to detach herself from the absurdity of the remark, said, 'I cannot encapsulate myself here, much as I have grown fond of the island.'

'Why, no my dear,' but the strange intensity of Llewellyn's features, the unusual penetration in his eyes, had Veronica pondering momentarily whether he had heeded her words, before Rothman's sigh broke the silence.

'Ah – the afternoon wears on, the weather worsens and we have a long journey ahead.' Rothman slapped the arm of his chair. 'Come Reynolds, we should prepare to depart.' He rose to his feet, 'I can truly say I have found my short stay here most interesting.' Glancing from Llewellyn to Veronica he added, 'I would like to repay your hospitality – you and your intended are cordially invited to my humble abode in Richmond – we must agree on a date that is suitable for you both,' with his eyes remaining on her he continued, 'should you feel inclined to leave the island, of course – Veronica.'

Llewellyn's eyes became crevices; a vein pulsed in his cheek. Quick to assess his agitation Veronica placed a hand on his wrist and fixed Rothman with a serene smile. 'I feel Mr. Rothman is something of a cheeky one; I am certain he speaks in jest, though I for my part would be honoured to accept his invitation, were I more certain of my schedule.'

Rothman returned an empty smile. 'Then perhaps it may yet be possible. Llewellyn will no doubt advise me.'

'No doubt he will.' Veronica switched her attention to Llewellyn, aware of the drop in Rothman's voice. Rothman was a good deal more than cheeky and his jest narrowly concealed a malicious edge, once more she sensed Llewellyn was in danger of losing his temper. He had become rigid, his eyes hard like stone, following Rothman's every step as the two guests exited the drawing room.

'Rothman's comment was intended for me. He belittles me Veronica,' Llewellyn muttered acidly. 'I regret inviting him; he has not distressed you too much?'

'Not at all.' Veronica stiffened as Llewellyn clamped his free hand over hers and tightened his grip. 'I think he is not so much belittling you, but engaging in game play. He has a tendency I feel, to amuse himself at other people's expense.'

'Perhaps,' Llewellyn exhaled heavily and drew in fresh breath. 'At least I can console myself in the knowledge that his departure is imminent, but I must express another concern…'

'Which is?' Veronica gazed at eyes widening into brown globes.

'Your safety. Please be assured that my butler, Dawson, will be at your disposal whenever you require him.'

'My safety?'

'No – no,' Llewellyn shook head. 'I think only of your security, your welfare – it is my wish that you treat this place as your home, relax within its solid walls – free from...'

'Free from what?' Veronica frowned, wrenched her hand from Llewellyn's grasp. 'Thomas, what on earth are you talking about?' Llewellyn thrust thumb and forefinger to his temple as if there were some kind of intense pain inside. 'I want only your happiness, Veronica, nothing else.'

"Then stop trying to cocoon me..." the words screamed inside her head, longing to boom into Llewellyn's ears but she held back, though only for a second, the urge had become too strong...

'Thomas you are trying to cocoon me, these castle walls you speak of should not protect me from myself.'

'It is a man's duty to protect the one he loves.' Llewellyn's eyes had turned misty, the severity had gone; his fingers caressed her hand. 'Please marry me, Veronica – say it will be soon...'

"But I cannot be protected, it is not what I desire – and I cannot marry you Thomas." This time the words didn't force their way out, because now Veronica understood the gravity of her predicament. Llewellyn wasn't stable – but at least in the morning he would be leaving, and if she could get through to Gibbings –

'I will marry you Thomas,' Veronica lied, 'and soon.'

'You will? God bless.' Llewellyn's eyes welled as he cradled her head in his arms, she was conscious of his odour for he was sweating profusely. 'When will it be?'

'Upon my return,' she said spontaneously. 'Upon my return. Now please Thomas, I feel tired, in need of a rest – if I may go to my room and lie down...'

'When will you return?' The lines on Llewellyn's forehead arched, along with his brows.

'As soon as I know my schedule,' Veronica said, calmly levering herself away. 'I will advise you. Now may I retire?'

'I would not detain you a second longer against your wishes – will we dine this evening to mark your momentous decision?'

'Yes Thomas, once I am refreshed.'

'Then, my love, I wish you a pleasant rest.'

Veronica turned to leave, sighed, and out amidst the shadows of the hallway a large shape loomed, not close enough to block her access to the stairs but close enough for her to make out its feature; the square jaw, the broken nose of the granite-faced butler, Dawson, who watched her every move.

Chapter Twenty Five

'Goodbye, Thomas, safe journey...' Veronica placed a kiss on Llewellyn's cheek, avoiding his lips while Llewellyn, visibly trembling, clutched her hands. 'Take care my precious and keep safe – Dawson will provide for your welfare.'

'Thomas, I have told you – nobody provides for my welfare...' but Veronica's words were lost on the high wind as Llewellyn and Dawson descended the slope towards the pony and trap waiting at the bottom. She watched Dawson assist Llewellyn into the trap and as he waved enthusiastically, she caught the butler's cold, hard stare.

Dawson will provide for your welfare, the implications of that remark were unmistakable, even her composure had been breached recently and now, as the wind lashed hair across her face with such force it stung and as it blew so hard she struggled to keep her balance, she contemplated her days, her nights in the castle under the auspices of this belligerent man. It was for Gibbings that she stayed to try to see her objective through, though now she felt her determination waver.

She stood at the castle entrance, waited until the trap joined the main track and then stepped inside. The hall, vast in its comparison with the smaller rooms that characterised the building, now exuded an air of intimidation. It had swept in with Dawson's arrival and solidified the previous evening when Llewellyn's unstable nature had finally become apparent to her, sending alarm bells tolling loudly within.

Truthfully Veronica had never known fear; not even the shipwreck had caused the trepidation that had manifested itself in her being, spreading like a germ, embedding itself in the fabric of the castle so that it enveloped her whole existence. She'd been completely immersed in her own confidence, unprepared for the effects of developments such as these. But the compulsion to take flight to the mainland was something she would fight stubbornly against.

She was proceeding through the castle, taking the stone steps to the first floor landing, entirely preoccupied with her own malaise, when Dorothea emerged from her room, the hem of her corseted pink dress swirling like a snake around her ankles as she stopped abruptly, appearing to block her path.

Veronica's first inclination was to square her shoulders, drive her strong body straight through Dorothea, sweeping her aside, such was her irritation.

But Dorothea's appearance became unusually placid, her dark eyes lacked their usual malevolence, and even her voice lacked acidity when she spoke. She seemed to sense Veronica's intentions, raising her hand. 'No Veronica stop, I need to speak with you; inside my room if you please. Do not charge me aside, I implore you.'

Veronica swung to her right, curtailing her momentum, drawing alongside Dorothea, opposite her door. 'What have you got to say that is worth listening to – do not try my patience, I am warning you...'

Dorothea stretched an arm. 'Please Veronica, step through – I promise I will not hit you from behind.'

Veronica sighed, brushed past Dorothea – 'You would be foolish even to try.'

'As I have found out at my own expense – please, take a chair.'

Veronica took a seat in a finely crafted, high - backed Queen Anne chair, her eyes fixed on Dorothea as she sat at her desk, turning her chair to face her.

'You may think I'm many things, Veronica – a many horned beast perhaps – you might think I'm mad – yes I can tell by your eyes that you do – but I can tell you this, my brother far exceeds me in that respect – and though he has endeavoured to conceal his ugly side from you, I surmise by your fatigued appearance that you have finally deduced as much.'

The lids dropped over Dorothea's hawkish eyes momentarily. 'You finally realise the danger here – what you have involved yourself in – and let me guess – on account of Gibbings, I suppose?'

Veronica bit her lip, crossed her arms, she felt exposed to everyone, including Dorothea.

'He saved my life.'

Dorothea smiled thinly. 'I'd vouch you could have saved your own.'

'He didn't know that.'

'But now you find yourself facing the ultimate peril?'

Veronica shrugged. 'Perhaps.'

'Ah, you concede at least that much – go to Gibbings Veronica, you have perhaps an hour before Dawson returns. I know of this man, make no mistake, he does not have our culture, he does not possess Hambleton's geniality, he is hard-boiled and dangerous which is precisely why my brother employed him and make no mistake that he will adhere to the instruction of my brother and he will impose a strict regime; can I make myself any clearer?'

Veronica felt the shudder that rocked her body in every nerve. 'I shall seek out Gibbings Dorothea, but are you not also in peril? You dismissed your brother's offer outright.'

Now Dorothea's eyes developed a dark sheen, just a suggestion of her usual malevolence. 'But for you it might never have happened. You brought forth this infernal lust within him, which has ignited the madness that always existed, not only in him, but in the depths of our family.'

Dorothea removed her hands from the arms of her chair, leaned forward and placed them on her thighs. 'Now Veronica you have become part of it. Gibbings is your escape.' She hefted her arm wildly, not in Veronica's direction, rather in the direction of Gibbings' cottage. 'And when Dawson returns, what then? That will be the real test of your character, will it not? I say no more.'

Chapter Twenty Six

Gibbings wasn't in the garden, and with conditions the way they were Veronica wasn't surprised. She glanced around but the driving rain obscured her view.

'Veronica...' she heard the shout hurry across on the wind and then through the grey veil of rain saw Gibbings hurrying towards her wearing his dark, hooded coat. 'Veronica I've been watching, waiting,' he panted as rain lashed his face. 'I need to talk to you.'

'At last...' Veronica wiped the rain from her eyes.

'Not here,' he said grabbing her arm. 'I can barely hear myself speak – my cottage...'

'Then we need to hurry – you have taken long enough; I take it you are now ready to speak about your problems?'

'I am.' Gibbings led her to his door, ushered her through, he watched the rainwater tumble from her hair. 'I'll get you a towel.'

Veronica shook her head fiercely. 'You will do no such thing, you will speak now of what troubles you.'

'You should take your coat off while I speak, you're wet through.'

'Yes and I will still be wet through when I leave, now go on,' she gestured.

Gibbings shrugged, gathered breath. 'I should explain I have relatives in Inverness, though I come from the south. I met a northern woman, a schoolteacher, fell in love and married her. Not long after Alice gave birth to a baby, Alexandra.'

Gibbings clasped his hands to his forehead, his eyes seemingly searching the ground before he raised them to meet hers. 'Anyway, we were on a steamer bound for Inverness, the three of us, when in high seas she struck rocks and it seemed to me that in seconds the bow plunged – we were forced overboard, I managed to get little Alexandra into a lifeboat but I swam round for Alice and she'd gone – gone beneath the waves.

'Last I ever saw of her.' He shook his head slowly. 'She didn't panic you know, she'd been so calm – in a way that was the worst thing – she didn't deserve to...' Gibbings eyes were misty as he looked at her, his words slow and sadly reflective – 'that's what started me with the lifeboat crew – I wanted to help others...'

'I'm sorry – I'm so very sorry.' Veronica stepped closer, biting her lip. 'And your daughter? What of her now?'

'My wife had a sum of money by inheritance; it was her wish that Alexandra be educated at boarding school – for her to have a bright future. That sum has been whittled away by boarding fees but the small amount I get here goes to her upkeep, though it gets harder to support her each school term. It's why this job is so important; I couldn't afford to get on the wrong side of Llewellyn, though now...'

Veronica snatched Gibbings' hand. 'Don't you see – I can help you. Oh John, why didn't you tell me before? I can pay for your daughter's education outright.'

Gibbings drew away, turned his back on her, forearm and forehead against the door frame. 'I don't want your money.'

'Why not?' Veronica demanded, 'Because I'm a woman?'

'It's not right.' Gibbings swung round, saliva between his white teeth. 'It doesn't happen.'

'John, it *does* happen, if you allow me to help, get rid of your dogmatic values, we can be away from here...'

'All right for you to say, but then what would I do?'

She shook his shoulders. 'John, help me, I am trying to help you. I could have turned and fled but I stayed to assist you. But now I need to pack my possessions, before the new butler Dawson returns – I have seen enough, heard enough to believe my very liberty is in jeopardy.

'Listen to me – Thomas – Llewellyn is not sane. Dorothea is not sane but he is worse, he has disguised his insanity whereas she displays hers openly.'

Veronica drew breath, let go of his shoulders and took a step away, her eyes never leaving his face. 'Time passes John, and all the while Dawson is returning with instructions to *protect* Llewellyn's *possession.*'

Gibbings squinted, gave a slight shake of his head, as if unwilling to accept the truth of her words. Finally he said, 'Is it that bad, can things be that urgent?'

'Of course it is John,' Veronica shouted as the rafters creaked with the strength of the wind, 'have you not the least idea?'

'Aye Hambleton has told me – and Dorothea, but I never thought...' Gibbings broke off, swung and slammed his fist against the wall. 'Very well Veronica, you have stayed to help me – put yourself at risk. Hurry back to the castle, pack your possessions while I pack mine.'

'Wait for me by the garden gate,' she said heaving open the door. 'We will not take the main track out, we will cut across the island – if Dawson returns and spots us – I do not trust him.'

'Hurry, Veronica.' The intensity in Gibbings' eyes was such that she met them for several seconds before a quick nod of her soaked red head saw her turn and set off at speed for the castle.

She was midway up the slope when she saw Dawson approaching the castle, flogging the pony in a way Hambleton would never have done and with his return her heart sank to despair. In theory he could not detain her against her will, and yet in reality she knew he would.

"Leave without your belongings," a small voice inside urged, but a deeper, more powerful one ordered, "*do not antagonise this dangerous man who acts for an insane one; stay calm, out-think him and bide your time.*"

Veronica yearned to be free of the castle, wanted to join Gibbings and flee to the mainland but the opportunity had passed; in truth, there had never been enough time.

And Dawson, tethering the pony, had already spotted her; she felt his unfeeling eyes following her to the castle entrance.

***

'You were a fool to return Veronica...' feeling the chill follow her into the hall, Veronica started at the sound of Dorothea's voice, and turning, found her reclining on the green chaise-longue inside its entrance.

'I have my possessions to pack,' Veronica retorted, head held high.

'You think he will let you leave now?' Dorothea's derision stopped her in her tracks. 'Dawson's instructions will be to contain you here pending my brother's return.'

'He cannot detain me,' Veronica uttered without conviction.

'You are a strong, determined woman,' Dorothea said grudgingly, getting to her feet, 'and for that I respect you, but you will not easily force your way past this man...'

Dorothea dropped the lids of her eyes, 'not without distraction ...'

'What do you mean by that?'

'You would do better to dry yourself off than to ponder upon that now. Dawson approaches up the slope; I can hear his heavy steps.' Dorothea ushered Veronica away. 'Dawson will pose problems only if you provide him with any and he will already have deduced your purpose in being out in such foul weather. It is better to avoid him as I intend to – as much as possible. Be ready for my call.'

Veronica looked back uncertainly before leading the way out of the hall, making her way to a room which now seemed more akin to a prison.

She towelled herself dry, and then thought of Gibbings – waiting for her by the garden gate no doubt, and in wild conditions.

She wondered how long he would wait, wondered what he would do now – and then pondered upon Dorothea's mystifying remark. Could she really expect any assistance from Dorothea?

Alone in her room Veronica sighed, and heard heavy footsteps along the passageway.

Chapter Twenty Seven

Gibbings waited in the rain, he waited for an hour as a steady stream poured from the hood of his dark cape, his few possessions packed in a bag deposited at his feet, before finally accepting that Veronica wasn't coming.

Following his revelations to her, his anxiety at leaving the island had dissolved into some kind of foolish hope that this beautiful woman who he secretly admired could somehow lead him to a better life, enabling him to fully provide for his daughter Alexandra. Now that hope had been dashed.

But as he'd stood there hunched from the rain, his feelings had taken a strange turn – he'd begun to wonder whether Veronica hadn't changed her mind, whether something or someone within the castle had changed it for her – wonder had turned into apprehension, an outright concern, an inner foreboding that he couldn't understand but nonetheless experienced.

He glanced across the field to the drawing room window where so often he'd been aware of shadowy figures watching, but now there wasn't a soul. The castle seemed closed around a woman he now thought he loved, but that he could become aware of as much in the hour he'd stood there was something he couldn't comprehend. Perhaps the feeling had always existed but he'd fought against it, on account of her background.

Now what did he do? Charge the castle, confront the big butler Dawson and force him to let Veronica go? If indeed he was holding her against her will.

But if he failed he might make things worse for her – surely at the moment no harm could befall Veronica. Mr. Llewellyn wouldn't want that – and yet she had said that he wasn't sane, and Dawson was a nasty man who'd carry out whatever he wanted.

Gibbings decided then that he wouldn't go to the castle – not yet – he'd seek out Mr. Hambleton at the inn, he would know what to do.

Gibbings scooped up his bag, hoisted it onto his shoulder and set out for the inn.

***

A single rap on the door heralded Dawson's uninvited entry into Veronica's room.

Unsmiling, he crossed close to her, outstretching an arm. 'Your coat madam – I will see that it is dried.'

'Really, Dawson, it will dry of its own accord,' Veronica said stiffly.

'I insist.' He snatched her coat from the stand.

'You do not have my consent to remove my clothing Dawson.' Veronica raised her hand slightly, stared into uncompromising grey eyes.

Dawson ignored her, taking large strides to the door as Veronica bit her lip, holding back her rising temper. 'Madam,' he said upon reaching it, 'your permission is not required. I have Mr. Llewellyn's authority to ensure that your comfort and safety are respected at all times.'

'I have already advised Mr. Llewellyn...'

'Those are his instructions to me,' Dawson interrupted brusquely.

'Then would you care to enlighten me, as to how far this *authority* extends?'

'Wherever it is necessary to enforce it.' The gravel voice was unyielding, flat and with a hint of warning.

'I dislike the word "enforce."' Veronica came slowly forward, hands on hips; 'In effect I am a prisoner within these walls, is that it, Dawson?'

There was just a twitch in the butler's rugged countenance. 'You are to be kept from harm; I am to protect you.'

'And if I do not wish to be protected? What then, Dawson?'

'A woman should be grateful for such protection. Will there be anything further, Miss Day?'

'You can return my coat; I might shortly take a walk.'

Dawson chewed on his lip, his stare hardening. 'In these conditions, madam, that would be inadvisable.' He slung her coat over his shoulder, pointed a finger, and uttered in a voice so low it was barely audible, 'Don't annoy me madam, you'll regret it.'

All endeavours at respectability abandoned, Veronica saw the exposed beast within. 'Is that a threat?' she called. But Dawson had closed the door with a thud, his heavy tread retreating along the passageway.

Veronica overcame an urge to march out. She had little doubt she'd be denied exit and her inclination had been to try to force one. But although strong, Veronica had little doubt that Dawson was stronger, with a volatile temperament to match; the facial movements within his granite - like countenance spoke as loudly as his words. She was not however, prepared to be confined to her room; after a brief rest to regain her composure, she would make that plain.

***

Hambleton had been resting in his room, his thoughts never far removed from events at the castle, when a light tap on the door roused him.

He heard Gibbings call his name, urgency in the voice, followed by another tap, louder this time. Hambleton drew back the latch, taking in the sight of the rain-swept Gibbings, eyes wide and earnest. 'I hope I'm not intruding on you but the landlord said to come straight up. I think something's happening at the castle and I didn't know what to do.' He exhaled heavily. 'I thought it best to come to you.'

Hambleton nodded. 'I advised him in such an eventuality to show you up; I have been expecting some development as it happens – have you spoken with Veronica?'

'Aye, you see that's why I think she might be in trouble,' Gibbings began at a gallop. 'We had a talk and...'

'Sit down.' Hambleton extended a hand towards a worn but comfortable looking easy chair and took a seat opposite. 'Tell me exactly what happened and not so rapidly, I cannot comprehend what you say.'

'Veronica came looking for me,' Gibbings began more slowly though still struggling for breath, 'though I'd already made up my mind to talk to her. I told her things about my life I'd never spoken about before – she told me that she could help and that we should both get off the island. I didn't like it at first but then she told me she was afraid of getting trapped in the castle. That Mr. Llewellyn wasn't right in the head – those weren't her words but it's what she meant – and that the new butler had been hired to keep watch on her – that he probably wouldn't let her out of his sight...'

He paused, head close to his knees, swaying from side to side in the chair. 'We agreed to leave the island, to meet at the garden gate. She went back to get her things and when she didn't show up I thought about charging right up there – but instead I came to you...'

Hambleton shook his head slowly, again chiding himself inwardly for falling foul of Dorothea's wiles, if he hadn't been rash this situation might have been averted. 'I fear I can do little to avert the situation...'

'But you can try,' Gibbings urged, nodding forcefully, so that drops from his rain flattened curly hair splattered the floor.

Hambleton frowned, contemplated whether there was anything he *could* do.

'Then perhaps the police?'

Hambleton forced a grim smile at Gibbings' naivety. 'Summoning police presence to the island is difficult at the best of times, the castle is a respectable establishment and we have no real proof that Veronica is held against her will...'

'They would believe your word as Mr. Llewellyn's last butler...'

'It will take more than my word, Gibbings, believe me.' Hambleton drew breath, gazed at the gardener solemnly. 'Very well Gibbings, I shall go to the castle, attempt to engage in conversation with Dawson and in so doing, endeavour to assess the nature of any threat to Veronica should it exist in Llewellyn's absence. We need more than mere supposition, Gibbings, to encourage policemen to this island.' Taking his coat from a peg on the door, he added, 'Pray that I find it, and Gibbings, you would be better off waiting here.'

'I'll accompany you if you wish.'

But Hambleton departed with a dismissive wave of his hand and not for the first time in his life, Gibbings whispered a silent prayer.

***

Llewellyn tweaked his moustache furiously; he was beginning to sweat and tremble; at precise, predetermined fifteen minute intervals throughout the day he had attempted to telephone the castle, each time to his increasing aggravation to be confounded.

The operator had been reporting impassively that there was a connection problem, as yet undiagnosed, though in all probability the line was down on account of the severe weather. But that information did nothing to allay his sense of trepidation. He had left matters at the castle, and most importantly Veronica's safety, in the hands of his new butler Dawson, a most pugnacious fellow.

His enemies however were not to be underestimated, his treacherous sister Dorothea for one – what if she had hatched some devious plot which had plunged the castle into chaos and ultimately threatened the safety of Veronica? Had Gibbings somehow wrought havoc within, angered beyond measure by his wise decision to have Dawson protect her against his incessant harassment of her?

The intolerable burden was proving too much for him, his concentration had evaporated; he could no longer concentrate on his business affairs, as pressing as he knew them to be they seemed of no significance when laid alongside Veronica's welfare. She was his world, nothing else was of comparison. The devilish elements that threatened her security needed to be eradicated – he should not be trusting all to Dawson.

Such action was the tell-tale sign of a coward. His facial nerves twitched, his throat seemed so taut he could barely swallow as he struggled to allocate his clients' business accounts to the correct folders, finally abandoning the task to a member of staff in his outer office.

He should never have forsaken his sweetheart, left her at the mercy of such despicable forces – if any foul play had befallen her, he personally would effect retribution.

Llewellyn's lips quivered into a smile at the thought as he hurriedly made from his office.

Chapter Twenty Eight

Veronica stood in the hall, watching the North Sea crash its waves against the rocks of a distant island, sending fountains of spray high into the air.

On such a turbulent day it was an uninviting scene, but one that distressed her far less than the prospect of being confined within the walls of the castle.

She sighed, crossed to the chaise-longue and took a seat, waiting for the footsteps she knew would quickly come. Barely had she sat, hands clasped around her knees, than the sound of his heavy tread resounded through the hallway. He held a large swab in his hands, with which he proceeded to wipe the windows.

Veronica placed an arm across the rear of the couch, sat back, her eyes on him. 'Your application to your task would be admirable, Mr. Dawson, were it not that your overriding priority is keeping observation on me.'

'Don't flatter yourself,' Dawson said gruffly, the swab sloshing against the windows more forcefully.

'Are you aware that Mr. Llewellyn is not of sound mind? You are in uncharted territory are you not?' Veronica asked the question casually, ignoring his remark. 'In a manner of speaking you could yourself become a prisoner of this island, much as you are instructed to keep me until his return - but what then? You are dispensable Dawson - you with your history of violence.'

Dawson swung round, water from the swab splattering the flagstones. 'What do you know of that?' he demanded, teeth clenched.

'My own intuition,' Veronica answered quietly. 'It is apparent in your features, your nose for one thing has been broken and reset very badly.

'You are a brawler Dawson, you are out of your depth in these surroundings and you feel it, yes? Oh but I guess he pays you well. Then does he pay you well enough? Your time within his service is limited I feel, because once Thomas and I are wed he will have no use of you. He desires no company other than mine.' Veronica laughed, flung back her head. 'And you think Dawson, you have control over me? Think again before it is too late – I am an internationally renowned concert violinist, you are from the hovels of London's lower life, I surmise. Who do you think will win in the master's tormented eyes, upon his return?'

Dawson seemed nonplussed, he'd dropped the swab, but his hands were balling into fists when the bell at the castle entrance clanged and Dorothea hurried past. 'I will answer the bell, Dawson; you seem somewhat agitated.'

'No...' Dawson bit his lip, spun round, was about to push Dorothea aside when Veronica smiled. 'He's facing up to a few home truths, aren't you Dawson. Have I given you cause to ponder on your future?'

'Tighten your mouth,' Dawson growled as Dorothea breezed through the hall to the entrance, unlocking the main door to face Hambleton.

'Listen to me, Hambleton and listen well.' Dorothea caught Hambleton's arm, her voice racked with urgency but so quiet he could barely hear above the crashing of waves below. 'The telephone is down, I suspect the whole island is affected but Dawson has no intelligence, he will not know that.

'You are to say that you carry a message from my brother, that being unable to telephone the castle he contacted you. Do you understand? He requires to know that all is well. That given the conditions there are enough provisions in the castle larder. In order that you can telephone Mr. Llewellyn and confirm, you will need to see for yourself – he will no doubt accompany you and upon his return Veronica will be gone...'

'And if he does not...' but Hambleton's question was curtailed by the emergence of Dawson on the castle step, his cold eyes wide and questioning.

'Mr. Hambleton carries a message from Mr. Llewellyn,' Dorothea said brushing past him. 'It seems the telephone line is disabled.'

'Mr. Dawson if I might come in?' Hambleton asked mildly. 'It is a trifle wet out here.'

Dawson exhaled heavily, stepped to the side, ushered Hambleton through to a hall now void of both Veronica and Dorothea. 'What is the message you bring?' he asked gruffly, marching through the hall and snatching the stem of the telephone from the top of a walnut cabinet. He placed it to his ear and cranked, before apparently satisfied the apparatus was faulty he replaced it heavily, glancing irritably at Hambleton.

Hambleton removed his hat, placed it on the cloak stand without invitation, brushed down his wet coat. 'In view of the conditions, Mr. Dawson, Mr. Llewellyn having been unable to contact your good self, requires to be reassured that provisions are sufficient to meet the needs of Miss Veronica. I am required to check …'

'They are sufficient; I have the cook's word.'

Hambleton coughed, traced a finger along the top of his upper lip. 'Mr. Dawson, in order to satisfy Mr. Llewellyn in the appropriate manner, I need to see for myself.'

Dawson picked up the swab that had fallen to the floor, slapped it on the cabinet beside the phone. 'Follow me.'

Following along the passageway behind Dawson, Hambleton cast a glance up the stone staircase at the top of which, he thought he heard Dorothea's hushed voice.

***

'Hurry now, head for the inn, and remember that it is not for you that I do this, rather to bask in my brother's demise.' Seeing the change in Veronica's expression and sensing she was preparing to challenge her Dorothea added quickly, 'Go now, before it is too late.' She followed Veronica down the steps, feeling the urge to push, though even carrying her bag she felt the vixen would be ready for her. But seeing Thomas reduced to the snivelling wreck he was soon to become was precious reward for her.

Slamming the entrance door behind Veronica, Dorothea marched back to the hall, in less than a moment Hambleton had returned closely accompanied by Dawson. The swiftest of glances passed between them before Hambleton bid them good-day and went on his way.

Dawson looked at Dorothea, his eyes narrowed with suspicion. 'Where is Miss Day?'

Dorothea raised her brows. 'I assume she is in her room. I followed her up the stairs. Good God man, she has you in such a state of high tension, I fear for your health.'

Dawson made as if to check for himself then did an about turn, picked up the swab from the cabinet and resumed washing the windows with noticeable aggression.

Behind his back, Dorothea gave a cold smile.

Chapter Twenty Nine

Veronica braced herself for the conditions. At the top of the slope the wind blew so hard she struggled for breath. She wore only a light coat to protect her from the rain, Dawson having removed her rainwear. But she was fit and strong, and even the bag she carried, containing her hastily scrambled possessions, wouldn't hinder her to any large degree.

But she was relieved to be leaving the castle; since Dawson's arrival there had been mounting trepidation, testing even her nerves, compounded by the transformation in Thomas' personality. Far from being a home the place had become a place of restriction and confinement, rendered that way by the personalities of those who resided there. She fully believed that Dorothea possessed no real interest in helping her escape, other than to confound her brother; without that desire they would have been at each other's throat, almost were. It was ironic that Dorothea should assist her departure.

And did she feel any sense of betrayal towards Thomas Llewellyn, the man who'd offered her a home there – whom she'd agreed to marry? Perhaps at a later stage there might be some, but the single entity governing her thinking was her desire to assist Gibbings with troubles that he wouldn't divulge – hadn't until that very morning.

Almost too late, she still didn't fully understand the nature of her escape, though it seemed Hambleton had had a hand. But now all that concerned her was leaving the island, with Gibbings; to chart a course for him that would create a sense of purpose, as well as ensuring the continuation of his daughter's education, and then to return to London in time to resume her musical commitments.

Somehow as she battled her way towards the village against the storm, the enthusiasm for doing that had waned. Why precisely, she wasn't sure - her stay on the island had turned as turbulent as the weather, she should be grateful it was over. Glad to be returning to the civility of the concert hall.

But she wasn't, not completely.

Ahead, just passing between the terraced houses which marked the end of the village street, Veronica caught sight of a figure running towards her and experienced an unaccountable surge of adrenalin as she recognised Gibbings. The head of his anorak flopping back and forth he came running up, taking both her free hand and the bag she carried in her right.

'You managed to get out – I thought you weren't coming – I didn't know what to do…'

'I think it had something to do with Mr. Hambleton,' Veronica said, her hands on his shoulders, 'and Dorothea of all people …'

'Aye, I know – I went to him, not knowing what else to do.'

'Thank you John.' Veronica kissed him softly on the cheek, thought she saw him blush, but with his dark tan she couldn't be sure. 'We must leave now before that awful butler realises…'

'There's Mr. Hambleton…' Gibbings pointed back along the track, from where the tall figure of Hambleton came, leaning into the wind, clutching his hat.

'I should thank him too, say goodbye.'

'Mr. Hambleton won't stay here now,' Gibbings stated. 'He only stayed over worry for you.'

Veronica nodded, bit her lip. 'I cannot see him wanting to make the trek across the causeway though – not in these conditions. How long will it take us?'

'Half an hour should do it, think you can manage in this weather?' he asked, suddenly concerned.

'I can do anything you can, John Gibbings,' Veronica replied, aware of the cockiness creeping into her voice.

'I would suggest you make haste, not stand around here talking,' Hambleton remonstrated, striding up.

'I wanted to thank you for your intervention,' Veronica said, touching his hand. 'What will you do now?'

'Much the same as you, I feel, though I feel I am not of an age to traverse the causeway. I will await the resumption of the telephone system before summoning a carriage. Now be off with you without further delay.'

'Will he be safe here, John?' Veronica asked anxiously as he led her away. 'There was some kind of distraction I know, and once Dawson finds out…'

'He'll be more concerned with finding you than worrying about Mr. Hambleton,' Gibbings assured her on reaching the village street. 'I need to collect my belongings from the inn, and then we'll leave.'

Veronica realised he was still holding her hand, she gave him a long searching look, feeling a strong sense of companionship – if companionship was the word, as she smiled into his brown eyes.

It took Gibbings only a minute to collect his bag, from whence they set off along the lane towards the causeway that would enable their departure from the island, and then as the road wound to meet it Gibbings froze, let go of her hand…

Before his eyes, the tide had come rushing in.

***

Dawson finished washing the windows, threw the swab away and proceeded upstairs to Veronica's room. Giving a single knock he pushed the door open, witnessing at once the disarray in her room. Cursing, he marched to her open wardrobe, only to find it bare. A few clothes strewn across her bed were all that remained, and her case had gone.

'Dorothea,' he roared foraging through the castle, 'where to blazes has she gone?'

'Dear me, what is all the commotion?' Dorothea stepped calmly out of her room, cigarette holder in hand.

'I asked you where she's gone, tell me, woman, before I…' Dawson lunged, grasping Dorothea's shoulders, forcing her back against the wall. 'I said tell me.'

'Take your hands off me, you oaf.' Dorothea struggled violently, her cigarette catching Dawson's chin, causing him to clutch it while his eyes burned cold fury.

'Compose yourself,' she said angrily. 'If she's taken flight I know nothing of it. I told you I followed her up the stairs. That is all I know.'

'You know more.' But Dawson didn't persist; he marched along the upper passageway, into the gallery then through to Llewellyn's room which provided an unobstructed view across to the village, but gazing out he saw only a deserted, windswept shoreline. He came back, striding furiously, demanding, 'Where would she have gone?'

'I know not, and I care not.' She turned her back on him, knowing it to be unwise but unnerved by the ferocity of the butler's twisted face.

'It is better you find her before my brother returns rather than waste your temper on me.'

Dawson scowled; she smelled his sickly breath on her neck but nothing more, as he pushed past.

The village, he thought, where else than to the village – and then perhaps the mainland. But if he were quick he might yet thwart her – haul her back physically and regain the trust he would surely have lost should Llewellyn return and find her gone.

Chapter Thirty

'Your hair is streaming, you're soaked to the skin, perhaps it would be better to find shelter when all said and done – here, take my coat...'

Veronica shook her head, sending a shower of rainwater to the ground. 'No, and as for shelter, with a thug of a man in all probability pursuing us, would you deem that wise?'

'Unless you're thinking of swimming,' Gibbings replied flatly, 'we have little choice.'

'Don't tempt me,' but the look in Gibbings' eyes dissuaded her from further comment.

'We can shelter at the inn until the tide goes out...'

'The first place the ogre will look. Can you not do better than that, John Gibbings? Or do you wish to remain here after all, with no prospect for you and your daughter?'

'There you go again.' Gibbings' eyes blazed with intensity, matching the turbulence that surrounded them. 'You seek to belittle me whenever you can, to tease me at your will – is it any surprise I distrust you?'

Veronica placed her hands on hips, narrowing her eyes as she stared into his. 'I find it implausible, that you, with your experience of the tide should overlook its flow, that is all. But if you are genuine in your desire for a better future, there is another option until it is viable to travel.'

'Which is?' Gibbings asked, voice and face full of resentment.

'Exactly what our friend Dawson will not be expecting, it is but a short distance though I suggest we make tracks.'

Gibbings coughed out the rain that was trickling down his throat. 'Veronica, this is no time for your riddles,' he said softly. 'You are infuriating in your superiority.'

'I seek not to infuriate, merely to confront a problem you are showing no signs of solving. Now come...'

Gibbings showed signs of resisting, but Veronica's hand clasped his and her strong arm forced him off balance. 'Do I have to drag you?'

She feared Gibbings would offer more resistance, but beneath his glowering look there seemed resigned acceptance.

The rain-swept peninsula was deserted but Veronica sensed that Dawson was not far off, as with Gibbings alongside and apparently content for her hand to remain in his she headed past the church to the gates of the vicarage.

Gibbings finally perceived her intention with a look of abhorrence. 'Veronica,' he spurted, 'now I *know* you've lost your mind; the Reverend Robertson is no more than an acquaintance. I'm no churchgoer...'

'Dawson will not think of looking for us here,' she said unlatching the gate. 'Once I have explained all he will shield us until it is time to leave.'

Gibbings glanced at her dubiously. 'I suppose I should admire your guts if nothing else,' he grumbled, allowing himself to be ushered through.

Veronica raised her brows and then looking over her shoulder caught sight of the hulking figure of Dawson in his long black cloak. He'd taken a short cut across land and finding the causeway awash, was figuring out his next move.

***

Rothman sat in the oak-panelled private members' lounge, but for once he was rigid in his black leather armchair, the palm of his right hand twisted around his face.

'You seem unusually perturbed,' Reynolds yawned, abandoning his habit of perusing his lunchtime paper and laying it down.

'Is it any wonder?' Rothman said. 'I warned you this would happen. Barely a single day has passed since Llewellyn's return from the island and already he has taken flight back there.'

Reynolds raised his brows, drew in breath. 'Perhaps it is easily explained.'

'Oh it is easily explained,' Rothman snapped with unaccustomed venom. 'He has lost touch with reality, old chap. He envisages his dream, for that is what it is, in peril. Having failed to make contact with him, I visited his office earlier with concern – his senior clerk is at a loss to explain his behaviour and it seems he found records at one time exemplary to be in a complete shambles. The poor fellow was at his wits' end trying to sort them out. Llewellyn mark my words is bound for the island and I sense disaster ahead.'

'Then there is precious little we can do,' Reynolds said retrieving his paper, 'than to await its materialisation; if our investment goes awry, then I am certain other opportunities will arise which will prove less costly.'

'For once it is not the investments I despair of. For such a remote desolate place the island spreads its tentacles afar.' Rothman leapt to his feet, rammed his hands into the pockets of his suit trousers and marched out.

***

She could not have escaped; for an instant the unacceptable notion that she just might have done so entered Dawson's head – the notion that the swirling tide might have engulfed her – that even in her death she might have outwitted him.

He spun round; through the pouring rain he spotted the entrance to the inn. The former butler, Hambleton, lodged there. Why the man had remained on the island he hadn't a clue, and then with a surge of fury he recalled the visit Hambleton had made and the part it had obviously played in her escape. Without another thought he headed for the inn.

***

Hambleton had packed, preparing for a return to the Capital, a usually orderly mind still reeling from what had transpired, when he heard the gruff, raised voice from the bar below, and heard his name mentioned along with Veronica's. He heard a fist come down heavily on the bar, 'I know they're here…'

And then footsteps on the stairs, the landlord's apologetic, worried expression, 'There's a man downstairs, Mr. Hambleton, ranting and raving. I don't want any trouble…'

But Hambleton had already heard the heavy tread of a second set of footsteps on the stairs and steeled himself for an unwanted but expected confrontation.

'It's alright, Thomas,' Hambleton said in as calm a voice as he could manage. 'I will speak to Mr. Dawson.'

The landlord shuffled, hesitated a second before making way for Dawson as the new butler charged in, an index finger cocked and accusing. 'Don't think I'm not aware of your part in this, where is she man – tell me or I'll…'

'Mr. Dawson, accosting me will serve you no purpose,' Hambleton said, retreating backwards. 'Your behaviour ill-suits a man in your position – and as you can see, the lady you seek is not here.'

'Oh, but *you* are Hambleton, you and your bloody interfering – I see your bags are packed. Your part in this is completed, is it?'

Hambleton looked into the heavy, glaring eyes. 'What I choose to do is my concern – as are Miss Veronica's affairs her own; you had no right to contain her within the castle and certainly no right charging after her like a madman.'

'She is Mr. Llewellyn's intended,' Dawson sneered, displaying his yellow teeth, 'and as such it is my duty to protect her, no matter what measures it may take. You should know about duty Hambleton.'

Dawson's big hands reached down, Hambleton felt himself being raised before the room spun and he was flying through the air. There was an agonising burning sensation as his head struck the underside of the mantelpiece and he blacked out.

Chapter Thirty One

The countryside flashed by, but not quickly enough for Llewellyn. As he gazed out of the rainy window at storm-laden skies he felt drawn back to the island by Veronica's sheer beauty and the threat posed to her by the gardener, John Gibbings. He could not bear the thought of them being in the same locality, even though his influence on her was about to be terminated. His new butler, Dawson, was a formidable chap who would protect his interests with an iron hand, unlike the doubting Hambleton who had been honoured with his position for far too long.

As long as was necessary, for once Dorothea had tired of her games and departed, (and depart she would,) wishing she'd accepted his offer, once she'd witnessed the sublime happiness that would evolve from his marriage to the delightful Veronica; then Dawson would no longer have a task to fulfil. Llewellyn glowed at the prospect of the two of them alone in their romantic hideaway, a castle all of their own. How many couples could claim that?

But first he needed to be there alongside her. The heat that burned within wouldn't be quelled until then. In fact his desire had increased since leaving his London office, growing stronger every minute that brought him closer to the island.

At Berwick he leapt into a carriage, barking his instructions and flinging his case into the back before the driver had a chance to assist. The man was chuntering something but Llewellyn's thoughts were too tightly locked on Veronica to enable him to listen.

It wasn't until he arrived at the causeway and saw the driver's hapless gesture towards an angry sea that Llewellyn comprehended.

The causeway was inaccessible, it would be for hours. This time the man's words brought a nauseating cloy to his throat. He'd come this far, within three miles and a matter of minutes from his beloved Veronica. Several hours to him would amount to a torture beyond his ability to endure.

He fastened his coat and grabbed his bag, searched along the grim shoreline. There were vessels moored in the distance, fishermen with anoraks huddled in a group. Llewellyn set out towards them.

The vicar seemed to gaze suspiciously upon them from his elevated position on the porch. Perhaps their bedraggled appearance caused a certain apprehension.

'Why Mr. Gibbings – John, this is a surprise, and the young lady, Miss Day isn't it? What on earth brings you here, and in these conditions, is something amiss?'

'We ask you to shelter us, Reverend Robertson. There is a man in pursuit who is not at all pleasant, may we come in?'

Robertson, a small man with a receding hairline, looked tentative, baffled, but waved them through. 'Here on the island? I know of no rogues here.'

He guided them along a dimly-lit hall. 'I will get you towels, you are drenched – and then perhaps you would reveal what distresses you so. Please take a seat. Try not to drip over the upholstery.'

Gibbings listened to Robertson's footsteps recede. 'He won't easily be influenced by your posh speech, or what you have to say…'

'We seek only shelter,' Veronica answered, aware of the harshness in her voice, 'until it is safe to cross to the mainland.'

Gibbings mopped rain from under his dark brows. 'Then we'll see if your bright idea works. The vicar seems more concerned with the appearance of his furniture, if you ask me.'

He glanced back out the window, Veronica saw his frown. 'I have told you, he will not think of coming here; Dawson is a foolish, ignorant man without an iota of intelligence. And is that resentment in your eyes – that I might regard you likewise?'

'You are playing with me, Veronica. I fail to see how you can find amusement in such situations,' Gibbings said moodily.

Veronica had turned her head towards the sound of Robertson's returning steps. 'Reverend you are most kind,' she said, taking the towels from the vicar's outstretched hand and thrusting one at Gibbings. 'Now I feel we must cast our problems upon you. You know my name, vicar; you may know something of me.'

'It would be an ignorant man indeed who knew nothing of such an illustrious individual, Miss Day.'

'Then you will know that I have frequented the castle of late with the permission of its owner.'

'I am aware Miss Day,' the Reverend eased himself into a high-backed chair facing the pair. 'In fact Mr. Llewellyn has visited the church on several occasions and has been most generous to our cause.'

'Then you will know he is no longer sane.'

'I beg your pardon Miss Day?'

'I learn from your expression that he has managed to conceal his insanity from you. There is a history of madness within his family and his sister is an example, I am in no doubt of that. As far as Mr. Llewellyn is concerned, I believe I am becoming something of an obsession for him, and I regard such as an indication of an unsound mind. His possessive nature has resulted in him employing a new butler, the very same as is pursuing me now, but there is much you do not know. We both require your shelter, at least until the tide leaves the causeway clear.'

Robertson was quiet for several seconds but his look had changed from mild benevolence to one of condemnation, and the hardening of his eyes told her where it was directed.

'Miss Day, I have resided in this locality for several years, many of them in my current capacity. I have yet to witness civil disruption of any kind – what you are describing is implausible to say the least; I have no reason to believe there is any threat to you other than that derived from your own imagination.'

Looking at Gibbings, he asked, 'John, would you state otherwise?'

Gibbings shrugged. 'I don't know Mr. Llewellyn as well as Veronica, but I've seen enough goings on to reckon she speaks the truth – Mr. Hambleton would surely agree…'

Robertson spread his hand, let out a tired sigh. 'But Hambleton is not here, and although you mean well John, I believe you are somewhat naive.'

'And for a clergyman you are insufferably rude. By that you insult my integrity and John's intelligence,' Veronica said angrily.

'Miss Day, I strive only to maintain peace and unity on the island. I find it difficult to believe that circumstances such as you speak of have developed here. I am rather busy with engagements to afford you any more time but the church is available to all. Once you have towelled yourself dry might I suggest you take refuge within its walls should you deem it necessary.'

'Your pomposity could cost us dear, vicar,' Veronica said bitterly, flinging the towel back at Robertson. 'Come John, I was wrong; we are obviously not welcome here.'

'You were right John,' Veronica admitted, slamming the vicarage door behind her. 'I had counted on the Reverend being more accommodating. I can be too headstrong at times.'

Gibbings shook his head. 'Reverend Robertson called me naive, but he is the naive one not even to consider what you…'

'Shush…' Veronica slapped an arm across Gibbings' waist. 'There he is – Dawson – and he's staring over here.'

***

Dawson thought he saw shadows sweep across the rain-lashed porch of the vicarage. He thumbed water from his eyes but saw nothing to confirm the image. But might the adjacent church provide the ideal retreat until the tide relented? Because if the woman wasn't at the inn, where could she go to seek cover but there? It was close to the causeway and the only notion he had. Dawson headed on, bull-like, towards it.

***

They sat on a small pew, tucked away to the side of the altar. 'I feel like a coward,' Gibbings uttered, an eye on the vestibule door, 'hiding like this, he's only a man after all.'

'A very dangerous one,' Veronica said quietly, 'and hired by a man of unsound mind.'

'You speak as though you have plenty of experience of men.'

In the darkness of the church Veronica's eyes blazed. 'That is precisely the kind of remark I expect of a chauvinist – a bigot,' she said, aware of the bitterness creeping into her voice.

Gibbings sighed as the door creaked, alerting them both, but it seemed caused by the high wind that was rattling the church.

'I have confessions to make, Veronica – I feel I must do so now, in case anything happens and I don't get a chance…'

'Try not to be so morbid…' Veronica's curiosity was aroused. 'Well?' she prodded, noting the thin crevasses appearing on his brow.

Gibbings took her hand. 'I have too long been resentful,' he spurted… 'and yes jealous of other men's attraction to you – like Mr. Llewellyn and the man with the posh car – I've tried to seem distant toward you, when I hadn't intended to be. I have fallen in love with you Veronica, but are you out of my reach?'

'Oh John…' but Veronica's speech was curtailed by footsteps along the main isle, and she realised in despair that Dawson's dark presence had been unkindly concealed by the dim church interior.

'She is beyond your reach,' Dawson barked. 'She is within reach only of my employer and master, Thomas Llewellyn.'

Veronica turned, clung to Gibbings as Dawson closed in on them.

Chapter Thirty Two

'I'll pay you anything you want.' Llewellyn delved into his inner coat pocket and snatched a wad of notes. 'I need to get to the island – the castle, I am the owner…'

'The conditions are too rough,' a heavily built fisherman, wearing a yellow anorak, said dismissively. But then glancing at his two colleagues seemed to reconsider.

'Anything you say.' He sniffed, snatched the notes and fingered through them, slapping them against the heel of his hand before tucking them into a trouser pocket. 'I guess we can cope; climb aboard.'

Llewellyn couldn't believe his luck. His mouth folded into a grin which became fixed as the vessel rose and plunged as it rode the stormy waves. Soaked in rain and spray he soon saw the castle ahead, a welcoming sight to his eyes on its high mound of rock.

Inside sat his sweetheart, soon to be surprised and delighted by his early return; with the gardener, Gibbings, soon to be banished and his malicious, devious sister soon to depart, it would be the ideal, magical haven.

He would shower Veronica with kisses as soon as he landed – implore her never to leave the island. Despite her statement to the contrary, what need was there?

The tide was too high for the vessel to land him ashore and he was forced to wade the last few metres carrying his bag, up to his knees in water; he didn't care for he was home and his love awaited him.

He climbed the slope to find the entrance open, the heavy oak door off the latch and swinging in the wind. Just a touch of annoyance crept in to mar his euphoria at his homecoming and just a touch more at the apparent emptiness of the place, emphasised by his echoing footsteps in the cavernous hall through which a dark draught swept, stronger than any he'd previously encountered there.

'Veronica, Veronica!' he shouted, sweeping through the ground floor, along the passageway and up the stone stairs leading to her room.

On reaching it his eyes transmitted a message he was unwilling to believe. Her wardrobe was open, empty apart from the odd garment lying at its base, as if her clothes had been ripped from the hangers in a hurry.

He placed his hands to his temples, they shook in disbelief. Sweating profusely, he stormed out.

Llewellyn swept through the castle in a blind panic. He hadn't expected this, he hadn't expected to find Veronica gone – and where was Dawson? In its empty state the castle resembled a mausoleum, except that it wasn't empty.

'The bird has flown its nest, dear brother.' The one voice he hadn't wanted to hear spoke from the rear. Llewellyn swung on his heels, a little too quickly – he needed the wall for support as he glared into the smirking face of his sister, standing in her long, dark frock, arms folded, her left hand caressing a glass of whisky.

'Those lovely green eyes never shone with desire for you. Were you so self-indulgent in your desire for her that you failed to see it?'

'Damn you Dorothea. What the hell has been happening here – where is Veronica, where is Dawson?'

Dorothea tossed her head, laughed and took a gulp of her whisky. 'Gone – has it not sunk into that thick skull? I should say that the man you employed as her "protection" might have contributed to her sudden departure.' Dorothea's smile evaporated, her face becoming bitter, her tone caustic. 'Dawson is a dim-wit, she simply out-manoeuvred him.' She gave a wide sweep of her arm. 'He is out there now, no doubt, in hopeless pursuit.'

'Damn you Dorothea, you instigated this.' The veins in Llewellyn's neck stood out gnarled and twisted. 'I can see it in your eyes; Veronica had no intention of leaving…'

'She had every intention,' Dorothea snarled. 'The desire in those lovely green eyes was for Gibbings – had been all along.'

Llewellyn's face contorted, his jaw clenched. His pupils seemed to enlarge until they became vast, unmoving brown globes in his head. He threw himself forward, arms making for her neck, his hands becoming claws as they grasped her throat.

She drew phlegm from the back of her throat, launched it at his eye and it produced momentary effect as his grip slackened enough for her to scramble free.

Dorothea fled along the hallway, aware of Llewellyn close behind, his voice raucous with curses, blending eerily with the howling wind.

If he caught her now he would kill her –

She turned, aimed the glass at his face but it was a clumsy action on the run, missing Llewellyn and smashing against the wall. Down the stairs two at a time she ran, then along the passageway to the hall, looming huge and her brother so close now she could smell his heated breath; a turn towards the main door and then out in the open; the wind whistling, the ground wet underfoot and slippery - and in her desperation she'd forgotten how slippery –

And then his hand on her shoulder, clenched and tugging, hauling her back, forcing her to turn, legs beginning to buckle as she lost her foothold - and then the damp smack of the ground and the sensation of tumbling, down, down, ever quicker –

Llewellyn watched transfixed as she came to rest at the bottom of the slope, motionless. Then with rigid, fixed steps he made his way down and approached her lifeless body. He kicked out at it, turned it over as her mouth fell open, blood oozing onto the cobbles.

He groped for her pulse, found nothing; her skin was paler than he'd ever seen it and the sudden stench from her body told him what he needed to know.

Llewellyn picked her up, shoulders drooping under the weight – waded into the sea and dropped his sister's body in. The heavy tide he was sure, would carry her out.

Chapter Thirty Three

Veronica clung to Gibbings. She had seen a way out. 'Come John, the rear door,' she said forcing him up.

She pushed him forward, pointing her finger towards the end of the eastern isle; Gibbings responded by running towards it, Veronica following, watching anxiously as he twisted the handle without success as Dawson's steps quickened behind, and then the door shuddering as Dawson's hand thumped against it.

'No you don't.'

'Get off!' Gibbings abandoned his grip on the handle, rounding on Dawson, thrusting the palm of a hand into his chest.

Dawson grabbed him, cuffing him with the back of a hand as Veronica's anger boiled. She lashed out, her fist catching Dawson on the lip and producing a red trickle. 'I warn you Dawson, I am not some helpless woman you can confine against her will – I am not Llewellyn's possession and if you persist with your present course I will fight you…'

Dawson had been knocked back a step, as enraged he wiped blood from his lip. 'You will do as I say, woman,' he growled, advancing quickly, snatching Veronica roughly by the thighs and hoisting her to his shoulder.

'Leave her be.' Gibbings shouted above the wind buffeting the rafters, and then a shout from the vestibule laced with the authority of a clergyman. 'What in *God's* name is going on here? Unhand that woman; have you no respect for the House of the Lord?'

'It is not *your* Lord that I am responsible to, but my master, Thomas Llewellyn.' Dawson's heavy brows levelled; 'Mind your tongue and stand aside.'

As Dawson faced Reverend Robertson, his back exposed, Gibbings clenched his fists together, drawing back his arms and swinging them as one into the core of Dawson's spine.

Dawson roared in anguish, lost his grip on Veronica and she tumbled from his shoulder towards the church floor. Gibbings gaped in that instant, expecting Veronica's head to hit the ground but somehow she protected it with her arms, rolling away from him.

The fissures on Dawson's cheeks cracked like porcelain as he recovered, scowled and launched himself at Gibbings.

'Get off him you oaf!' Veronica sprang to her feet, leapt on his back, tightened both arms around Dawson's neck; she heard him choke as in desperation he whirled, swinging her against the wall.

Winded, Veronica slid to the floor as Dawson bent low, clasping his knees, panting for breath. She grabbed Gibbings' outstretched hand and he pulled her to her feet; she looked up to find the Reverend heading for the rear door, keys jangling in his hand. 'Quick, through here…'

Gibbings and Veronica plunged through the vestry door, Dawson close on their heels.

***

Llewellyn spared no remorse for his dead sister, she had contrived against him from the outset. This situation was her doing and she had paid the penalty; she'd had the opportunity to leave the castle with ample remuneration and refused – preferring instead to conspire against him. So justice had been done but it wasn't fully effected yet – there was another equally abhorrent figure to deal with – the gardener Gibbings, a most treacherous servant who had contaminated the pure mind of his beloved Veronica –

His objectives were twofold – to account for Gibbings, but overwhelmingly to rescue Veronica, so that their future happiness would be sealed forever. Gibbings must never again be allowed to taint the mind of his intended.

He had to have taken her. If Dawson hadn't already done so he would find them and rectify the situation.

In the castle basement, carved deep into the molten rock which formed the building's base, was the remains of an armoury which had once formed the core of the castle's stronghold. When he'd acquired the castle, Llewellyn had discovered several weapons still intact and though the pistols were no doubt unusable, the sabres he'd found were perfectly preserved in their sheaths.

Delving in the basement now, he selected one, drew it and held it close to his nose with a quivering smile. The perfect solution to the problem; the perfect weapon to effect Gibbings' demise.

Llewellyn didn't bother securing the castle entrance way, the thought didn't enter his mind. Out in the driving rain he marched down the slope. Somewhere in the village he'd find them, he was sure - they were trapped on the island after all.

***

Veronica thought ahead, marching to the outer door and tugging the handle, before turning towards Robertson for the key.

The noise of Dawson's fist intensified and then the door began to bulge as he applied his shoulder to it. Gibbings cast a sharp glance back. 'It won't hold for long.'

Robertson nimbly slid the key into the lock and ushered them out into the open, locking the external door after them. 'There is a small chapel at the rear of the church garden,' he whispered. 'God willing you will be safe there until you are able to commence your journey.'

'And if not?' Veronica raised her voice above the sudden crescendo of the wind. 'Are you now so certain of the innocence of this island?'

'It was free of violence until your arrival, which is all I know.' There was an edge to Robertson's voice, resentment on his face as he strode towards the rear of the vicarage.

'Foolish man, his principles blur his vision,' Veronica uttered with enough velocity for him to hear. 'Come John, it seems we have no refuge other than the chapel.'

The gravestones stood stark, greying monoliths in a storm, a reminder if any was needed of the peril they were in, but anger clouded Veronica's mind, fury at the Reverend's intransigence, at the way the thug, Dawson, was pursuing them in blind ignorance, in the cause of his "master," who was insane.

If it wasn't for John Gibbings she would regard the shipwreck as the disaster it should have been. But now, even though in great peril, his words loomed large, words she hadn't a chance to answer. *"Are you beyond my reach, Veronica?"*

"Beyond her reach?" he was every bit within it. Those recollected words shafted arrow-like through the anger she felt, as thoroughly soaked from the driving rain they hurried through the undergrowth to the chapel.

'John Gibbings,' she said, breaking open the door with her foot, 'you *are* within my reach – I am in love with you, I have fought against it as much as you – though this is not a particularly ambient location to admit such…'

'Damn the location, Veronica, and your highly polished language. All I want is you - and security for my daughter.'

'You shall have both.' Veronica allowed Gibbings to embrace her, to draw her close. Outside, within the vestry, Dawson would soon break through. Well let him come, she would be ready.

***

Llewellyn had the sabre, he had the means to eliminate Gibbings and dispose of the body in much the same vein he had Dorothea's.

For Gibbings was the only entity which stood between him and his dream –

The cluster of buildings that constituted the hub of the village lay ahead; he only needed the correct one – and it couldn't be that difficult. The inn would be his first port of call, and from there he'd branch out – if he needed to.

The door to the inn was ajar. He pushed it open, the bar was empty and so he climbed the stairs to a room at the top; in the dim light he made out a figure he thought he recognised, that of a man slumped in a chair, a swab to his head, with a tall thin man at his side attending him.

But he gave it no thought, because the ones he sought weren't there.

He heard the tall thin man shout, but his words didn't register – he stumbled down the steep stairs using the railing but not conscious of its support and then outside towards the square where a blast of wind buffeted him. But it had no effect, because a voice was guiding him within, venomous, calling out the name "Gibbings" – he was here in the vicinity and should be accounted for.

Veronica was here and she should be rescued –

At the crossroads the vicarage lay ahead, but he didn't give it thought, he passed it by along with the church – and then he stopped.

Contrasting with the howl of the wind there was a deeper sound, the thud, thud, thud, of a door being struck, could this be Gibbings?

Perhaps Veronica had managed to find refuge – and perhaps any minute he might break through –

If so, he was on hand to rescue the love of his life.

Chapter Thirty Four

Llewellyn drove his tiring body into the wind, forcing his legs to the limit of their endurance; his arms were beginning to flail but his right hand clung steadfastly to the sabre.

Dawson heard his floundering steps in the aisle. 'She's through here,' he grunted, 'with the gardener, but I'm about to change that.' With one further thrust of the shoulder and a splinter of oak he'd broken through.

Dawson hurried into the small box room to find it empty, its outer door swinging back and forth in the storm. Beyond the church the grounds looked empty, descending into undergrowth, with wild heather and bracken rustling furiously in the wind.

'We must find them – and quickly,' Llewellyn gasped, 'before harm comes to Veronica – this is not of her making.'

'I fear,' Dawson sneered, 'she needed little persuasion to flee.'

'It is all that wretched gardener's fault.' Llewellyn wiped rain from his mouth. 'You should have paid more attention to his activities; you were hired to protect her.'

Lofting his head as waves thundered in the distance, Llewellyn raised the sabre, the fingers of his free hand fumbling with the sheath, then finally baring the blade he said angrily, 'Let it not bother you unduly however – I shall soon account for him.'

***

'The smell is rancid, the air full of decay; can you not smell it, John Gibbings?'

'Would you suggest we open the door?' Gibbings asked, raising his head to watch the rain stream down the chapel's greasy windows. 'Shall we see how long it is before they find us?' He sniffed. 'Women!'

'Men...' with all their witless sarcasm.' Veronica turned her head slowly, forcing a smile as they sat huddled in a recess of the long-disused chapel. 'You realise if he finds us the "game," as they say, is up?'

'We cannot run with nowhere to run to,' Gibbings snapped.

'Kiss me, John Gibbings.'

He sprang forward. 'What?'

'Well, what else will we do to wile away the time?'

Veronica coiled an arm around his neck, held him close, her kiss gentle on his mouth; she felt his rigidity. 'John,' she asked, inching apart, 'is your desire not as great as mine?'

Gibbings sighed, wrenched himself from her grasp. 'This is not the place – and I should be protecting you not hiding like some defenceless animal while Llewellyn's damned henchman closes in – desire has nothing to do with this.'

'Does it not? Does your attitude not derive solely from the fact that you are the man and I am the woman – do you think that should count for anything?'

Veronica traced a finger down Gibbings' cheek and said softly, 'I can see that in your eyes at least – it does.'

Gibbings said nothing, but his brown eyes exuded an added hue that reflected his resentment.

Veronica sat forward, and clasping her hands around her calves studied him. 'Do you think that the gravity of our demise escapes me – how long before the causeway becomes clear to cross?'

Gibbings shrugged. 'I could tell by the light were it not for this storm, the time must be approaching. Damn this man Llewellyn that he should ever have come here.'

'And damn me…'

'Damn you *no…*' Gibbings let out a great sigh. 'You are the one good thing that's happened – it's just that I feel so powerless to help you.'

'Then let us take our chance – up and go – I trust your judgement, John Gibbings, it cannot be long before the waves relent.'

Veronica held out her hand, allowed Gibbings to pull her up. She met his eyes and asked a question. 'What is it, John?'

'Even with your hair a mess, you look so beautiful.'

She pushed him onto the porch, and together they prepared to brave the storm.

***

The waters were receding as Rothman reached the causeway, though the debris deposited by the heavy waves rendered it barely passable. But he didn't let that deter him. He couldn't, despite the possible damage to his prized motor vehicle – for the circumstances that had induced his lengthy drive to a location he had no desire to return to, were dire enough to pierce even his conscience.

Rothman had witnessed the change in Llewellyn, from shrewd City businessman to hopeless dreamer – he had seen the deterioration in his appearance, his attitudes and even his increasingly bizarre bodily gestures. And the focus of his dreaming was the enigmatic Veronica Day.

A woman of extraordinary beauty, refined, unconventional in a way that he himself was; with first class breeding but with an air of mischievousness entwined. Was it her attractiveness that had so beguiled Llewellyn, or was it something inherent in the man himself?

Some form of madness waiting to manifest itself with Veronica the unsuspecting trigger?

It was, he thought, the latter.

Whatever the truth, he sensed the change in Llewellyn spelled peril for Veronica. Why, when he'd departed the island just a few days past with such nonchalance should that disturb him so?

He'd an image to live up to; that of a wealthy, sophisticated but carefree young man, an image entirely at odds with his current course of action –

Veronica Day –

There was no denying it, he felt aroused at the very thought of her.

His tingling skin, as he approached the village wasn't a result of the unusual chill – he accepted as much but fought against the conclusion – excitement and Veronica Day seemed inextricably bound.

The castle lay ahead, looming dark against low grey clouds, its turrets engulfed in mist.

Uninviting, unwelcoming in the gloom, stark and uncompromising, and yet Rothman could feel the adrenaline swelling his veins.

He abandoned his Rolls Royce at the bottom of the slope, negotiating the wet cobbles with less caution than he should, reaching the entrance to find the main door flapping back and forth like cardboard in the wind.

An air of foreboding swept over him the moment he stepped inside; the draught that funnelled through the hall approach seemed more akin to a cold wind.

And the whine of the wind was the only sound that met Rothman's ears as like the uninvited guest he was, he searched through a castle void of any life.

Concern mounted to new heights the moment he reached the basement room that had served as an armoury in days long gone; its door wide open as was every other in the deserted former fortress – but this was different, because within the box-shaped room, amidst weapon encasements, wherein most of the explosive fire-power had been rendered useless by age, one case stood empty, the wooden cover hanging from its hinges. The positioning of the retaining brackets told him a sabre had been taken.

Llewellyn had been here. He'd seen his luggage lying unopened on his bed, a weapon had gone – and where now was the king of the castle? More to the point where was Veronica? Dorothea? The intimidating new butler Dawson? Just what had happened?

Veronica was resilient, but she was more than that, and in a sense she'd become an incumbent of the castle under false pretences – it was patently obvious Llewellyn wasn't the attraction for her –

Had there been an attempt to confine her; had she tried to escape?

Had Llewellyn tracked her? Was that the reason the weapon had been removed from its mounting – and where were the others?

Rothman negotiated the treacherous slope down from the castle, reaching the bottom cobbles with the intention of driving to the village and then a dark shape riding the waves – a human form, made him start.

Limbs broken, grotesquely disproportionate to the body, soaked clothing covering its bulk like a shroud – and then a fearful apprehension that this figure so suddenly appearing before his eyes might be Veronica.

Rothman's heart stopped and then resumed beating with an alarming irregularity as he approached the shoreline. He waded in, stooping down amidst the spray that showered his face, took the body in his arms and rolled it over - to stare directly into Dorothea's wide-open, lifeless eyes.

Here was a relief he shouldn't have felt – a woman was dead. But what cruel fate had determined her demise?

Could a similar fate have befallen Veronica? Rothman dare not let that thought take hold of him as, leaving Dorothea's body on the shingle, he returned to his motor vehicle and headed for the village.

Chapter Thirty Five

Veronica looked up, saw the two figures looming against the background of the church – one slim and ungainly in his stride – Llewellyn. How his stance had changed – no longer the dignified lord of the castle, and behind him, the thick set ogre, Dawson, his bearing prowling, aggressive; that of the foraging animal.

She tapped Gibbings' shoulder, crouched and then saw the pair searching steadily through the undergrowth that shielded them.

'We can make for the causeway,' she whispered. 'They haven't laid eyes on us, let's go.'

Gibbings shook his head, keeping his eyes on the two men closing in. 'I'm staying put…'

Veronica grabbed Gibbings' arm and tugged him towards her roughly. 'This is no time to play the hero, now come …'

'How far do you think we'll get?' Gibbings glared at her, resisting, 'You forget how well I know the island, I can lure them into a false trail, then double back while you keep yourself down, get away unseen…'

Veronica eyed him dubiously. 'You know this island well enough to forget the tide was out…'

'I need to do this,' Gibbings said, his dark brows meeting. 'It is the only way.'

'Such foolishness.' Veronica ground her teeth as she swept rain from her face. 'Play the hero if you must but I am not crossing the causeway without you.'

'You won't have to; trust me, now go…'

Veronica sighed, kept herself low, the lie of the land as it sank between the church and the chapel, populated by dense heather and bracken, was on her side. She headed for the causeway.

***

Dawson's attention was drawn to the figure rising from the undergrowth; that of the lean, curly-haired gardener, Gibbings. But where was the woman; why was he alone?

He looked east and west, and then just a glimpse of a redhead scurrying through the undergrowth told Dawson what he needed to know –

'I see the wretched gardener,' Llewellyn shouted, 'but where is Veronica, what has he done to her?'

'He has done nothing.' Dawson scanned the wild heather, got a better look at her lithe, rain-soaked body through a thin clearing. 'She's trying to flee. She's swift, but she will not escape...'

'She runs from me.' Llewellyn clutched his hands to his head. 'Why does she do so?'

'We waste time with idle chatter about such matters...'

But Llewellyn's wide-eyed gaze had become so centered on Gibbings that he failed to hear Dawson's departing words. Gibbings was the reason she fled, it hadn't been because of him – Dawson would reach his beloved Veronica, pacify her, so that she returned to him with renewed desire and heart. But the rough land would soon slow Gibbings down, he could track and catch him – and then – Llewellyn glanced down at what was contained in his right hand, produced a glazed smile – he would effect suitable retribution.

He set off in pursuit with stiff leaden steps while Dawson ploughed after Veronica.

***

Veronica reached the road, looked back and saw that the plan hadn't worked. She saw the oaf of a butler begin chasing her, felt the sheer futility of her flight, but John, damn the man's dogmatic stand – had demanded she did so. Loathe as she had been to comply, the man's sense of integrity over-ruled her doubts – and she loved him – and –

But her thoughts were interrupted by Dawson's heavy tread, thud – thud – thud – for despite his bulk, the ogre was gaining ground. It was the wind and rain of course that hampered her lighter frame, but while she was running what was happening to John?

Thud, thud, thud - like the blacksmith's blow on an anvil.

This couldn't, shouldn't be happening. Veronica Day stopped running, turned and stared directly into the approaching Dawson's eyes.

***

'Stop running you wretched man, turn and face me!' Gibbings heard Llewellyn's hoarse shout, turned and saw the man threading clumsily through the undergrowth after him, but he couldn't see Dawson and that much alone made him halt in his tracks.

That he was the bigger danger to Veronica Gibbings had little doubt, if Dawson had spotted him and taken off after her –

Without Dawson chasing him his plan had failed. Gibbings scanned the landscape without so much as a glimpse, his apprehension rising like the high tide; and yet as Llewellyn approached eyes glazed in a wild stare, froth from his mouth merging with the driving rain, Gibbings was confident of his ability to contain him, but then too late he saw the blade rise in his right hand, felt the cold steel cut into his throat.

Rothman was approaching the church when he heard the shout carry high on the wind. His view was hampered by the rain splattering his offside window, but as he reached across to wind it down, some distance ahead, as his wipers cleared the rain in waves he saw Dawson closing in on Veronica.

The big butler's bulk almost eclipsed the tall, elegant woman but what alarmed him was that she seemed bent on confronting Dawson.

Abandoning his interest in whatever transpired in the church field he slammed his foot hard on the accelerator, splashing along the road towards the couple.

Dawson wasn't aware of Rothman's approach, the howling wind having drowned out the motor's humming drone, but it would have changed little because the controlling element in all his senses was the all-encompassing purpose of inflicting upon the woman who'd so ridiculed and embarrassed him the beating she so deserved. Sometimes women needed to be put in their place – especially haughty women like this one.

He no longer cared what his deranged master thought – it was as plain as day now that the man who had brought him here was mad – completely mad. There was no future in Llewellyn's employ, but Dawson's anger wasn't about to be vented on him –

Ahead he saw her stop, turn and face him, her hands on hips, her eyes like green emeralds in the stormy day where light faded and the sky had turned brown. Had the woman lost her senses? No, this was typical of her, even now she taunted him – and it served only to drive his fury to new heights.

Rothman must have been twenty yards away when he saw the big man grab Veronica's shoulder, saw her raise an arm, saw the back of her hand flash across his face, saw his head drop, saw that right hand strike him again – somewhere around his chin, and then watched as he recovered and caught hold, raising her from the ground, flinging her in his anger across the street, her body colliding with the column of a gas lamp.

Rothman saw Dawson march towards her, his shoulders hunched, decided in that instant what he would do –

He slipped the Rolls Royce into top gear, hit the pedal – Dawson's hands were reaching down when the vehicle hit him – towards her throat, but they got no further – a brief yell blended eerily with the howling wind as his body was propelled through the air, landing motionless in coarse grass after rebounding from a cottage wall.

Rothman paid him no further heed as he jumped from the vehicle's running board alongside Veronica's prostrate body.

'Where did you come from?' She gazed up through half-open glassy eyes. 'Thank you. But I could have managed.'

'From where I stand, dear lady, I very much doubt it.'

Veronica shook her head dismissively. 'I am alright.' She looked over at Dawson's body. 'Do you think he's…'

'Dead? Do you much care?'

'I do not.' Veronica allowed Rothman to pull her to her feet, brushed herself down, and then as her smashed senses recovered, 'John,' she cried with sudden urgency. 'Have you seen John?'

Rothman turned sharply, recalled the voice he'd heard in the field – but it hadn't been the gardener's voice –

He left the car at the point it had struck Dawson and turned to run – and found Veronica ahead of him.

Chapter Thirty Six

Veronica reached the church field yards ahead of Rothman, racing to the point at which she'd left him a few long moments earlier. The clouds had lifted slightly, broken into dark fragments which pursued each other vigorously across the sky, and for an instant the sun broke through, striking a curved object that lay amongst the heather. A steel object smeared with blood. For a second Veronica froze, her eyes slowly following the trail of blood that led to John Gibbings' throat.

She glanced back at Rothman, stooped, placed her hands tentatively around the wound as he crouched beside her, taking hold of Gibbings' hand before sliding her fingers to the man's wrist. 'His pulse is weak, his breathing is shallow and I doubt that he hears us. He needs a doctor, and quickly – are there any in this godforsaken place?'

Veronica forced her eyes away from Gibbings' stricken body, glanced towards the vicarage, 'The Reverend will know…'

'I'll find out,' Rothman got to his feet, headed for the vicarage.

'He can't stay here,' Veronica called after him, 'not in these conditions, tell him what's happened, that I'm bringing John…'

'What?'

'Go on –run…' Veronica ushered him forward, took Gibbings in her arms, gently cradling his neck, and then rose to her feet. 'I can manage Mr. Rothman; it would be a great help if you would hurry to the vicarage and not impede my progress by standing gawking.'

She watched him finally turn tail and head for the vicarage, following carefully in his wake with Gibbings in her arms.

Robertson held the door open and this time he reflected genuine concern. 'Through here; I have a bedroom at the back, lay Mr. Gibbings upon the bed.' He followed Veronica through as she gently lowered him down. 'I'll staunch the flow as best I can, but Doctor Ferguson needs to attend these wounds, they're much too close to the artery for my liking.'

'Where can I find Doctor Ferguson?' Veronica wiped her eyes and it wasn't rain water this time.

'The mainland I'm afraid, just across the junction to the causeway. I'm sorry, the phone line is down but at least the tide has receded.'

'I have a motor car. It will not take me long,' Rothman announced. 'Will you accompany me, Veronica?'

She shook her head. 'I need to remain with John.' Veronica cast a glance over her shoulder, but her view of Gibbings was restricted by Robertson, now applying more pressure to the wound. 'But thank you for returning, Mr. Rothman.'

'Byron, please.' Rothman smiled and made his way to the car.

'Please hurry.' Veronica was unable to return his smile, providing him with a grateful nod of thanks before watching him drive away.

'I cannot believe this is happening,' Robertson muttered. 'In all my years spent here – what has happened to cause Mr. Gibbings these injuries?'

'I tried to explain that Mr. Llewellyn was no longer sane,' Veronica said, revealing the circumstances with thinly disguised bitterness providing an edge to her voice. 'What you treat now is a result of that fact.'

Veronica moved alongside Robertson, laid a hand on Gibbings' brow, felt the heat –

'Will he recover Reverend?'

'I pray that he will. He has lost much blood.' Robertson placed the towel tightly against the wound. 'But it is to the doctor that you should address such questions...'

Robertson paused. He looked Veronica directly in the eye. 'Where is Mr. Llewellyn now?'

'Oh my God!' Veronica felt a wave of anxiety rush through her stomach. 'I was concerned for John, I have not thought to search – and the blade remains in the grass. I must remove it...'

'No Miss Day...' Robertson grabbed her arm, 'that would not be appropriate in the light of what has happened here.'

'Damn what is appropriate, if Llewellyn has gone this far, if he is able, he will not hesitate to strike out again – we may all be in danger.'

Veronica shrugged Robertson off, rushed to the door, ran down the field, through the heather to the area where she'd found Gibbings. Blood marked the spot but that was all.

The blade had gone, Llewellyn must have retrieved it, and to have done so he must be in sufficient health as to use it.

Through squalls of rain she looked left and right, forward and behind, to no avail. She cursed herself for not considering the danger, but her concern for John had outweighed everything – now as she trudged back up the field, stopping at intervals to search around, she was filled with a mounting unease – that they could become besieged by a madman with a violent weapon in his grasp.

She reached the deserted street and ran to the door. Further down on the opposite side Dawson's body lay unmoved. He was, she was quite certain, dead. He at least, they did not need to worry about.

***

Llewellyn examined the sabre; Gibbings' blood had been washed off by the rain – much to his satisfaction. He had an abhorrence of the sight of it – it was the reason he'd fled the scene.

But he'd dealt with Gibbings in the way he'd intended. The wretched man had been foolish enough to attempt to wrestle the sabre from him, but one swift blow from its sharp blade must surely have severed an artery, by now he would be dead.

No more would he poison Veronica's precious mind –

And yet he'd watched in shock and disgust as Veronica had hurried to the scene, with Rothman in her wake – that had been a surprise, but nothing like the disturbing experience of watching her caringly cradle the dying man in her arms and carry him to the vicarage.

He'd carried out his actions for Veronica, to enable her to become free of Gibbings' venomous influence, and yet it seemed that even in his death that influence remained; she was his world but could no longer be so with his poisoning mind inside hers. And to carry him that far she must possess the strength of the Devil.

He'd acted too late – there was no other course of action than to terminate Veronica also.

At least in her death she would be free.

Llewellyn emerged from behind the chapel and made his way uphill.

***

'I have done all I can for the time being, he continues to bleed but not as profusely. The doctor should be with us shortly. I take it there was no sign of Mr. Llewellyn?'

'Nor the blade – I fear he is not finished yet...'

Robertson shot Veronica a look of alarm. 'Then are we to remain prisoners here?'

'I will not be subjected to the whims of a madman.'

'I beg your pardon, Miss Day?'

'It is against my nature to be cornered like a wild animal.'

'I must advise Miss Day, against any talk of this nature,' Robertson stammered. 'You have witnessed the extent of Mr. Gibbings' injuries caused by Mr. Llewellyn's use of the blade. It would be foolhardy in the extreme ; besides there has been enough bloodshed on this island…'

'Which might have been prevented had you listened to me in the first instance. Now it is past the point where I am prepared to concede to this man.'

Robertson shook his head despairingly, before a drone a pitch lower than the howling wind drew his attention.

He marched through to his front lounge and peered out the window. 'Your friend is back and he has the doctor with him.'

Veronica ushered them in, she watched the doctor clean and tend the wound, was relieved when he stood up and said, 'Your friend needs rest, it is a matter of shock as much as the severity of the wound itself. But he should be fine.'

The doctor adjusted his collar and tie, frowned. 'I understand there is a dangerous man at large, the nature of this wound confirms as much. I shall of course notify the constabulary upon my return to the mainland. In the meantime I urge you all to exercise extreme caution. Circumstances such as these, have, to my knowledge, never arisen here before.'

'There is a man lying in the grass by the cottages,' Veronica said bluntly. 'I fear he is dead.'

'That is so,' Rothman cut in, a glance at the doctor. 'I advised Doctor Ferguson and he examined the scoundrel on the way through.'

'Veronica,' Rothman uttered as soon as the doctor had departed, 'I feel you should allow me to drive you from the island. This is not a safe place…'

'I shall leave the island when John does and not before,' Veronica said adamantly. 'Doctor Ferguson says he needs a rest. I will ensure he gets it.'

'He is welcome to rest here at the vicarage until he is well enough to travel, as are you, Miss Day,' Robertson announced, albeit edgily.

'That is most generous of you vicar,' Veronica acknowledged, aware of the unease in his voice. 'I am sure we will not trouble you for long.'

Veronica cast her eyes down, took in Gibbings' appearance as he lay motionless on the bed. He was sleeping but his breathing appeared less shallow and this gave her heart.

'Veronica, if I might speak with you as a matter of urgency,' Rothman whispered in her ear. 'Alone.'

'Be my guest,' Robertson said, having overheard. 'The front parlour,' he indicated, his arm outstretched, his brow knotted.

'Mr. Rothman, please be brief.' Veronica closed the door behind them. 'I would want to be beside John when he awakes.'

'I cannot understand your fascination for the gardener, Veronica, any more than I could Llewellyn, but though I feel your lack of passion for him was evident, it seems the same cannot be said of this Gibbings fellow. You are aware that a fusion of such diverse backgrounds seldom works?'

'I fear that it is seldom given a chance.' Veronica turned her back, crossed to the window and arms folded, stared out at a deserted, stormy scene, no sign at the moment of the mad Llewellyn. 'I for one am not an enthusiast of this rigid class structure, if that offends you Mr. Rothman then I am sorry but it is the way I am.' She swung to face him. 'Now, have you anything further to say?'

'Indeed dear lady.' Rothman approached her, leaning forward, his face close to hers. 'Your values are most commendable, but your philosophy is flawed. I can much better serve your interests than the gardener. Together we would make a fine couple.' He gazed at her head, touched it with the palm of a hand. 'Why, even our hair seems to match up. I would be honoured Veronica, to have you as my wife.'

Veronica bit her lower lip, edged past him. 'I feel that it is not possible, Mr. Rothman, indeed, it seems there is little more between us than the colour of our hair. What has brought you back is your vision of me, is it not? And since you cannot know me that vision is only skin deep.'

Rothman spread his hands. 'I returned out of concern for you and it seems such concerns have proved well founded. In any event, would you not concede that your perception of the gardener is similar to mine of you?'

Veronica swallowed, met his stare. 'I believe there is a difference Mr. Rothman, if there is nothing more, I must attend John…'

'I implore you to reconsider.' Rothman followed her to the door. 'There is no future in this relationship.'

'That is for me to decide.' Veronica paused, her hand on the lever. 'I would thank you to remember as much.'

'Then at least allow me to remain lest my assistance is required; by remaining here you put yourself at great risk – Llewellyn has already accounted for his sister, along with seriously injuring the…'

'Dorothea?' Veronica interrupted, her brows knit tightly together.

Rothman lowered his eyes. 'I took her body from the sea, laid it on the shore. I am certain it was his work…'

'I see.' Veronica shook her head. 'I cannot prevent you from remaining here, Mr. Rothman. I must attend John.'

She hurried through to the rear of the vicarage, sat at the side of Gibbings' bed, aware of Rothman's presence in the doorway. Gibbings' eyes flickered open momentarily and her spirits rose, though his return to consciousness was fleeting and those spirits were dashed with the suddenness of a ship striking rocks.

Despair was creeping through her veins; Llewellyn was no longer sane if ever he had been. And what had been *her* part in this? He'd seemed fully in control of his senses when they'd first met, quite an honourable gentleman. Had she encouraged him for her own ends, to a point where his sanity had been challenged? Was she in some way to blame? Not solely for his demise but for the ensuing violence on the island? Had the problems on the island been of her making as the vicar had seemed to imply?

If so it was her duty to confront Llewellyn, thus averting more bloodshed.

Chapter Thirty Seven

Her sense of responsibility, for so long overlooked, could no longer be denied. She would seek out Llewellyn, go to him. The burden was hers, and by bearing it she would help John.

It was the only course of action.

Llewellyn had watched the doctor enter and he'd seen him depart; he'd watched from a distance as he'd examined Dawson's lifeless body. He'd seen the shake of the head which told it all.

So Dawson was dead; he was alone – but that was the only way. Only he could drive the Devil from Veronica – and there was but one way of doing it –

And he didn't have to wait long; he was elated about that. Because all of a sudden he saw her emerging from the vicarage, her lovely red hair blown in fine wisps around her neck and face.

He couldn't believe it would be that simple – she had delivered herself to him. His eyes met hers and his mind struggled to focus, yet she wasn't wearing her sweet smile as she walked towards him, directly into his path.

His grip on the sabre tightened, the handle fitting like a glove in his hand –

The blade so silver and pure –

And then she spoke. He cocked his head; he hadn't expected that, for no words seemed necessary.

***

'Put the saber down, Thomas; you no longer have use for it.'

Llewellyn raised the curved tip to the bridge of his nose and seemed to gaze upon it lovingly, angling his head from side to side. 'I do Veronica, for it has not yet finished its good work.'

'And what work is that, Thomas?' Veronica continued her walk towards him, her voice cutting through the wind. 'You think I am the "target" for that good work do you not; the voice of reason has deserted you?'

'You have been harmed by the gardener, irreparably I fear. Though your soul will rest in peace, unlike the wretched man who has so tainted you.'

'You cannot hold anything against John Gibbings.' Veronica kept her eyes steady, aware of Llewellyn's hands leveling the blade. 'I alone am responsible for my actions. There has been no misguiding force, no unholy influence Thomas. If anyone deserves your wrath it is me.'

The sabre began to shake in Llewellyn's hands, he was close enough now should he suddenly surge forward, to pierce her stomach.

'Veronica my dear, you were as pure as newly laid snow – until he contaminated your mind with impure thoughts. Sadly there is little more to say, no further use for words.'

So little time to decide what to do; she could tackle him for the sabre but one thrust would put an end not only to her but John also –

She clasped her hands together, held them out. 'It is not too late, Thomas – I have seen the folly of my ways, and shall return with you to the castle; forgive me, Thomas, and toss that thing aside.'

Llewellyn trembled, rain glistened on his face and his eyes fell on the blade. 'Even were I to do that, the accursed gardener would remain.'

'I have told you, Thomas,' Veronica said taking a step forward, 'it is not the gardener who is responsible. It is me. You are not well, Thomas, let me look after you – let John Gibbings be, you have almost killed him as it is; if you pursue your course there will be nothing left.'

'You would return to the castle with me and become my bride?' his eyes swelled, their whites bright against the smoky sky.

Veronica gave silent assent, forcing her eyes to meet his.

'Then I will get the vicar, he will marry us now…'

Veronica shook her head despairingly. 'Thomas, this is hardly an appropriate time…'

'Veronica!' She heard the call from behind, it made her breath catch in her throat. 'Stay away from him – I beg you, he will kill you!'

'No - no he won't.' *Damn!* Veronica kept her eyes on Llewellyn, his face had so little movement and colour it might have been plaster, but it had exuded a kind of doughy pleasure and she'd thought she'd managed to pacify him.

Now the stony look of non-comprehension was back in his eyes as he stared past her towards the onrushing Rothman.

'Byron! No! Stop!' Veronica held out an arm, refusing to yield ground, it might have been the unaccustomed use of his first name, but nonetheless it brought Rothman to a halt.

'What is *he* doing here?' Llewellyn hissed through his half-open mouth.

'He came back to help,' Veronica said quickly, the barest of backward glances at Rothman.

Waving down Rothman and now within striking distance of his blade, Veronica said to Llewellyn, 'I must speak to Mr. Rothman alone – he needs to understand…'

'Understand, Veronica?'

'That you need taking care of,' she said resolutely, 'and that it is my desire to see to it.'

'Veronica…' Rothman protested, 'what kind of lunacy is this?'

'Please, Thomas, one moment and I shall return.'

'And together we return to the castle?'

Veronica hung her head, 'Yes.'

'Very well, one moment.' But Llewellyn's grasp on the sabre was as intense as ever as he stood hunched, rainwater and froth oozing from his mouth.

Veronica hurried Rothman to the vicarage entrance, ushered him inside and closed the door as Llewellyn's dark shape hovered outside.

'You cannot contemplate going with him; you will not return…'

Veronica sighed, placed her hands on Rothman's shoulders. 'He is quite insane, but at least I have pacified him and he will do me no harm. You have come this far, do not ensure further bloodshed now, I implore you. Stay with John, look after him.'

'Just a short time ago, that was what *you* were intent on doing.'

'Just a short while perhaps, but the situation has changed and I see things from a different angle. I feel now, I have no other course of action than to accompany him.' Veronica removed her hands from his shoulders and turned to go, her head down. Rothman grabbed her arm but she shrugged him off, not bearing to take one more look at John, not bearing to think about what the future held.

***

Llewellyn kissed the blade as Veronica returned slowly towards him; his dream had been reborn, like a phoenix rising from its ashes. His beloved Veronica was coming back to him, but she needed protecting from the evils that surrounded her. Nothing would touch them in their castle stronghold and were it ever to try, then his trusted weapon would deliver the ultimate response. He swung the sabre from right to left, felt it cutting through the wind and saw Veronica flinch.

'Veronica, I did not mean…'

'Thomas,' Veronica drew in as much air as she could, breathed out only slowly, 'please drop that awful thing.'

'I cannot trust the forces that surround you, my dear; it is for your protection that I carry it.' Llewellyn kissed the blade. 'It will prove our staunchest ally, should they dare besiege us.'

And yet a few short moments ago you would have killed me with it.

'Then at least hold it at a distance from me.' Veronica Day closed her eyes, returning to the castle with this man's final remnants of sanity disintegrating before her very eyes would be like entering the jaws of hell.

But how great had her contribution been to this great character metamorphosis? Should it be her fate now to endure life in the castle with a man devoid of all rationality?

But she had thwarted the bloodbath; John would be safe. That was her achievement and also her main concern. For soon the policemen must surely arrive – her despondency lay in the fact that she hadn't provided John with the ending she'd so desired, she'd failed him – but in so doing she'd failed Llewellyn also, because he'd trusted her and that trust she'd known from the start could never have been returned –

'Why, Thomas, you are shivering.' Veronica touched his free hand. 'It is only the rain that brings the chill; we shall soon be in the warm.'

She felt his hand clamp around her wrist with all the strength of someone without sanity, closed her eyes to the rain, and her mind to painful thought.

Chapter Thirty Eight

'Where is this place - what's happened?' Gibbings flicked his eyes open, searched around the room as he tried to raise himself and found the red-headed man standing over him; there was a pain in his neck that seared through his upper body.

'Lay still,' the man standing over him insisted. 'You need rest.'

Gibbings closed his eyes momentarily as a growing awareness overcame him. 'Veronica,' he murmured, and then louder with more coherence, 'where is she? Is she safe?'

His scrambled senses had recovered sufficiently for him to be able to read Rothman's expression. 'What's happened to her, for God's sake?'

Rothman's lips remained tight, Gibbings struggled to raise his back against the iron bedstead, 'She's not…'

'She went with Llewellyn,' Rothman said tiredly, biting his lip, wiping a smear of blood and seeing Gibbings' look of horror he added, 'there was little I could do. It was her choice – and Llewellyn was brandishing the sabre…'

'Saber? So she's in the hands of the mad man and we sit here like useless gnomes – he's going to…' Gibbings struggled to leave the bed and the sound of straining strings brought Robertson from his study. 'I hardly think you should be exerting yourself, Mr. Gibbings, the doctor has said …'

'Damn what the doctor said, we just can't stand by…' Gibbings narrowed his eyes, stared at Rothman. 'What are you doing here anyway – I thought you'd…'

'I came back –' Rothman interrupted moodily. 'Veronica has asked that I watch over you and that is what I intend to do.'

'Just who's looking after her?'

'It certainly cannot be you; you are in no fit condition.'

'Then why have you failed her? Why have you returned?'

'Enough of this talk.' Robertson pushed Rothman aside, adjusting Gibbings' pillows. 'Lie down please; this is not serving Miss Day's interests. The policemen will soon be here, the matter is best left in their hands.'

Rothman left the room, irritated beyond measure, what right did a mere gardener have to question him? He hadn't foreseen Veronica doing this, had been appalled by what she'd done, but was powerless to prevent it.

Rothman tapped his fingers impatiently on the window ledge, Robertson of course was right. This sorry business was best left in the hands of the police, no matter how much the gardener might lay blame at his door. The problem was, the longer it took them, the greater Veronica's plight. Through the wind and rain that rattled the panes, the sound of wheels and trotting horses broke the air and Rothman's spirits rose just a little.

***

Veronica felt Llewellyn's free hand clasp hers, fought back the agony of it and tried to keep her mind from contemplating an awful future inside the castle's bleak walls. But her time inside it must surely be short, the policemen would come to arrest Llewellyn and how would the prospect affect her conscience?

Still, in the midst of her plight she struggled, she struggled with it…

'My life is complete my love. I have you and the castle and together we will enjoy our lives as one…'

'Yes, Thomas.' Veronica looked into Llewellyn's unseeing eyes, turned her head away; they were heading along the coastal path towards the castle, and she watched the angry waves driving onto shore.

Llewellyn had no grip on reality – every single strand had gone, as if swept away by the storm.

He was still talking, his voice high-pitched in its attempt to rise above the wind, but she wasn't listening. She'd trained her thoughts on John Gibbings and whether she'd ever see him again. The castle was a fortress, there was no easy way to gain entry if that entry was denied – and denied it would be. There was little point in deluding herself.

Approaching the castle slope Veronica took a look back but the panoramic coastline was deserted, save for the gulls and turnstones, and something lying on the shoreline. Veronica narrowed her eyes, unable to determine what it was.

Llewellyn's features were enveloped in a rigid smile as his unmoving, unblinking eyes stared up at the castle shrouded in an unnatural afternoon darkness. It was a darkness that seeped through Veronica's bones, bearing down, inevitably entombing her mind, forcing her towards Llewellyn's plane.

Soon to be beyond help, but it was of her making.

Thomas, allow me to walk out of this misery - set my conscience free, that I might rejoin John...

But she knew there was little point in her plea progressing any further than her own mind. Llewellyn wasn't about to listen to anyone or anything. And then, close to shore, at the foot of the castle approach, a sight that made her want to shield her eyes, though she couldn't – she gazed down anyway at the lifeless form of Dorothea, spread-eagled on the ground, dark curly hair tousled across her face, arms askew, eyes wide and unseeing staring upwards into the blanketed grey skies.

'Thomas.' Veronica grabbed at his arm. 'Oh Thomas, we cannot leave her there – whatever has happened, we cannot leave her like that...'

'I will arrange for her disposal my dear. Do not distress yourself, I implore you.' Llewellyn sniffed, raised his head towards the castle slope, raised his arms and spread them out. 'Ah, our castle, our wonderful haven awaits.'

Veronica bit back tears; entering the castle hall now, the draught seemed colder than she could recall.

***

'Officer, the man is mad, completely mad, and Veronica is at his mercy. You must act soon before she is...'

'One thing at a time, Mr. Rothman.' The lean-faced Sergeant Taylor fixed Rothman a severe stare. 'There is a man lying dead in the street.' Taylor drew up a chair, clasped his hands together, 'You have not fully explained your part in this.'

'The thug of a butler had his hands on Veronica. Good God man, the madman's henchman would have killed her. And as for Llewellyn, he is probably in his castle now, as mad as a hatter, with Veronica in peril.'

Taylor fingered his chin. 'Mr. Gibbings has no recollection of what might have transpired to cause the man's unfortunate demise. The Reverend Robertson saw nothing, in essence there is little hard evidence to substantiate your claim - and are you seriously expecting me to believe Miss Day simply "walked" into Mr. Llewellyn's arms?'

Rothman placed his hands on Taylor's chair. 'I do not know what possessed her to act in this manner, only that she is in danger, and that by delaying and asking pointless questions you are placing Veronica in even greater danger.'

Taylor got to his feet, adjusted his tie and frowned. 'Very well Mr. Rothman,' he said turning to his three officers standing in the hall, 'but you are to remain in our custody until this unfortunate business is concluded.'

'I am more than willing to accompany you to the castle if it means helping to ensure Veronica's freedom.'

'I said nothing about any such accompaniment,' Taylor said, beckoning his officers and striding to the door. 'Nonetheless it is probably the simplest option.'

Gibbings heard the slam of the vicarage door, puzzled for a moment at the silence that hung over the place and realising what had occurred, struggled from his bed.

***

Llewellyn locked and bolted the castle door, his back turned towards her, the sabre tight in his hand; it was a chance she knew. She had strength, perhaps enough to fight her way out, and with it an element of surprise, and yet his insane mind might relish the contact, might actually be inviting it, and his frenzied reaction could then lead to tragic consequences either for her or for him –

And it had been her choice to accompany him, born of the guilt that his affliction might in some way be attributable to her –

Shivering from the draught she turned, stepped away, abandoning any thought of confrontation.

Llewellyn spun round. 'There my dear.' He clutched the key in his fist and then slipped it into his pocket. 'We are safe within our fortress and nothing can harm us here.'

'Then you can put the weapon down, Thomas. It is making me nervous, and then perhaps you can light some fires. It is a little cold in here.'

'Yes, yes, I should put the sabre down.' He stared at the curved blade with glazed eyes before returning his unseeing stare to her. 'And I will instruct Hambleton to prepare the fire…'

Veronica grimaced. 'Thomas, Hambleton is no longer the butler; I fear there is nobody in this place but us.'

'Nobody?' Llewellyn's eyebrows arched as he spun round bewildered, looked aimlessly around and then swung back clutching his forehead. 'Mrs. Simms…'

Veronica shook her head. 'Mrs. Simms left when Mr. Hambleton resigned.'

Llewellyn blinked in rapid succession. 'There was another fellow – oh yes, Dawson…'

'Dawson is…' Veronica checked herself. 'Dawson is not here either – there is only ourselves, as indeed you wished it to be, now please put that awful thing down and light the fires.'

But Veronica needed only look into the unresponsive eyes to know there would be no fires lit, no food cooked or served, and neither would he relinquish his hold on the sabre –

Llewellyn had his dream, but that was all it was. He was now faced with the bare bones of reality.

Chapter Thirty Nine

'Can't you drive any faster, man?' Rothman glared at the driver of the carriage from his seat in the rear, receiving a stony glance in response.

'The track is rough on the horses' hooves. Have some concern for the animal man.'

Rothman leaned forward, his face flushed. 'Do not address me in that tone of voice; I shall most certainly speak with your superior.'

'You might find yourself doing that in any event,' Taylor remarked brusquely. 'You are a detained man – a man under suspicion,' and then looking away and folding his arms, 'you would do well to remember that.'

Rothman was speechless with indignation but there was little point in further conversation with the abrasive little man. Ahead the castle seemed to rear up through the unabating rain. It appeared foreboding, impregnable on its high mound of rock, and Rothman stiffened.

But something else also lay ahead – to their right – he saw Taylor frown, saw him lift an arm. 'Stop the carriage,' he barked, leaping out before it had been reined to a halt; running across to Dorothea's body he crouched over it, turning sharply to Rothman. 'She was swept in on the tide,' Rothman shouted above the wind. 'I pulled her clear; alas it was too late…'

Taylor got to his feet and closed up on Rothman. 'Why wasn't I informed of this?'

'I was more concerned with Miss Day's welfare, as I am now; this wretched woman is already dead.' Rothman turned and jabbed an arm wildly at the castle. 'And if we are not swift, Miss Day might suffer a similar fate.'

'Are you saying?' But Taylor dropped his words and marched ahead perhaps spurred on by Rothman's angry gesture. Rothman caught up, matched him stride for stride. The sergeant and his men seemed incompetent, probably not used to dealing with anything other than the odd pick-pocket.

And this was a whole different proposition.

***

'Let us sit together in our cosy castle, Veronica.' Llewellyn stretched a hand towards the couch. 'You have returned to me – to your rightful place and all is well.'

Veronica tensed but remained standing. She looked down on

Llewellyn as he sat, hunched forward, still with the sabre in his grasp. 'It would be better if you would provide some of the basic comforts, for example heat and food if you could manage it. If we are to live in the castle for any length of time we will need provisions.'

Veronica raised her head to the ceiling, sighed; his facial indifference said it all.

The sheer absurdity of her position, her feeling of guilt that she was in some way to blame was as preposterous as her action in deserting Thomas – in marching out into the wilderness and taking the hand of a man who obviously suffered the same personality disorder as his sister.

A stout rapping on the castle's solid oak door, its volume increasing as it echoed through the castle, had Llewellyn springing to his feet, his head turning so sharply it seemed his neck would snap. He jerked it back again, looking lop-sided at her, as if trying to assess the situation but incapable of doing it.

'I will answer the door, Thomas.' Veronica had reached the hall, aware of the sudden hustle of Llewellyn's feet behind; he was alongside her in an instant, his pupils darting from side to side, almost protruding from their sockets in the dim light highlighted by the whites of his eyes.

'You cannot do that Veronica, I cannot allow it.' Llewellyn used his free hand to clasp hers, dragging her with him towards the small window overlooking the entrance. He grimaced as his thigh struck the monk's bench and for a moment his hold on her was broken as he clutched his leg, retaining the sabre by the tiniest thread of his index fingers.

She seized her chance, pushed him aside, causing him to lose balance completely, and then kicking the sabre beyond his reach ran towards the door. It unbolted readily enough and she heard shouting and hammering outside, and through it all, Rothman's cultured tones strained with urgency. But the door was thick and the voices muffled, and hope and expectation turned to despair as pulling at the handle she realised that Llewellyn still retained the keys.

Llewellyn rose to his feet, his face contorted, his brow furrowed, the dark eyes incensed.

'You would try to trick me – your intended?' He rushed headlong towards her, almost tripping over the sabre in his blind anger. 'You will pay for your treachery…'

Veronica had no time to think. He was upon her, striking her below the throat, the impact sending her reeling against the door. She felt the sharp pain in her back and bit her lip, but as he prepared to strike again she kicked out at his injured thigh, stopping his advance abruptly. She grabbed his injured arm, swung him round and then calling on all her strength hurled him across the hall's flagstone floor where he lay on his back.

It was at that moment Veronica knew she was stronger than him, even in his deranged state, she could force a conclusion and quickly.

She walked forward and looking down upon him held out her hand. 'Thomas, give me the key or I will take it myself.'

Suddenly with a madman's agility Llewellyn sprung up, stumbled away across the hall, forced the Gothic window open and then turned, facing Veronica, his face bitter and twisted. 'My dear Veronica, you have the strength of a demon and that is what you are – my vision has been clouded by your spell. Your beauty is no more than a mask.'

Without looking over his shoulder Llewellyn tossed the key through the opening. 'This castle will become our tomb.'

Veronica strode to the window, looked down towards the volcanic mound to the rear, saw the key glistening in a fleeting moment of sunlight, and sighed. 'You are merely postponing the inevitable Thomas; you cannot contain me here indefinitely. If the policemen do not force a way in I will find a way out. You cannot stop me.'

'Oh but I can…'

Veronica turned, alerted by the gravity in his unnaturally low voice, and winced as the sabre flashed, slashing deep into her calf. She felt a warm, sickly pain.

Slipping to the ground, she felt the weight of Llewellyn's boot on her back. 'You will have the slow, tortuous death you deserve.

'Every quarter of the hour I will slash one of your limbs my precious, until I reach your divine hands.' And then holding the quivering sabre against her neck he added, 'and ultimately your throat.'

Chapter Forty

'What was that? I thought I heard a cry.' Rothman turned in alarm to the trio of policemen repeatedly ramming the door. 'It's no use, we'll never break through this without some kind of ram, we must find another way...'

Taylor looked grim. 'We would need to travel to Berwick for that kind of equipment. I very much doubt we could obtain the equipment before the tide returns across the causeway.'

'Then we have no alternative, we must find a way in.'

Taylor pushed a hand across his chin, surveyed the castle frontage and shook his head. 'The place looks impregnable, what on earth has befallen this island?'

Rothman was in no mood to dwell on such melancholy considerations. 'If nobody else will, I shall scour the surrounds for another method of entry.'

Taylor turned to him. 'I remind you that you are a detained man.'

'There is a life at stake sergeant.'

'Perhaps even two.' Taylor grunted and turned to his two colleagues. 'Search the exterior thoroughly; we need to force entry quickly.'

But nothing in Taylor's expression could convince Rothman of the effectiveness of his words.

***

John Gibbings could stand the tension no longer. The pain in his neck and upper body seared but was nothing like the concern he felt for Veronica. He was bare from the waist up, save for the bandaging applied by the doctor. His coat had been placed on the rack in the hall and that was all he took now as protection from the fierce elements as unnoticed by Robertson he slipped out of the rectory.

Veronica had walked away with the madman, in doing so she had been saving him and he had been lying there when every crevice of his mind screamed out that she was in mortal danger.

No longer though; no longer.

By the time Robertson had realised what had transpired Gibbings was halfway towards the castle. Taylor's carriage was visible at the foot of the castle approach, the pony seeming restless in the storm. How stupid he'd been, if he hadn't been so stubborn all of this could have been averted – the bloodshed, the peril that Veronica was in – but she was of a different breed, like the man with the red hair – Rothman, was his name – in truth they were made for each other.

But at least he had the chance to put things right.

The figures around the castle entrance were more definable now, high up on the slope, scurrying back and forth to no avail, while one hammered on the door.

Didn't they realise that from their position the castle was impenetrable – that only if the madman allowed them access would they ever get in.

And what were the chances of that?

None at all.

If there was any chance it would be at the rear, where the Gothic windows looked out across the gardens, closer to the ground. The rock that formed the castle's foundations could be scaled with difficulty, but once having done that there was a small chance he might be able to force entry.

Ignoring the policemen and the one he recognised as Rothman, Gibbings diverted from the path, cutting across fields at the rear of the volcanic mound.

The climb was wet and slippery; the rock fragmented and interspersed with clumps of green moss made ascent all the more hazardous. The rain fell intermittently now, but in squalls, the strength of the wind threatening his stability.

The pain in his chest as sharp as the blade that had pierced it, Gibbings edged across the rocky castle base until he was beneath a dining room window, and only then did he realise the futility of his task: the narrowness of the windows reinforced by the thick central strut running down its centre ruled out any chance of his breaking in.

Despairingly Gibbings glanced at the ground, his eyes falling upon a silver object laying on the wet rock. He examined it between his fingers, his pulse quickening as awareness dawned.

Llewellyn whirled as the trio burst in, his flailing sabre catching Taylor's arm. Taylor let out a yell as Gibbings surged past him, driving his fist into the pit of Llewellyn's stomach, and as Llewellyn doubled up, snatched the weapon from his hand.

Gibbings glanced as Rothman pushed past, rushing to Veronica's aid, clutching the wound. 'My darling your leg, let me tend it.' Rothman threw off his trench coat, ripped the sleeve from his shirt and bent down to her.

Veronica shook her head, groaned. 'No, help John,' but Rothman appeared not to have heard, wrapping the cloth tightly around her leg while the scuffle continued behind them.

'That should stem the flow, darling, I feel the wound is not as severe as it seemed...'

'Yes, yes – now please go and help John.' Veronica pushed forward, struggled against him as Rothman seemed unwilling to remove her leg from his grasp, stemming any resistance she could offer.

With Taylor reeling in agony, Gibbings felt the wrath of Llewellyn's insane anger. A wild forearm caught him on the chin, knocking him sideways as Llewellyn seized the chance to retrieve the sabre from the floor.

Gibbings began to fall, colliding with a stone column, saw the sabre rise in Llewellyn's frenzied hands and, as the madman closed in, expected at any moment the fatal strike.

But just as it seemed that strike would come, Llewellyn wheeled away in the direction of Veronica and the attentive Rothman.

Veronica saw him coming, thrust herself up, found the strength this time to wrench free from Rothman's grasp and as Llewellyn plunged towards them lashed out with the leg Rothman had been attending. The kick was powerful, catching Llewellyn below the groin. Recovering, Gibbings seized his chance, diving forward and grasping Llewellyn's thigh.

The madman lost his balance, was drawn backward into Gibbings' hold, falling heavily, his skull thumping into the flagstone floor. He managed to raise his head, but was restrained by two of Taylor's officers from regaining his footing.

Veronica sighed, finally her ordeal was over. She glanced into Gibbings' eyes and as he rose to his feet, saw him meet her gaze for an instant before casting his own eyes down, draw a deep breath and turn away towards the groaning Taylor.

Rothman's arms were around her, helping her up, his expression full of concern – but it wasn't his concern that she wanted – longed for.

***

'Ghastly business,' Taylor muttered, then staring at Llewellyn, 'stay with this man until I can arrange his removal.' Looking to the others he added, 'With the exception of Mr. Rothman you are free to leave the castle, but I must request you all remain on the island until this unfortunate business is concluded. Mr. Gibbings, I thank you for your contribution, even if it was somewhat foolhardy; I will transport you to the rectory, the vicar will no doubt be anxious as to your welfare.'

'I'll be all right.' Gibbings turned away. 'I need no further attention.' With a brief glance over his shoulder he headed for the door.

'John wait,' Veronica called after him as Rothman placed two restraining hands on her arms.

'Please don't exert yourself my dear. You must come with me and lie down.'

'I will *not* lie down –John...' she called over Rothman's shoulder, 'where are you going – wait.' She glared at Rothman. 'Let me go!'

'He is not for the likes of you Veronica, please...'

'Do as she says, let her go,' Taylor said sternly, walking towards him. 'You are not currently a free man. I need to speak with you on the subject of the dead man in the main street, and of the body on the shore. Please desist in restraining Miss Day.'

Rothman yielded reluctantly and Veronica met Taylor's eyes briefly before hurrying after Gibbings. 'John I said wait!'

Gibbings had begun descending the slope, he took a step further and then half turned, halting on the cobbles. 'If that's an order, Miss Veronica.'

'Oh John, please don't revert to that nonsense.' Veronica placed a hand on the drawbridge framework, steadying herself.

Gibbings looked at her bandaged leg and the blood slowly seeping through the makeshift bandaging. 'You shouldn't be out here, not with your leg like that, you need rest.'

'My leg will be fine John. I will be fine thanks to you.' She drew breath, forced herself away from the support, took his hand, searched his eyes. 'What is it John, what's wrong?'

Gibbings shrugged. 'It won't work Veronica, it isn't right.'

Veronica squeezed his hand. 'Is that what you think John? Before this happened you were ready to leave the island with me – what's happened to change things? And it doesn't involve Llewellyn and this damned place. Don't you try to tell me that.'

Gibbings' eyes finally met hers, with a dark severity. 'I belong here, you belong – oh to hell!' Gibbings struck the wall with his balled fist in a rare display of anger. 'I don't know where you belong, but it isn't here with the likes of me – nice fine places with nice fine people…'

Veronica clenched her teeth, so tightly a sharp pain seared the veins of her neck. 'You haven't listened to a word I've been saying these last few days.' Her anger disturbed her sense of balance as a violent gust of wind took her sideways, her shoulder striking the drawbridge surround; her leg, complaining from the impact, began to buckle beneath her.

She was aware of Gibbings' sudden movement and his facial agony as he took her in his arms and carried her inside the castle hall, laying her gently down on the chaise-longue.

Gibbings paid scant attention to the others as he left the hall and Veronica covered her eyes; it hadn't been the pain caused by her collision with the wall that caused her reaction but the thought that she might never see him again.

Again he'd come to her aid, once more she'd been unable to bridge the gap that continually seemed to separate them –

'My darling, I said you needed rest.' Rothman was at her side, kneeling over her, taking her hand. 'Now you can appreciate the wisdom of my words. Rest my love for you are in dire need of it.'

'I am in need of only one thing.' But Veronica's lips were stiffening and her words fading as she lapsed into unwanted sleep.

Chapter Forty One

Hambleton's head ached; he'd come to on the bed where the landlord had managed to lay him, and then as his memory slowly, tortuously pieced together events of the past few hours, he'd dragged himself up, waving aside the landlord's protestations and hurried across the square where he'd encountered a distraught Robertson.

'I fear something dreadful has happened, Reverend.' Hambleton paused, took in Robertson's ashen appearance. 'I can see that it has – what is it, man?'

Robertson buried his face in his hands for an instant, shook it forlornly. 'Never since the Saxons pillaged could this island have encountered such violence…'

'Never mind that man – Miss Day – there was a madman in pursuit of her…'

'That madman is no more.' Robertson turned sideways, pointed along the street indicating Dawson's body. 'But there is more than one madman here.'

Hambleton realised at once. 'Llewellyn – what has he done to her?'

The Reverend raised his head to the leaden sky, sighed. 'She went with him willingly – Llewellyn had a sabre, used it on Gibbings.'

'You say – willingly?'

Robertson nodded. 'I believe to protect Gibbings. Gibbings received a nasty gash to his chest. He was resting in the vicarage but while my back was turned I fear he took off in pursuit.'

'Then I must hasten.'

'There are policemen in attendance. You should leave it to them.'

'No, I cannot. I feel a part of this unfortunate affair.'

Hambleton turned away, bowed his head into the wind and proceeded towards the castle.

***

Llewellyn had been bound to a chair. Robbed of his weapon he looked a withered sight, staring ahead with unfocused eyes; the dark suit he'd worn since leaving the city, askew and ragged from his encounters.

Rothman could scarcely remove his eyes from Veronica, lying on the chaise-longue, her lovely face turned upwards towards the ceiling, her splendid green eyes closed, while her red hair cascaded over the side of the couch. When he managed to raise his head he became aware of Taylor's scrutiny. You have questions to answer,

Mr. Rothman, now is as good a time as any.'

Rothman released an impatient sigh. 'If you are referring to the rogue on the main street I have little to say; the beautiful lady here was in extreme jeopardy from his thuggish hands when I struck him with the car. It was not my intention that he should die, I acted solely in Miss Veronica's interests.'

'Nevertheless it remains an act of violence, even were what you say to be true, it cannot be overlooked.' Taylor chewed his lip, turned, crossed to the window and looked down on the woman's body on the beach. 'You say you found her washed to shore…'

'She is my accursed sister.' For a moment Llewellyn's lips sprung to life, his eyes lost their glazed appearance. 'This man played no part in that – she slipped, her wretched body lay lifeless at the foot of the slope. It was I who cast her into the sea.'

'You speak of a most dangerous man, forgive me for my unannounced arrival but I felt the need to return to my former abode.' Hambleton sighed, looked at Llewellyn before gazing into Taylor's eyes, feeling him studying the crusted blood on his temple. 'Yes, Sergeant Taylor, I believe this is the work of the evil man Mr. Llewellyn employed to replace me when I tendered my resignation. I overheard your remark, Sergeant, but I have very little doubt that Mr. Rothman acted in a most noble fashion; had he not done so I believe Miss Veronica's fate would have been dire indeed.'

Llewellyn had once more seemed absent and detached, but now he directed his gaze down on the sleeping Veronica. 'I sought only the lady's protection, to cherish her and to love her…' his mouth twitching with bitterness he added, 'but I find her to be truly cursed. She deserves to be slain for she is tainted with evil…'

'I find this whole business most abhorrent.' Taylor thrust his hands in his pockets, glanced at each in turn. 'I shall need to consult my superiors. However in the light of what has been said and what I have witnessed, it seems I need to reconsider whether there has been genuine foul play in respect of the two deceased. Therefore I intend detaining nobody apart from Mr. Llewellyn. Though I would, at this stage, repeat my request for you all to remain on the island.'

'Then please consult your superiors at the earliest opportunity,' Rothman said through tight lips, thrusting a hand roughly through his rust coloured hair. 'I have no desire to remain on this wretched island any longer than necessary.' He cast his eyes down on

Veronica, 'and I am certain that Miss Day would agree. Now if you would excuse me I need some fresh air.'

But the desire for fresh air was not paramount in Rothman's mind; rather it was the need to press home to Gibbings the folly of any thought of romantic attachment with Veronica. He'd already detected that Gibbings thought she was above his station, now was the time to convince him. He'd seen the gardener trudging back towards his tiny cottage from his viewpoint in the castle hall.

***

The futility of the situation had struck Gibbings long before he'd heard the rap on his door. What future was there for them? She was an accomplished musician while he was a lowly gardener. And besides, the upheavals on the island had begun with her arrival. He wasn't a superstitious man normally but he saw it now as a portent of what might be if he were to leave with her.

And he knew he couldn't depart with her, no matter what his emotions screamed at him. The red-headed man, Rothman, had returned for her and was more suited to her standard of life than he was.

He'd never be able to accept that she'd returned to the island for him. Surely the excitement for her lay in Llewellyn before his madness overtook him and the place was plunged into chaos. Surely if not for him she would never have kept her fascination for the place.

The rapping on his door began again, more intense this time – and there he was, the man with a much greater claim to her affections than he could ever have.

'Mr. Gibbings – I come with a message for you, and also to enquire personally as to your welfare.'

But there was little true concern on the redheaded man's face as Gibbings held the door ajar, the thin smile and disinterested eyes told him that. 'I'll be okay,' Gibbings said flatly, and then, 'what message?'

Rothman gave his thin smile. 'You're a first rate chap. The lovely lady Veronica is most appreciative of your valiant efforts – might I step inside?'

Gibbings sniffed. 'I cannot offer you anything.'

'Perhaps not, but my demands are few.'

Gibbings shifted uneasily, feeling the intruder taking in the contents of the sparsely furnished room. 'So what's this message then? Pass it and then get out.' He bit his lip; bitter bile clogged his throat as he glared at the elegant figure before him.

Rothman removed his gloves and settled on a couch, its upholstery worn and crusting, his eyes locking on Gibbings with a sudden intensity. 'Miss Veronica is about to leave the island, her ordeal, thank heavens, is at an end; she sends her regards and warm wishes as to your future.' Rothman leaned forward, clasping his palms together. 'I feel it would not be in your interests to attempt to accompany her, there is little long term future in…'

'I have no intention of accompanying her.' Gibbings fought back the tide of indignation that fuelled the bile in his throat. 'You can pursue your interest in her without interference from me.' Gibbings watched Rothman colour, then rise and stiffen, before bidding him a curt good day and marching out on the return journey to the castle. So Veronica had sent Rothman to deliver her message; so much for her concern and feelings for him.

He closed the door that Rothman had left ajar and contemplated an uncertain future on the island.

Chapter Forty Two

At first Veronica saw the ceiling as a cream sky she lay beneath, a sky through which a pale sun shone blandly and then through which a familiar face appeared as if drifting down from the heavens.

Her body shuddered with shock before a reassuring hand touched gently on her shoulder and she saw the ceiling for what it was; the sun became a dimly lit chandelier and the ethereal presence transformed into the more human form of Hambleton.

'Veronica, please do not fret, you have been sleeping and the nightmare you have recently had to endure, I feel is finally over.'

Veronica curled a hand over her forehead, gazed at Hambleton, took in his concern and then craned her head. 'Llewellyn is gone?'

Hambleton nodded, stooped beside her. 'The policemen took him away; I fear he is quite mad.' In a quieter tone he added, 'I feel that you should leave the island as soon as you are able, there is nothing here for you any longer.'

Veronica held his eyes. 'I will leave when John Gibbings does and not before.'

Hambleton gave a slow shake of his head. 'I feel that will not happen my dear, you must realise that whatever affections you hold for him are wasted – there was a time I thought differently but I do so no longer. John will not leave this island; he no longer possesses the will to do so.'

Veronica pulled herself up, ignoring the pain in her leg and with arms across her chest she paced to a window overlooking distant islands. 'What future is there for him here?' she asked, her back to Hambleton. 'He will waste away, the castle will become an empty shell - and John along with it.'

'That may well be so,' Hambleton said tracing a finger along his lip, 'but there is nothing you can do; it is time for you to accept that. Resume your musical career my dear, you appear to have lost interest in it if I may say so and that is such a waste. In some ways this island is partly to blame.'

'I will second that.' The crisp tapping of Rothman's boots echoed around the hall, he glanced at Veronica before resting his gaze on Hambleton. 'You will allow us a little time in private, my man?'

Veronica unfurled her arms, turned and placed her hands on hips. 'There is nothing that cannot be said in his presence. Please stay Mr. Hambleton.'

'Very well, I did not mean to appear rude.' Rothman nodded

towards Hambleton but his apology was tempered by the edge in his voice. 'I happen to believe that Mr. Hambleton is right, that your career is suffering as this desolate place holds you in its grip; but there is little here for any of us.'

Rothman pursed his lips, it hadn't been what he'd wanted, but Veronica's refusal to dismiss Hambleton had left him with no choice. He desired Veronica Day more than any woman he'd met in his life, and he needed her out of the clutches of Gibbings. There was something in his dark, brooding, good looks that posed a threat to his intentions –

'I propose that we leave this island the moment Sergeant Taylor gives us word, I have a motor car, the finest in production; it will speed us on our way.' Glancing between them, he saw the apprehension in both. 'I implore you – common sense demands that we leave here.'

Hambleton's gaze fell to the floor but when he returned it to Rothman there was resolution in his eyes. 'You intend driving to London?'

All Rothman needed do was nod, but it was Veronica that he craved for and looking to her now his eyes expressed as much. 'And you my dear Veronica?'

He saw the slow bow of her head, not convincing but it was as much as he could hope for, and confirmation that she would be accompanying him.

***

Veronica Day felt Rothman's eyes upon her, they seemed to burn into her and follow every movement she made. 'My dear, you still appear fatigued, which is hardly surprising considering your ordeal.' He thrust forward a smooth hand. 'Would you care to join me in the parlour while we await this damned sergeant's clearance on what should be patently obvious?'

Veronica met his gaze briefly. 'No forgive me, I am rested enough, I shall take a short walk.' She glanced around at the cold stone walls and trembled. 'I no longer feel comfortable here; it is as though we are uninvited guests now that Llewellyn has been taken away. We have no right to be here no matter what…'

'But dear lady…'

'Please excuse me.'

Veronica swept through the hall at speed. Rothman's boots

resounded behind her but she paid no attention. Though her leg still burned she managed to negotiate the slope with scarcely a limp, but there was the perception of Rothman's footsteps behind, pursuing her relentlessly. She bit her lip, the pain she could deal with but Rothman's company was another matter.

'Veronica, please…' inevitably he caught up, wrapping his hand around her upper arm, 'please desist - reconsider, it is foolhardy to face the elements in your condition…'

'Mr. Rothman please!' Veronica swung round, forcibly broke his grip with her left arm. 'I will determine what is foolhardy and what is not. And as for my 'condition,' there is nothing the matter other than a minor injury to my leg. Please allow me to continue unhindered.'

She turned, walked the remainder of the slope at pace, but in a cocktail of anger and despair realised that Rothman had been undeterred by her stance. 'My lady, it is not such a minor injury, as you know full well. I tended it. I feel it my duty to accompany you on this foolish walk, particularly as the weather is so inclement.'

'I am very strong, Mr. Rothman, I can manage.'

Rothman baulked from the indignation in her eyes but with renewed bitterness she realised she wasn't going to be allowed the solitude she so desired. She heard his impatient sigh. 'You are right my dear Veronica, we are like uninvited guests in this godforsaken place, that is why I join you now.'

'Your mind runs a ragged path, Mr. Rothman; do you seriously expect me to believe that?' Veronica stopped abruptly, placed her hands on hips, she was tall enough to look him in the eye without inclining her head. 'But I ask that you follow that path rather than joining me on mine.'

'Which is to the door of the gardener, I do not understand your affections for this peasant chap.'

Veronica brushed back her windswept hair, leaned forward to him. 'As a matter of fact Mr. Rothman, I was intent on doing no such thing, and even if I had of been what right have you to belittle him?'

'He belittles you. He talks of you in terms that do not befit a lady so why should I pay him the honour of being termed a gentleman?'

Veronica swallowed and then hardened her eyes to combat the moisture which threatened to form droplets. *Because it wasn't true.* The man who had come to her aid against the maddened Llewellyn and paid the price, just couldn't do that. Her anger found its voice, the composure she prided herself on finally gave. 'You devise untruths for your own purposes Mr. Rothman. In short you tell lies.'

Rothman's features, so smooth and youthful suddenly developed twitches revealing tiny fissures. 'I will not be spoken to like that by a woman. It is an insult of the highest order.'

'Then it befits you, please leave me in peace.'

'I came from London at great haste to rescue you from the clutches of that madman Llewellyn and you treat me like this...' Rothman's mouth shaped into a bitter twist as he grabbed her shoulders.

'Mr. Rothman,' Veronica said coldly, 'I did not ask you to come, and if you do not remove your hand from my shoulder I will strike you, and if I do so I will hurt you, please do not make me...'

Rothman's temper hanging by a thread suddenly snapped as he gave an angry push, the sheer force of it sending her falling to the uneven ground behind the castle.

Veronica fell on her injured leg and a pang seared through like hot liquid; Rothman stood over her, his anger unabated as she winced with pain. She wanted to spring to her feet, to teach him a lesson, but her agony was so great that all she could do was to produce a wide-eyed defiant gesture.

For a second it seemed that the incensed Rothman, having lost all control might lash out with his foot, but from the direction of the bungalow came a shout that distracted them both, and before he'd a chance to react to the source of that shout he was struck full in the chest.

Gibbings was upon him as he fell, his fist striking first on the chin, and then landing on his nose producing an instant stream of blood.

Before he could strike again Veronica scrambled between them. 'No John – leave him.' Wrapping her arms around his waist she managed to wrestle Gibbings off. Rothman, his elegant grey suit ruffled and muddied, managed to regain his footing, pointing a trembling finger first at Gibbings and then at Veronica. 'Don't think I'll let this be,' he shouted, his chest heaving, 'the peasant here may have no money to call his own, but you will, you vixen, I'll have you know I'll sue you for every penny.'

'You can try Mr. Rothman, oh yes, you can try.' Veronica

stepped between the two men, 'But with immediate effect you'd best be on your way, unless you would like the same treatment from me. You will not be fortunate twice.'

Rothman glared, shouted some obscenity and then wheeled away, leaving Veronica and Gibbings to watch him go.

Above, the heavens opened once more, and the rain poured down.

Chapter Forty Three

Veronica Day narrowed her eyes, watched Gibbings panting and saw him lower his hands to his knees. 'Once more you hurry to my aid, I thank you. How am I going to manage without you?'

Gibbings fixed her with his brooding stare. 'You will manage well enough.'

Veronica inclined her head and watched Rothman disappear around the volcanic mound that formed the castle's base. 'However you need not have bothered, I could have fought him off.'

Gibbings looked derisively. 'From what I saw that looked bloody unlikely.'

'There is no need to swear.' Veronica brushed her windswept hair from her eyes and gazed back to him. 'I was complacent, that is all.'

Gibbings bit his lip, but it failed to stem his irritation. 'You are the most ignorant, arrogant woman I have ever met. The island will be well rid of you.'

Veronica placed her hands on hips. 'Is that what you truly think? Is that your heart speaking now, John Gibbings? Well at least there is some fire in your belly.'

'Go back to your concert halls Veronica, to your privileged existence and then this island can return to peace again.' Gibbings swung away angrily but she caught his arm and pulled him round to face her.

'You speak of ignorance and arrogance, but is that not what you display now, that you presume these things to be uppermost in my desires? You cast aside my feelings for you, my willingness to help you provide for your daughter, whose interests you hold so close.' She raised her voice above the wind that buffeted them both, 'Answer me John, is that not what you accuse me of?'

'That's enough, Veronica; this island has been besieged by madness, by violence, since your arrival here.'

'Oh, has it, indeed?' Veronica let go of his arm. It was her turn to let out a dismissive laugh. 'Are you trying so hard to find cause to refute your feelings for me?'

He was heading for the cottage but she kept pace, her voice relentless in his ear. 'Was it my fault I was shipwrecked? Was it my fault that Dorothea and Llewellyn shared an inherent madness? That this madness coincided with his obsession for me, an obsession I didn't realise until too late – or that Mr. Rothman would return pursuing his own lust?'

Veronica fought back her rising emotions. 'I want to spend my life with the man who saved it – is that ignorance – is that arrogance, answer me!' She reached across, grabbed Gibbings shirt and shook him – 'Answer me, damn you, is it?'

'I cannot leave this island Veronica, can't you see?' Gibbings' voice became hoarse. 'There is nothing for me on the mainland…'

'In effect John, you have lost your livelihood here – what else is there?'

'Perhaps nothing, but I cannot face the mainland, I have been too long separated from it. I stay.'

Veronica shivered and hugged her waist. 'Are you going to shut the door on me John, or allow me inside? I cannot bear to go back to the castle at the moment – not with that wretched man there – I shall wait until he has left.'

Gibbings turned, his hand gripping the knob. 'And yet only recently you were so reluctant to leave it that you sent that "wretched man" to deliver your farewell message.'

Veronica frowned. 'What on earth are you talking about?'

'You know full well.' But Gibbings relented, pushed the door open, and without facing her added, 'Don't tell me you didn't know he called on your behalf.' He strode into the washroom, produced a towel, 'Here, dry your hair…'

Veronica snatched at it and glared at him. 'If you mean Mr. Rothman I had no knowledge. I was too weary to be aware of anything. Do you really believe I could allow somebody else to pay my respects to you?'

Gibbings swallowed, her green eyes had a fire in them, an intensity that unsettled him. She finished toweling her hair, flung the fabric back at him. He caught it and sighed, indicated the couch, 'You can sit if you want.'

'It isn't only my hair that's wet, John Gibbings, I'll soak it through.'

Gibbings lowered his eyes. 'A lady like you should not be in such a condition, you should dry yourself fully in the washroom – I can provide fresh clothes until yours are dried out.'

'And what of you?'

'I am used to the wet. Do as I say, dry yourself. I will find you something to wear – and when your clothes are dry you will be able to leave this place for good…'

Veronica raised her brows, took steps towards him. 'Such authority, and what I ask do we do in the meantime, exchange not so pleasantries? We make a fine couple do we not? You with your gashed throat, and I with my hacked leg. And none of this would have happened if I hadn't come here – none of this disruption – none of this violence – all would have been peace and serenity, that's what you believe isn't it? Do I frighten you, John? Am I some wicked witch who has cast her spell over the island?'

'You're beginning to sound like Dorothea...'

'Then perhaps it's the island, not the people who reside on it, that is root cause of the problem – perhaps it would be better if we both left as was our intention...'

'I've already told you – no.' Gibbings strode into his bedroom, a few minutes later returning with a pile of clothes, thrusting them at her and pushing open the washroom door. 'There is no future for us.'

'Very well, shield your heart with your stubbornness, there is nothing more to be said...' Veronica flung the clothes on the couch. 'Goodbye then, John Gibbings.'

Without looking back she marched out. It was a waste of time talking to Gibbings – in fact the whole episode had been a waste of time; she should never have returned to the island. It had been for Gibbings' benefit, though not wholly a question of that. No matter what she felt for Gibbings and it could no longer be denied that she felt plenty, the call of the north east coastline had played its part, until the shadow of the castle had engulfed everything.

And in truth was that what had happened? Had she, Gibbings, Llewellyn, Dorothea, Hambleton, even the departed Dawson been sucked into its grip? It sounded absurd, but did malevolence exist within its cold walls that absorbed and manipulated the personalities of the characters within?

But it mattered not now; she would be returning to recitals she had no desire to perform, and despite it all, outside of the castle walls there would be emptiness in leaving the island that would not be filled by returning to her world of music. She'd made up her mind not to return to the castle, that the policeman Taylor could come searching for her – her time within its walls had expired.

To her left the fields ran down to the sea, beyond that were the distant islands she'd seen through the castle windows. She wondered what she'd find there – perhaps somewhere within their confines another hulking castle – or perhaps something more pleasant – something remote but peaceful.

This part of the coastline was strewn with boulders, her normal energy absorbed by her tribulations Veronica had no desire to venture further. She climbed one, perched upon it and clasping her hands around her knees looked back at the castle, stark in the gloom as ever, dominating the island, brooding, soon to be empty of all inhabitants not knowing what its future held or what future incumbents would be unfortunate enough to dwell within its walls.

She turned, stared straight ahead and focused on the islands. Even from a distance she could see white crested waves lapping around them, the foam and froth. In spite of the stormy conditions there seemed a peace about the place. She wondered whether John Gibbings had ever been there, surely he had –

John Gibbings – she would miss him.

Footsteps on the shingles behind made Veronica turn, surely not Rothman again – she couldn't face that –

'Haven't you had enough of the rain today?'

Veronica crooked her head, smiled. 'I had until I saw you.' She placed a hand on the boulder and withdrew it. 'I, like you John, am not afraid of the wet.'

Chapter Forty Four

Veronica clasped her hands together, placed her elbows on her knees. 'Those islands in the distance, what do you know of them John?'

Gibbings shrugged, sighed, 'What do you want to know?'

'Tell me what I might find there, they look so peaceful, if a little rain-swept.'

'You'll find nothing there to interest you, only a few ramshackle cottages – derelict now, an old lighthouse and a load of puffins. Nobody lives on them anymore.'

'How lovely it sounds.' Veronica slapped his thigh, jumped to her feet. 'Take me there.'

Gibbings followed the line of her eye across to a trio of motorboats anchored at the water's edge. 'Too rough to sail in these conditions.'

Veronica shook her head and smiled at him. 'Where's your sense of adventure, John? The wind is slackening and the rain lessens.'

He glanced at the boats, scratched the back of his head. 'But the sea remains rough, and the boats belong to old Tom Higgins. Shouldn't be taking them without his permission…'

Veronica walked over to them. 'Well he isn't here to ask, I'm sure he wouldn't mind.'

'You don't know him,' Gibbings scoffed but he followed her, one eye on the turbulent sea. He blew out his cheeks. 'I could get called to the lifeboat…'

'Yes, you could in which case I could go alone.' Veronica selected a boat, prodded it with her foot and swung to face him. 'I could sail this, and if by chance I get into distress you'll need to rescue me, all over again.'

Gibbings placed a hand on his brow, drew it down slowly. 'That's blackmail.'

'Perhaps, but your sense of duty would induce you to come to my aid.'

Gibbings caught her quiet smile, the flash of amusement in her green eyes; he shook his head. 'This is no laughing matter, I will never understand you.'

Veronica grabbed his hand, held it tight. 'You understand me well enough John Gibbings; you choose to hide the fact behind a mask.'

Gibbings grunted and inspected the craft Veronica had probed with her foot. I suppose with good fortune this will serve our purpose.'

It had been tied to an iron post. Gibbings undid the strap and pushed the vessel away from shore as Veronica leapt aboard, and soon its small bow began plunging into heaving waves which sent their angry froth cascading into the boat's hull.

Gibbings removed a hand from the vessel's steering arm and reached down to a grey pot which he flung in her direction. 'Bail it out,' he yelled, 'or we'll submerge before we're midway!'

Veronica needed little telling. She'd clawed the pot out of mid air beginning to scoop from the gathering pool with a clinical rapidity.

As Gibbings guided the boat closer to the islands Veronica turned, fixing them with her gaze before swinging back to him with a coy smile. 'I do believe we're going to make it, John, we make a fine couple do we not?'

But Gibbings had spotted the sudden tidal surge; he thrust out an urgent finger. 'We won't if we can't shift the water. Bail woman, bail.'

Veronica followed his line and saw the swell approaching, whipping the tide into a frenzy. She applied herself with renewed vigour but at that instant a voluminous wave struck the boat broadside, all but lifting it from the water. 'It's no use!' Gibbings shouted, his voice hoarse. 'The waves will turn us over...'

Veronica flung the pot into the sea and crouched forward. 'Then we'll have to swim John, we're almost there, don't fret so.'

'Then how do we get back?'

Veronica shrugged, then raising her voice above the roar of the sea, 'Don't concern yourself with that now ...'

Another big wave caught the vessel, whipping it sideways. Veronica saw the sea swelling up on her, caught Gibbings' eye and on his beckoning flung herself over the side. She began her strenuous battle with the tide knowing that land lay only fifty metres distant but not knowing whether Gibbings had followed suit, and although every ounce of her being willed him alongside her, a strange emptiness told her he wasn't.

Veronica wanted to turn, to check his whereabouts but the frenzied conditions forbade it, all of her energies were channelled into the fight to reach land. She reached the shingle, crawled ashore and heaved herself up. Breathing deeply she swung round, heart pounding in her ears she scanned the angry waves, but of Gibbings there was no sign. Only the harrowing sight of an empty boat tossing in the storm met her eyes.

Her despair grew by the second as she wiped moisture from her eyes; amidst the dawning realism that produced an all-encompassing sadness came the ultimate irony – she was left to face the fact that she hadn't saved him the way he had her. If she hadn't have insisted on this foolhardy journey in such atrocious conditions this would never have happened. John would not have been swept away by the tide – he who had saved her life and in return for which, because of her own stupidity, had lost his.

Veronica Day lost track of the time she'd spent on the shore; in the distance across the sea the spectre of the castle lay before her, darkly brooding, though it might merely have been an impression on a canvas – her mind had become a void through which no thoughts or feelings could travel.

She began wandering aimlessly, scrambling up grey cliffs before reaching coarse grass where she came upon a long abandoned single storey dwelling standing on the edge of a gully. Its neglected state was reflected in the condition where the few remaining tiles lay in the broken guttering, and in the once white-washed walls, now a forlorn grey. The drab frontage was dissected by a rotting timber door hanging from a single rusty hinge to reveal a rain-soaked and time ravaged interior with debris and fallen masonry strewn over an eroded slate floor. Her soaked clothes seemed to weigh as heavily as her spirits as she wandered into the shell of the building and slumped on a rotting window ledge, head in hands. The rain that poured through the dilapidated roof gradually reduced to occasional droplets before any sound of it was replaced by that of footsteps.

She was afraid to glance up for fear that it wasn't him – until a voice, tired and relieved filled her ears, rejuvenating her tired mind, her spirits rising and seeming to float on the moist air –

'Thank God you're all right, Veronica, I searched the coastline …'

'Oh John, I'm so thankful you're safe!'' She was on her feet, drawing his lithe body into an embrace, cradling his face in her hands. 'I thought – oh my – I thought you'd drowned. She drew her head back, searched his dark eyes. 'I thought I'd lost you.'

'I never thought I'd see you again.' Gibbings placed an arm around her shoulders, drew her out of the tumbledown dwelling, across the gully and up onto the rocks overlooking the sea. 'The tide carried me across the bay, I was fortunate I wasn't thrown against the rocks and killed, the force with which the waves swept me.' He hugged her against him. 'Anyway we both made it, now all we have to do is get back – the boat, luckily, was washed ashore, I managed to secure it to some old moorings.'

'Back, John? I'm not so sure.' Veronica gazed across the water to the castle, dominating the island from its rocky base. Somehow the place doesn't look so foreboding from here. She swung round, clutching his hand, the skies had broken, rays of sunshine swept the coastline in waves, while the breeze, still stiff, ruffled her long red hair.

He was regarding her quizzically. 'What do you mean – not so sure?'

'You never really wanted to leave, did you John? So we have a compromise, we'll leave the island and live here – together.'

Gibbings screwed his eyes, shook his head and repeated her words. 'Live here – where?'

Veronica tightened her grip on his hand, led him back up the cliff and from the summit pointed to the derelict cottage with her free hand. 'There…'

'But it's a ruin for God's sake.'

'Exactly, obviously nobody wants it. I am not without funds John, as you are aware; renovated, it will make a fine home with our own small garden at the side. I cannot imagine how it was allowed to fall into such disrepair.'

Gibbings pulled her to him, his arms tight around her body. 'Because people grow old and when they're gone there's nobody wants to live on islands such as this anymore. The lure of the mainland and all that…'

She placed her arms round his waist, hugged him. 'But I do, John – and you belong in these parts…'

'Why Veronica? Your career, your music…'

'I have told you. I might love playing the music but it was a career I was born into. I feel neither compulsion nor desire to return to it.'

She drew a deep breath, taking in the return of warm summer air. 'Perhaps the occasional performance, but oh John, we can be so happy here. Meanwhile, I can ensure your daughter's education, and what a respite from her studies a haven like this would provide. I look forward to meeting her.' She held him at arm's length, widened her eyes. 'John, please say you'll agree.'

He met her appealing gaze with a solemnity that told her he'd say no – that her idea was much too preposterous, that she possessed too much imagination, not enough practicality.

'We'll need help, plenty of it,' he said at length, cuffing his hand around his jaw before breaking into a smile, 'but no doubt we can find it – alright, yes.'

She clung to his neck in delight, kicked her legs in the air. 'Just you, me, the puffins and the sea breeze – that's all I want, John Gibbings.'

Gibbings hugged her to him, kissed her softly on the lips; she felt the warmth of his body and then as he drew away watched his face stiffen. 'What is it John?'

'You'll be going away.'

Veronica nodded slowly. 'Yes, people to tell, things to arrange, but you'll be accompanying me, will you not?'

He drew back, shaking his head. 'I'll need to arrange for help if we're going to rebuild the bungalow. I can remain at the cottage while you're gone, there's nothing to stop me now, and when you return we can remain there until our home is ready.' He clutched her hands. 'Are you sure you really want this Veronica?'

'With all my heart, and when I return it will be with the funding for our home – and we will create our own bliss. I shall not be long away John Gibbings...'

Gibbings led her across the cliffs down to the bay, where the boat stood glistening in the afternoon sunlight. 'It'll be alright, the vessel's taken a soaking, but she's seaworthy.'

'I have only your word for that, but what difference will another soaking make?'

She paused before stepping inside, giving the castle a long, lingering gaze.

Epilogue

To Thomas Llewellyn's strained eyes, the inside of his castle seemed to have shrunk. The windows were higher, smaller and barred. He couldn't smell the sea air, he couldn't hear the waves, and he could barely see the sky through the thick, glazed windows.

But such matters were of secondary consideration, for his world had shrunk in relation to the size of his castle – gone was his precious princess, banished from his presence for being disloyal – not worthy of his consideration. She had betrayed his love and devotion; an evil presence and so he had cast her out, along with his scheming butler, the name of whom he could no longer remember – and most significantly of all, that despicable gardener – a treacherous fellow he'd felled with a blade for daring to entice his chosen one from his side.

Damn them all, they were gone now, let their bodies rot. He would survive alone in his castle, a stronghold of strongholds –

He heard a click, the turn of a key. How could his key be on the outside of the door? And how dare his servant enter without his consent – but ah, at least he'd brought his food –

'Put it down man,' he snapped, 'and then leave me in peace.'

He thought he saw his servant snigger, damn the man for his incivility, he would have him replaced forthwith.

Llewellyn ignored the knife and fork provided him and thrust his supper into his mouth with both hands.

www.ingramcontent.com/pod-product-compliance
Ingram Content Group UK Ltd.
Pitfield, Milton Keynes, MK11 3LW, UK
UKHW041257180426
11947UKWH00008B/527